Praise for the Asperger's Series
The Question of the Missing Head

A Mystery Scene Best Book of 2014

"[A] delightful and clever mystery."

—*Publishers Weekly*

"Delightfully fresh and witty … Pure heaven."

—*Mystery Scene*

"In this well-crafted story, the Asperger's element … provides a unique point of view on crime solving, as well as offering a sensitive look at a too-often-misunderstood condition."

—*Booklist*

"Copperman/Cohen succeeds in providing a glimpse not only of the challenges experienced by those with Asperger's, but also of their unique gifts."

—*Ellery Queen's Mystery Magazine*

"Cleverly written and humorous."

—*Crimespree Magazine*

THE QUESTION OF THE
FELONIOUS
FRIEND

THE QUESTION OF THE
FELONIOUS FRIEND

AN ASPERGER'S MYSTERY

E.J. COPPERMAN

JEFF COHEN

MIDNIGHT INK
WOODBURY, MINNESOTA

FIRST EDITION
First Printing, 2016

Book format by Bob Gaul
Cover design by Ellen Lawson
Cover illustration by James Steinberg/Gerald & Cullen Rapp
Editing by Nicole Nugent

Midnight Ink, an imprint of Llewellyn Worldwide Ltd.

Library of Congress Cataloging-in-Publication Data
Names: Copperman, E. J., author. | Cohen, Jeffrey, author.
Title: The question of the felonious friend : an asperger's mystery /
   E. J. Copperman, Jeff Cohen.
Description: First edition. | Woodbury, Minnesota : Midnight Ink, [2016] |
   Series: An asperger's mystery ; 3
Identifiers: LCCN 2016008351 | ISBN 9780738743516 (softcover)
Subjects: LCSH: Asperger's syndrome—Patients—Fiction. |
   Murder—Investigation—Fiction. | GSAFD: Mystery fiction.
Classification: LCC PS3603.O358 Q46 2016 | DDC 813/.6—dc23
   LC record available at http://lccn.loc.gov/2016008351

Midnight Ink
Llewellyn Worldwide Ltd.
2143 Wooddale Drive
Woodbury, MN 55125-2989
www.midnightinkbooks.com

Printed in the United States of America

*For our real friends: Jeff Pollitzer, Ken Cohen, Lou Grantt,
Jennifer E. Beaver, Matt Kaufhold, and so many others.
You're in these pages even if you don't know it.*

AUTHORS' NOTE

You'd think two authors would be enough to argue, compromise (remember that, Congress?), and finally create something that will end up as the book you hold in your hands or on your screen. Or maybe are listening to with your ears. This is getting complicated. Anyway, you'd think two people would be enough for all that. But you'd be off by a fairly large number.

First of all, Terri Bischoff of Midnight Ink had to read the first Asperger's mystery, *The Question of the Missing Head*, and like it enough to publish it and ask for more. She has read and edited all three of Samuel's questions so far, and we always love to hear what she has to say, mostly because she likes what we write, which is always a nice thing.

But the book doesn't stop there (that was a pun). Thanks to Nicole Nugent for editing the manuscript and turning it into something coherent. Your work is never taken for granted, Nicole.

And the volume eventually has to have a cover, which might be what attracted you to this book in the first place. So thank you to Ellen Lawson for the cover design, to James Steinberg/Gerald & Cullen Rapp for the cover illustration, and to Bob Gaul for the book format that makes it readable, or at least more readable than when we submitted it.

If you do happen to be hearing rather than seeing these words, our sincere thanks to Mark Boyett for bringing Samuel and all the other characters (and there are a LOT) in these volumes to life. We are in awe of your talent and love to hear the audio versions from Audible as soon as they're available.

To the people who put up with us while we're writing 1,000 words a day—Jessica, Josh, Eve, and everybody at HSG Agency—yes, we know how difficult authors can be. Not us, of course, but authors. And we appreciate all you do for us. Mostly by not killing us and creating some incredibly complicated scenario to cover it all up.

But our readers (and we're pretty sure we know each of your names) are the people who keep this series going. Your loyalty and interest have been amazing, and the connection to Samuel, Janet, and Vivian is remarkable. Especially to those on the spectrum who have contacted us: We can't thank you enough. But consider this and subsequent books our attempts to do so.

—*E.J. Copperman and Jeff Cohen*
February 2016

ONE

—

I received a text message.

This in itself was unusual. I had only recently purchased a cellular phone at the urging of my associate Ms. Washburn. I have some anxiety about it because I am given to misplacing some objects I own, and had taken to keeping the iPhone in my front trouser pocket and patting my thigh on occasion to confirm its continued presence there. It is a comforting ritual and one that I do not consider inappropriate or odd.

The fact that the cellular phone was now buzzing, an indication that a text message had been received, *was* odd. Only three people have been given the number to my cellular phone: my mother, Ms. Washburn, and my friend Mike, who drives a taxicab. All of them know of my distaste for text messaging, which is an illogical pursuit. Texting does not increase the speed of the information being communicated. It actually slows the exchange, as a simple telephone conversation can be conducted in much less time. Answers to questions will come instantaneously in a conversation. By text, they can take minutes or longer.

Ms. Washburn surely had not sent a text message to my iPhone. She was sitting at her desk, only nine feet to my left, and was engaged in billing some clients whose questions we had recently answered. It would be ridiculous for her to send a text when she could simply look up and speak to me directly.

My mother had not sent the message, either. For that matter, neither had Mike. The number being displayed on the screen, which identifies the incoming caller, was not a familiar one, although its 732 area code indicated it was a local one, at least narrowing the location of the caller—or the caller's phone number, as a cellular phone might very well be calling from anywhere—to central New Jersey.

Ms. Washburn looked up from her work when my iPhone buzzed. "What's that?" she asked. "Is someone calling you, Samuel?"

I shook my head. "It is a text message," I said.

Ms. Washburn looked puzzled, an expression I have learned to recognize and have seen on a number of occasions when I have said something Ms. Washburn did not understand or was not expecting. "I thought you didn't like texting," she replied.

"I don't." I looked at the screen and considered whether it made sense to unlock the phone's system in order to read a text message from someone I probably would not know. "Some telephone solicitors might use text messages."

"Why don't you read it and find out?" Ms. Washburn asked. Sometimes when she asks a question like that, it makes me see the simplicity of the situation. There was no danger in reading a text message; it could not corrupt my iPhone's software simply by existing.

I opened the phone's systems and read the text. Is THIS QUESTIONS ANSWERED?, it read.

The question itself illustrated one of the many problems with the concept of a text message. It was difficult to answer, and would have been considerably more clear and quickly disposed of in a traditional conversation.

Was *what* Questions Answered? Obviously, the person sending the text wanted to know if he or she had reached my business, but had not asked the question in a fashion that was designed to elicit that information. If I were to answer what had been asked of me, I would have to determine exactly what the sender was asking.

"What does it say?" Ms. Washburn asked.

I pondered the question. Questions Answered, the business I'd started one year, two weeks, and three days earlier, had its own telephone number, which was assigned to the landline only inches from my right hand on my desk (an extension telephone was located on Ms. Washburn's desk). So to be exact, if the text sender was asking whether he or she had reached my business, the answer would be that he or she had not. Instead, the texter had reached me personally and that was not the same thing. Ms. Washburn was part of the business and she had not been contacted in this fashion.

But since Questions Answered is my business, and since its concept is that I will personally answer questions for clients if the question is interesting (and the client is willing to pay my fee), the argument could be made that reaching me was equivalent to reaching the office. After all, even on the landline, only Ms. Washburn or I can speak at once. In order to contact both of us, it would be necessary to employ speakerphone.

"It is a text message asking if this is Questions Answered," I told Ms. Washburn. "I'm not sure how to respond."

She smiled in a familiar fashion. Ms. Washburn believes that my Asperger's Syndrome, a particular set of personality traits some see as a "disorder," leads me to overanalyze some situations, and it seemed that was her opinion at the moment. "Tell them yes," she suggested.

Rather than explain my reasoning to her, I responded via text to the person who had contacted me. It is. Do you have a question?

To my relief, the response came only eleven seconds later. I have many questions.

I did not see how that was going to be useful information. "Should I tell the person to call the office phone?" I asked Ms. Washburn. "If we keep up like this, it could be a very long time before we know what the point of the conversation might be."

Her brow wrinkled a bit. "But you're concerned about speaking to a new person on your personal line," she said. It was not a reminder, but an analysis. Ms. Washburn is very good at interpreting my words and anticipating the issues that might give a person like me some anxiety. Since her first day at Questions Answered, during which we had encountered the Question of the Missing Head, she had proven herself intuitive, intelligent, and invaluable.

"That's correct," I said. "Suppose this person has some nefarious purpose."

Ms. Washburn stood up and walked to my side. "I doubt someone trying to do you harm would start by asking if they had reached Questions Answered," she said. "Suppose they want to hire us."

The phone buzzed again. I looked down and saw the same message repeated.

"Why don't you call the number?" Ms. Washburn said. "That will give you the upper hand." I could not be certain if her tone contained some irony. But her suggestion was quite practical.

I called the number listed from the mysterious texter and listened to the phone ring three times. A voice, male, immediately asked, "Is this Questions Answered?"

Ms. Washburn, who probably was able to hear what had been said, nodded her head, indicating I should say it was.

"This is the cellular telephone of one of the people who works at Questions Answered," I responded. "How did you get this phone number, and why did you not call the business number that is listed on our website?" Ms. Washburn had created a website for the business five months before.

A sound came through the phone that was clearly generated by the person calling but was not really speech. It sounded like, "Nnnn-nnnnnnnnnnnnnn."

Ms. Washburn looked a little concerned. I was not really sure how best to proceed, as that was not a communicative sound.

"How did you obtain this telephone number?" I asked again. I confess, repetition was the only course of action that came to mind.

"Nnnnnnnnnnnnnnnn…"

Ms. Washburn picked up a small pad from my desk and wrote on it, *He might be on the spectrum.*

That meant my caller could be someone with Asperger's Syndrome or a related "disorder" classified under the autism umbrella in the Diagnostic and Statistical Manual of Mental Disorders, a publication from the American Psychiatric Association. The DSM-V, as it is best known, no longer recognizes Asperger's Syndrome but would undoubtedly identify me as someone whose behavior is consistent with autism in some form.

I consider such classifications demeaning, frankly, but the issue at hand was the caller, and what Ms. Washburn was suggesting seemed likely.

Since I had heard the caller's voice, I knew he was capable of speech. It was possible, then, that my aggressive response to his original question with queries of my own might have upset the planned conversation he had expected. Perhaps a different tactic would yield better results.

"This is Questions Answered," I said into the iPhone. "Allow me to introduce myself. I am Samuel Hoenig. With whom am I speaking?"

There was a six-second period of silence, after which the caller said, "I'm Tyler Clayton. I have a question I would like to have answered. May I come to your office at 735 Stelton Road in Piscataway, New Jersey?"

Ms. Washburn's suspicions were proving correct—this was definitely someone whose behavior would indicate a degree of autism. "You may," I answered. It would be best not to present Tyler Clayton with a question, so I added, "Tell me where you are and I will provide directions."

Unfortunately I was met with the repetition of, "Nnnnnnnnn..."

Ms. Washburn, eyes narrowing, walked to my right, through our offices, which are in a space previously occupied by a pizzeria called San Remo's. She moved to the area in front of the vending machine (diet soda for Ms. Washburn, spring water for me, and green tea for Mother) and looked outside.

"Samuel," she said. She pointed toward the front window. I walked over to her and looked where she indicated.

Standing in the parking lot outside Question Answered was a man in his late twenties, if I were judging properly. He was a large man in every sense, tall and hefty. He wore black-rimmed eyeglasses, denim blue jeans, and a t-shirt bearing the logo of Hewlett-Packard. His hair was not recently washed. His left arm was flapping nervously at his side.

His right hand was holding a cellular phone, and he was staring intently at the offices we occupied.

I looked at Ms. Washburn and she nodded again.

"Come in, Tyler," I said. "We are here to help if we can."

We watched as he looked at the phone, then seemed to take a moment to collect himself. Ms. Washburn gestured that we should move back toward our desks, presumably to spare Tyler the embarrassment of being watched. I did notice before I turned that his left arm had ceased its vertical movement at his side as Tyler began walking toward the front door.

It took him longer than anticipated to come inside the Questions Answered offices, but I did not look to see if he was hesitating at the door. My philosophy since opening our doors the first day has been that clients should come in because they truly desire the service we provide and not due to any extraneous coercion on the part of the business. I have done some advertising in *The New York Times* and the *Home News-Tribune*, strictly to inform people that the service exists. The same was true of the few online ads Ms. Washburn had placed. I make no claims and offer no promises.

Tyler entered through the front door, then looked up, seemingly startled, at the bell attached to the door that rings when anyone enters or exits. The bell had been left there by the owners of San Remo's Pizzeria business and I had kept it to be sure I would not, in the heat of researching a question, fail to notice when a potential client might enter.

"Don't worry, Tyler," Ms. Washburn said. "That happens whenever the door opens."

Tyler looked at her, his head swiveling in her direction quickly. He seemed overwhelmed by everything in the room, which was surprising, since all the office held was a desk for me, one for Ms. Washburn, the drink machine, an overstuffed easy chair for my mother when she visited, and the unused pizza oven the previous tenants had left behind.

"Come in," I said. "Do you have a question?"

Tyler Clayton did not look either Ms. Washburn or me directly in the eye. I understood that, since it has taken a good deal of training and practice for me to make eye contact in conversation. He stared at his shoes, which were made by New Balance and were black.

"I … I … yes," he said. Then he nodded repeatedly, not so much affirming what he'd said as simply burning off nervous energy.

"Please sit down," Ms. Washburn suggested, gesturing toward Mother's easy chair. I suppressed the urge to object, as I am not fond of having strangers sit in the chair we reserve for my mother. Suppose she dropped by unexpectedly? Where would she sit?

My concerns were nullified, however. Tyler shook his head slightly. "I'll stand," he said.

Now I was a bit confused. I had been planning to sit behind my desk, the usual position I take when considering a question. But I am aware that there are some circumstances under which it is impolite to sit if another person in the room is still standing. I was not certain whether this was one of those instances.

Luckily, Ms. Washburn, to whom I look for many of my social cues when working, sat down behind her desk. "That's your choice," she told Tyler. "I hope you don't mind if Samuel and I sit down."

Tyler ignored her last statement and kept looking at his shoes. "Who are you?" he asked her. "I didn't know there would ... would be two people."

I was about to introduce Ms. Washburn, and perhaps to suggest that Tyler be more polite toward her, but she spoke before I could. "I'm Janet Washburn," she said. "I work here at Questions Answered too. Would you prefer to talk only to Samuel?"

Tyler looked up, but not at either my face or Ms. Washburn's. He seemed to focus on the pizza ovens, and he studied them with great care. "No. It's okay if you work here."

"What is the nature of your question?" I asked. There was no point in discussing Tyler's obvious difficulties. I assumed he had some support system in place. Someone had clearly driven him to our office, as he had not been standing near a vehicle when we first saw him, and the idea of Tyler driving a car was difficult to believe. He would probably stare at the gas pedal and pay no attention to the road. Or perhaps I was assuming his behavior in the office would be similar to that in a moving motor vehicle.

"I work at the Microchip Mart," Tyler said.

"That is not a question," I pointed out.

"No. No, it isn't." Tyler's hands started to flutter at his sides.

I looked at Ms. Washburn, who was watching Tyler and looking concerned. If I were sure it wouldn't cause him to become more agitated, I might have suggested that Tyler call the person who had brought him to our office and ask to be driven home.

"It's okay, Tyler," Ms. Washburn said. She gave me a quick glance with an expression I could not interpret because it passed too quickly. "Samuel can help you if you just ask him a question."

I was not certain that claim was accurate. I accept questions to answer based on my own interest in the topic, since I will be less efficient researching a topic I find dull and I do not wish to give a client any less than my best effort. But now that Ms. Washburn had made the assurance to Tyler, I felt it would be unwise to contradict her before I knew what it was Tyler had to ask.

"A question," Tyler repeated. It is a tactic I sometimes use—repeating what has just been said in order to find a few extra seconds to think. "A question."

Ms. Washburn was clearly trying to signal me about my attitude toward Tyler. She turned her head toward me in a position he could not see and smiled broadly and obviously, then tilted her head in Tyler's direction. It took me four seconds, but I realized she was indicating I should seem more avuncular or at least welcoming toward our potential client.

"Yes, Tyler," I said, looking at him and forcing a smile. It was a moot point, as Tyler was still staring at the pizza oven. "What is your question, please?" I often add the word *please* when I would prefer to simply get to the point. Mother says it makes the person I'm talking to feel less stress. I am unaware of any stress I am causing, but I take Mother at her word.

Still, my tone or the situation itself must have caused Tyler some anxiety. His hands flapped harder and his eyes rolled up in their sockets. But he did manage to take a deep breath, which was a little comforting.

"Is Richard Handy really my friend?" he asked.

TWO

It took more than two minutes for Tyler Clayton to become calm enough to discuss his question, which I found a bit confusing. I understand that people whose behavior places them, in the eyes of mainstream society, on the autism spectrum sometimes have difficulty making friends. I can rely on only a very small number of people as my own friends, particularly if one excludes family members. My mother is a close friend.

But the concept of not knowing whether a person is a friend or not is more subtle and complex. I have heard of some people with Asperger's Syndrome and others with autism being taken in by duplicitous people posing as friends either to humiliate or defraud the person with the "handicap." It is challenging for some of us to determine if the allegiances with which we are presented are real or feigned, since we spend so much of our time acting in the way we have been taught rather than the way we would naturally behave. Emotion is a difficult concept.

"Who is Richard Handy?" Ms. Washburn, notepad out and in use, asked Tyler.

Tyler seemed to collect himself; he shrugged his shoulders and inhaled deeply through his nose. He continued to stand, but averted his gaze from the pizza oven and fixed it on a point three feet above Ms. Washburn's head. It is a tactic I was taught in social skills training when I was a teenager.

"Richard is the assistant manager at the Quik N EZ," Tyler answered, his voice almost a mumble. I strained to hear, but did not move my chair closer to him or urge him to speak up. I wanted to do one of those things, but saw Ms. Washburn watching me closely and believed her tension might have been in anticipation of my causing Tyler additional stress. "He calls me 'my friend' whenever I go in for a soda or a soft pretzel."

I considered the statement. People, particularly those who work in retail businesses, will often refer to customers as *my friend* in conversation as an honorific or as a means of creating what they hope will be a rapport with the customer that will lead to increased sales. If that was all of Tyler's evidence, this might become an extremely easy question to answer.

"Does he do anything else that would indicate he thinks of you in a way other than as a customer?" I asked. Ms. Washburn grimaced a bit, leading me to believe I could have phrased that question more tactfully. I had thought my wording was quite sensitive, actually.

Any inadvertent transgression was unimportant, anyway; Tyler seemed not to have been offended. He looked up at the ceiling for a moment. "Yes, of course," he said. "If I thought that meant he was my real friend, I'd be stupid."

I looked at Ms. Washburn to indicate that Tyler was being less delicate about his own feelings than I had been. She did not react.

"What other evidence is there, then?" I asked. "What made you think Richard Handy is your friend, and why do you have doubts about his friendship now?"

"Can I still sit down?" Tyler asked.

Ms. Washburn indicated Mother's chair again. "Of course. Please."

Tyler flung himself onto the chair so heavily I winced. I did not want him to cause any damage to my mother's chair. It creaked a bit, but otherwise seemed unharmed.

I was about to ask Tyler about Richard Handy again when, again looking over Ms. Washburn's head, he added, "Richard played video games at my house once. He said he was into S and S, too, but we never played together."

Ms. Washburn looked at me with an expression I could not read.

"You play Swords and Sorcerers?" I asked, more to give her the information than to get any from Tyler, in case she was not aware of the term. The role-playing game and others like it are not uncommon among those on the autism spectrum. I do not play them myself, but I have spoken to a number of people like me who do. They find the possibility of taking on another identity liberating. I find the idea of being someone other than myself, even when pretending, terrifying. As a child I wanted to go trick-or-treating as myself.

"Yeah, online. I belong to a group of five people and we play every Wednesday from five in the afternoon, Eastern Time, to eleven p.m., Eastern Time. I'm a necromancer named Skullkiller."

"Does Richard Handy play with you?" Ms. Washburn asked.

"No. Richard plays with a group in person, in Somerset. I don't do that." Tyler made the prospect of playing a game with other people present sound like a somehow shameful act.

"But he did come and play video games at your house," I said, hoping to bring the conversation back to the relevant issue.

"Uh-huh. We played Assassin's Creed and the Elder Scrolls," he said. The names held no particular significance for me, but I did not believe the specific games played were relevant.

"Was it his idea or yours to play games together?" I asked. I saw Ms. Washburn nod; that was a question she wanted answered as well.

"Richard suggested it," Tyler said. "He saw I was buying video game magazines in the Quik N EZ and he asked me if I played."

"And you answered?" I said. It seemed odd, given Tyler's predilection toward avoiding conversation.

"The third time he asked, I could," he said. "So Richard asked me what games I liked and then he said we should play together sometime."

"Is that the only time you saw him outside the convenience store?" Ms. Washburn asked.

Tyler did not seem to have absorbed the question. "Then he asked did I have a PS4, and I said yeah, I had one, so he said could he come over and see it, and I said yeah, and then he came over and we played Assassin's Creed and the Elder Scrolls." On the armrests of Mother's chair, his hands were balling up in fists.

"Tyler," Ms. Washburn said, "listen to me. Is that the only time you saw Richard outside the convenience store?" She began to type on her computer keyboard, although I could not see what she was trying to accomplish, as her screen was turned away from my vantage point.

"We chose those games because Richard had played Assassin's Creed and I had it, and we could both play the Elder Scrolls online at the same time," Tyler went on. His "special interest"—an area in which he was especially well versed and could be considered "obsessive" by some—was clearly video games.

I decided to try to penetrate his defenses by beginning with the subject he found endlessly fascinating. "Who won?" I asked.

Tyler actually looked me in the face for a moment, then looked away, back at the pizza oven again. Perhaps he was wondering why an agency that answers client questions had two pizza ovens, and why there were not in use. "Won?" he asked.

"The video games. When you played with Richard, who won?" If I could isolate the incident in his conversation, I might be able to steer Tyler back to information that could help me answer his question.

"They're not that kind of games," he said.

"Oh."

"Richard was good. He could blow through a level if he wanted to or he could work at it and make it last if he thought it was interesting. Sometimes he'd play for two hours and not say a word to me at all." Tyler's eyes, although not trained on Ms. Washburn or myself, were bright. He clearly admired his companion's ability to focus.

But his continuing dissection of Richard Handy's video game skills was not going to help me answer his question. Frankly, if Ms. Washburn (who continued to perform some task on her computer keyboard) had not prematurely promised Tyler we would accept his question, I probably would have rejected it. Human interaction is hardly my area of expertise, and I firmly believed this question could easily be answered by Tyler himself by simply asking Richard if they were friends. That would be direct and simple.

"Tyler," I said, "what else did you and Richard do outside the convenience store?" Perhaps asking him that way would trigger better information. On the basis of what Tyler had told me to this point, I felt I could have made a very good guess about his question—Richard Handy did not seem to value Tyler as a friend—but I had no definitive evidence.

"Outside the Quik N EZ?" Tyler repeated.

"Yes."

"There's just a parking lot there," he said, obviously confused. "There's not much you can do in a parking lot, especially if you want to play video games. You could play on your phone, I guess, but . . . "

"Tell us about other times you saw Richard when you weren't in the Quik N EZ," Ms. Washburn suggested.

"Oh. That was the only time."

"What kind of game system does Richard own?" I asked. I was forming a theory and thought the information might help develop it.

"Um, I don't know," Tyler said. His hands started moving on the arms of the chair again. "He wanted to come see mine."

"Do you live alone, Tyler?" Ms. Washburn asked. I assumed this was an avenue to another question, because I doubted Tyler could live on his own. I live in the house where I grew up, where my mother lives, but I could get a separate apartment if I wanted to. I was not as certain that Tyler could manage it.

Tyler's eyes widened a little and didn't roll, but they did dart from side to side, as if he were looking for an escape route. "No," he mumbled. The more uncomfortable the question seemed to be, the less audible Tyler's speech became.

He did not elaborate, so I asked, "Who lives with you?"

I prepared myself for a very soft response, and that was what Tyler offered. "Mason."

That did not help very much.

"Who is Mason?" Ms. Washburn asked.

"My brother." Tyler started to chew on his lower lip.

"Did Mason drop you off here?" Ms. Washburn asked. She very casually hit a key on her keyboard and I heard the printer, on a table behind her, begin to operate.

Tyler was looking at a point very near the ceiling. "The first Grand Theft Auto was released by DMA Design in 1997," he offered. "There have been eleven stand-alone games and four expansion packs in the series so far."

It is not unusual among those with Asperger's Syndrome or an autism spectrum personality to have a very strong special interest, and it is equally common in that group to speak only about that topic to the exclusion of all others. My own interests, in criminal justice, the

New York Yankees, and the Beatles, are subjects I prefer to discuss ahead of most other things, but I have learned that "neurotypical" people tend to become bored when conversing about only one subject, particularly when it is not one of their own choosing. Why they would not want to hear about the history of the New York Yankees or the recording sessions that produced the music of the Beatles is a mystery to me, but observation has confirmed that it is true.

But when Tyler shifted his topic back to that which he found most comfortable, it was hard not to conclude he did so because he desperately did not want to discuss his brother Mason at all.

Ms. Washburn, however, either had not realized this or was determined to press on under any circumstances. As she stood up to retrieve the document in the printer, she asked, "Is there a way we can contact Mason?"

"Nnnnnnnnnnn…"

Tyler had reverted to his least communicative state. His head was back on the chair and he would have been staring directly at the ceiling of the Questions Answered office if his eyes had been open. His arms were not flapping, but only because he had clasped his hands together and was holding them motionless with such force that his knuckles were white and his fingers were beet red.

I was not capable at that moment of placating our new client. His behavior, in fact, was making me anxious enough that I felt my own hands start to move nervously, my fingers flexing as if I were playing an invisible piano. I was not so upset that I was in danger of what Mother calls a "meltdown," but it was difficult for me to focus on the question at hand.

I began to mentally concoct an all-time New York Yankees lineup, which was difficult because only nine players from over a hundred years of teams could be included. Surely Babe Ruth would be included, but he would not bat first. Who would be the right leadoff hitter?

"Tyler," I heard Ms. Washburn say, "in order to answer your question, we will need you to fill out this client intake form." This surprised me, as I knew we had such a form on file and did not understand why Ms. Washburn had felt the need to type a new one.

But her action had the effect she must have intended: Tyler's eyes focused, his hands stopped moving, and he took the form, which Ms. Washburn had mounted on a clipboard. Ms. Washburn gave Tyler a ballpoint pen and he immediately set to work on the form.

The action appeared to calm him; Tyler was being asked questions about himself and responding, and the medium was a cleverly chosen one. Tyler had the control over the pace and style of his answers. He worked for eleven minutes quite happily at the one-page form Ms. Washburn had composed.

When he had completed it, he handed the clipboard back to Ms. Washburn. "Is that all I need to do?" he asked.

I was about to mention his paying half the fee in advance, as is the standard procedure at Questions Answered, but Ms. Washburn said, "Yes, that's all for now," before I could bring it up. "Do you have a way to get home?"

Tyler looked embarrassed and shook his head from side to side, but not as a negative. He was clearly just working off the energy that his emotion was generating. "I can call my sister," he said. He reached into his pocket and produced a cellular telephone.

It occurred to me that at a younger age than I, and with more difficulties related to his place on the autism spectrum, Tyler Clayton had obtained a cellular phone long before I had. It was a slight source of embarrassment, but I decided not to concentrate on it.

Before Tyler could dial his phone, however, the front door opened and a woman of approximately thirty-two walked in. She had very curly hair and large brown eyes. "Tyler?" she said as soon as she entered. "I think it's about time to go."

The woman walked toward Tyler and Ms. Washburn, who were standing at the center of the room. I stood and approached from my desk. "Sandy," Tyler said, "I was just calling you."

Ms. Washburn extended a hand. "Are you Tyler's sister?" she asked.

The woman we now knew as Sandy nodded. "Sandy Clayton Webb," she said, taking Ms. Washburn's hand. "I hope he hasn't bothered the two of you too much."

"He hasn't bothered us at all," Ms. Washburn said. I would have disagreed, but felt that would have been seen as an insult. "I'm Janet Washburn and this is Samuel Hoenig. Tyler has asked us to answer a question for him."

"Sandy knows about it," Tyler said. "You don't have to tell her."

"Tyler," his older sister scolded. "Don't be rude."

"Was that rude?"

Despite Ms. Washburn's introduction, I felt it was reasonable to approach Sandy and say, "Allow me to introduce myself. I am Samuel Hoenig, the principal operator of Questions Answered." Before Ms. Washburn had become a full-time employee, I had introduced myself as the proprietor, but since she was now working with me and had become a vital part of the operation, I had altered my title accordingly.

Sandy reached for my hand. Despite my usual slight revulsion at the thought, I took it and said, "I was not offended, Mrs. Webb."

"It's Clayton Webb, with no hyphen," she said. "The fact is, I divorced Mr. Webb last year." I am not sure why she thought that information was relevant to the answering of Tyler's question. I resolved to ask Ms. Washburn what she thought after Tyler and his sister left.

"I'm sorry to hear that," Ms. Washburn said. She was in the process of divorcing her husband, Simon Taylor. I did not ask Ms. Washburn about the proceedings unless it was completely necessary, as when she once had to take off half a day of work when consulting an attorney.

Sandy waved a hand. "Don't be. Best thing I ever did."

"Really?" Tyler asked. "You cried for three hours when you told me about it."

Sandy hid the grimace well but not so well that it was invisible. "I think it's time for us to go," she said. "You have group in an hour, Tyler."

Tyler looked at me. "I go to social skills therapy in a group session that includes three other people who have autism spectrum disorders," he said. "Jim O'Malley, Ken Martel, and Molly Brandt. What part of the spectrum does your disorder fall on, Mr. Hoenig?"

"Tyler!" his sister admonished.

I chose not to explain that I saw no shame in the question, nor that I do not consider myself to have a disorder. "I was classified in high school as having Asperger's Syndrome," I told Tyler.

"That's not a diagnosis anymore."

"I am aware of that. It was eliminated in the DSM-V."

Sandy looked positively mortified. "I am so sorry, Mr. Hoenig," she said.

"There is no reason to be," I assured her. Then I looked at her brother. "Tyler," I said, "there is a very important question I must ask you if I am to help you answer the one that brought you here. What is your favorite song by the Beatles?"

This is a tactic I use frequently when meeting new people; it helps me understand their personalities in ways I would not normally be able to access. My knowledge of the music recorded by the Beatles helps me make assumptions about the strangers I meet. Some people find the question odd, but it always serves me well.

"Beetles don't sing songs," Tyler said. He looked confused.

Clearly he was taking me too literally, which is not unusual among those with personalities that are classified as on the autism spectrum.

"Not the insects," Ms. Washburn explained. "The band called the Beatles."

Tyler stole a glance at his sister and his hands flapped a little at his sides. Sandy started to shake her head negatively.

"There's a band called the Beatles?" Tyler asked.

That was the moment I decided to answer Tyler Clayton's question. Clearly, he needed my help much more than I had previously understood.

THREE

"So this young man wants you to find out if some other young man is his friend?" My mother stood up from the kitchen table and walked to the sink. She placed her dinner plate on the counter and reached for the faucet.

"Mother," I said, "you cooked. I'll wash the dishes." We own an automatic dishwasher, but Mother rarely uses it. She says it does not do the work adequately. I stood and brought my plate to the sink, then began to wash the dinner dishes. "And yes, Tyler Clayton wants me to find out whether Richard Handy is actually his friend."

"Why doesn't he just ask?" Mother smiled a bit as she sat back down. No doubt it had been her intention to draw my attention to the dinner dishes by pretending to wash them herself. She sometimes uses subtle methods to focus me on a task.

"As I explained, Tyler is a young man with behaviors that—"

"Behaviors that would place him on the autism spectrum," Mother said. There were only two dinner plates, two glasses, and two sets of utensils to wash. Mother had cooked a pasta dinner, and since I do not eat mine with sauce, the pots were mostly clean. Mother's bore the marks of the Paul Newman sauce she favors, which I tried to block out. It makes my stomach a little queasy to see leftover food. "But you said he can speak."

"Tyler is capable of spoken language, yes. But that does not immediately lead to the conclusion that he is socially adept enough to ask another person that question."

"Why don't *you* ask him?" Mother said as I began to dry the dishes with a towel we keep for just that purpose in the cabinet under the sink. "That will answer Tyler's question and you'll be done with it."

I nodded. "That would be true, if I were to try to do a fast job instead of a thorough one. Suppose Richard lies about being Tyler's friend. My job is to answer the question, not to get Richard to answer the question."

I placed the last dried dish in the drainer on the counter. I could have put it away in the cabinet above, but Mother says even a towel-dried dish still has some moisture on it and needs a little time to become completely dry. I do not argue with her on issues of housekeeping.

"What does Janet think?" she asked as I sat down again.

"Ms. Washburn suggested we ask Richard Handy the question, as you did," I reported. "But after I explained why that would not provide us with an accurate answer to the question, she said one of us should watch Richard and Tyler together when neither of them was aware of our presence and observe the interaction."

"So that's what you're going to do?"

It was a difficult question. "Not necessarily. That would at best provide us with an opinion about the question. It might be correct, but it might not. Tyler requires a factual answer. He especially needs to be shown objectively whether Richard is or is not his friend."

Mother looked puzzled. "Is that possible?" she asked. "Is friendship something that can be measured and proven mathematically? Isn't it just a feeling?"

23

It is often helpful to use Mother as a sounding board for a question that ventures into areas with which I am not especially comfortable. In that way, she serves much the same function as Ms. Washburn, but she has her own perspective. I can frequently present both women with the same set of facts, and even if they have the same opinion, they will present it differently.

In this case, I was entering into two areas with which I am not always sure-footed: emotional interaction between people and others identified as having an autism spectrum disorder. I have some difficulty dealing with those who are classified in a similar way as I, and it is not clear to me why that is the case.

"Friendship can be considered a feeling a person has when interacting with someone else," I said, agreeing with Mother. "But it is also an accepted state of relationship. I can say that Mike the taxicab driver is my friend because he has proven to be helpful to me on numerous occasions without asking for anything in return."

Mother's eyes sharpened. "So that's what a friend is? Someone who serves a purpose for you and doesn't require payment?"

This was dangerous territory. Mother has made no secret of her opinion that I should "mingle," as she says, with more people than the few I trust. She believes it is a failure of mine that I have only two people—Ms. Washburn and Mike the taxicab driver—whom I consider friends. I see no reason to populate my life with more people than I need. When I was in school, I found that many peers considered me odd and were wary of me. I was wary of them because they seemed shallow and inconsequential. Since earning my degree I have almost always worked on my own. That was true until Ms. Washburn became an associate at Questions Answered.

"You know perfectly well that we have differing opinions of the merits and dangers of friendship," I told Mother. "I'm not going to let you start that conversation again for two reasons."

"One is that the Yankees have a game starting in ten minutes and you want to watch it," Mother said. "What's the other?"

She was right about that, of course.

"The other is that I dislike arguing with you, and since we have had this conversation to the same impasse on more than one occasion, I see no reason to repeat the experience." I stood up, prepared to walk into the den where I could watch the baseball game with the sound turned off. The chatter of the announcers and the roar of the fans distract me from the sequence of situations that make up a baseball game.

"You don't think I can change your mind?"

"I think not."

Mother chuckled. "You're probably right."

The Yankees lost the game, five runs to two.

———————

"I thought you said we weren't going to do this," Ms. Washburn said.

We were sitting in her car across the street from the Quik N EZ convenience store in Somerset, New Jersey, that Tyler Clayton had specified was the one where he had met Richard Handy. Having found an online photograph of Richard, we had a general idea of his appearance. We were waiting for Tyler to appear, as he had said he did every day at eleven a.m., according to the form Ms. Washburn had created for him to fill out.

"Sometimes it is best to enact a somewhat flawed plan than to have no plan at all," I noted from the passenger seat. I have an active license to drive a vehicle, but I rarely do so. Ms. Washburn drives when we have to leave the Questions Answered office.

"You mean you couldn't think of anything else," she said.

"That would be another way to characterize the situation, yes."

Ms. Washburn had a camera ready with a telephoto lens attached. We did not have access to any sound equipment that could pick up conversation from this far away, and I was not sure I would have used it if we had. The idea of eavesdropping on a private talk—and we had not told Tyler we would be watching because we did not want our presence to alter his behavior at all—was distasteful. I did wish I could, as Ms. Washburn had put it, think of something else to try.

She must have been thinking along the same lines as I was, at least in part. "If we can't hear them, how will we be able to answer Tyler's question?" she asked.

"For the time being, we will observe body language and other visual cues," I said.

"That's not your strong suit, is it?" Ms. Washburn asked sincerely.

"No. My Asperger's Syndrome makes it difficult for me to interpret the attitude a person exudes through behavior," I admitted. "But my social skills training over the years and my work with Dr. Mancuso have helped me develop that skill to some extent. And I have another asset."

"Me," Ms. Washburn said.

"Precisely."

A short silence followed lasting seventeen seconds. "Samuel, I want to tell you about my divorce," Ms. Washburn said.

My fingers might have fluttered a bit, although I have taught myself to use my left hand, thumb and middle finger at the temples, to deal with stress, replacing the hand flapping I had done as a younger person. I am not comfortable discussing personal issues with anyone, and perhaps less so with Ms. Washburn, with whom I work every weekday.

"I don't mean to make you fidgety," she said. "Don't worry. I'm not going to tell you anything intimate."

That was a relief, but her use of the word *fidgety* was troublesome; was that how she saw me?

"The thing is, I want you to know you didn't have anything to do with the fact that Simon and I broke up," Ms. Washburn went on. "My working at Questions Answered just supplied the last reason to argue. We'd been in a bad place for a while."

I had been concerned because Ms. Washburn had told me of her divorce almost immediately after accepting full-time employment at Questions Answered. I knew her husband Simon Taylor was opposed to her working with me, as he had told me so in very specific terms. But the timing appeared to be too large a coincidence to accept.

"Are you saying that because you want to spare me any feelings of responsibility?" I asked. "I assure you, I did not try to cause your marriage to end." My mother believes I harbor romantic feelings for Ms. Washburn and had, until recently, admonished me fairly regularly that she was "another man's wife."

"That's exactly the opposite of what I'm doing," Ms. Washburn assured me. "I'm telling you it had nothing to do with you at all. If I hadn't come to work at Questions Answered, I'm certain I would still be going to court in two weeks to divorce Simon. Wait."

I was not aware I had been ready to do anything that required waiting. "What is it?" I asked.

"Tyler." Ms. Washburn pointed across the street. "That's him, isn't it?"

I followed the path of her finger toward the Quik N EZ across the street and there was a young man resembling Tyler approaching the store. "Check through your lens," I suggested.

Ms. Washburn picked up the camera and looked through the viewfinder, not at the LCD display on the back of the unit's body. She has told me she can get a clearer look that way, and as a professional photographer, her judgment is certainly the one to which I would defer in all things related to imagery.

"That's him all right," she said. "He's going inside."

I could see that the young man across the street had been entering the convenience store, so that comment was not especially useful. The pertinent information was that the young man was indeed Tyler Clayton. "Can you see through the window if Richard is visible?" I asked.

"I checked before. If he stays at the counter, I can see him."

I waited twelve seconds before asking, "What can you see?"

"Tyler's second in line. He's behind a Hispanic woman with a package of diapers."

"Did Richard acknowledge his presence?"

"Not yet. But he might not have seen Tyler. He's concentrating on the cash register and the woman."

I considered the task we were undertaking and a thought occurred to me. "If I were watching you and your husband through a window, would I know you were divorcing?" I asked Ms. Washburn.

To her credit, she did not turn away from the viewfinder. "What are you talking about?" she asked.

"The usefulness of body language. In some cases it can help interpret an encounter between or among people. In others, it can distract or misinform. It is difficult to know which we are witnessing at the moment."

Ms. Washburn continued to look through the lens. "Tyler's about to reach the front of the line," she said. "Do you want me to shoot pictures?"

"I don't think that will be necessary," I answered. "We will not have to provide Tyler with evidence that he saw Richard. He will know that occurred."

Ms. Washburn did not answer directly. "He's at the counter and talking to Richard," she said.

"How is Richard reacting?"

"He said something back, and the other guy at the counter laughed a little," Ms. Washburn replied. "I wasn't watching Tyler directly at that moment, but I don't think he was laughing."

"Not a good sign," I said. There have been times in my life—principally in school—when peers would say something either to or about me intending to be amusing. Others have sometimes agreed with that assessment, but I rarely have.

"Tyler is buying a soda," Ms. Washburn reported. "And he is paying with a card, probably a debit card, because he had to punch in a PIN number."

I understood the impulse to avoid using cash—you never know who has handled it before you obtained the bill or coin—but even I wouldn't have bothered with an alternate form of payment for something so inexpensive. "I assume Tyler does not want to handle cash, or is considered too careless to have any with him," I told Ms. Washburn. "Is he trying to engage Richard in conversation?"

"Yes, he is, and it's a problem," she said. "There are people behind him in line, and Richard is pointing to them. I think he's telling Tyler to get out of the way."

"Is Tyler doing so?" I asked. It was frustrating not being able to see at the same time Ms. Washburn could. Perhaps if we ever tried this again I would bring a pair of binoculars.

"Finally, yes. But he does have some cash on him, because he's leaving a bill in the tip jar on the counter." Ms. Washburn gasped. "Whoa."

"What is it?" I asked.

"Tyler just tipped Richard a hundred dollars on a soda that cost a buck and a half."

FOUR

"We have circumstantial evidence, and we need more than that," I told Ms. Washburn.

"I don't think it is just circumstantial," she countered. "I think there's no other explanation."

We were back in the office of Questions Answered, each at our assigned desk. After Tyler had left his enormously generous tip for his assumed friend Richard Handy, he had left the Quik N EZ market and walked away. Tyler had a part-time job at a local electronics shop but would not be working this week except on Saturday, he had told us.

There had been no further contact between the two young men, although Ms. Washburn reported that Richard had quickly snatched the $100 bill Tyler had left in the tip jar—really a small plastic cup left on the convenience store counter—and pocketed it for himself. His colleague behind the counter, she said, had not appeared to protest the move at all. "It's like they have it down to a science," she said. "It's happened before."

We had seen no point in staying away from the office if the two men were not going to meet again on this day. Tyler's question about

Richard as a friend would be answered, in my opinion, only by compiling relevant facts based on the interaction between the two young men. One encounter lasting less than a minute was not enough, I thought, to consider the question answered.

Ms. Washburn seemed to disagree.

"We saw the way Richard joked about Tyler to his buddy behind the counter," she said now. "We saw how Richard basically dismissed Tyler from the store, and we saw why Richard might want Tyler to think he's a friend, because Tyler hands out incredible tips that he can't possibly understand are inappropriate. Richard's playing Tyler, clear as day."

I don't like to disagree with Ms. Washburn, but when considering a question I am not moved by emotion; my work has to be based strictly on that which I can prove. So I attempted to make that point.

"The set of circumstances we saw can easily be interpreted in numerous other ways," I said. "Perhaps Richard was under pressure to keep the line moving. He said something funny which Tyler, because of his neurological difference, either did not understand or simply did not find amusing. He left the oversized tip in the jar because he has a limited grasp of the value of money or because he did not pay attention to the size of the bill he was using. That too is a possible scenario."

"There's nothing in what you said that indicates Richard is Tyler's friend," Ms. Washburn said. She was typing away at her keyboard, a little more forcefully than usual, I thought.

"That is true. It is also true that there is nothing in what we observed that proves he is not."

Ms. Washburn stopped attacking her keyboard and looked at me. Her expression was not one I could readily interpret. "Do you realize you're acting differently with this client than you have with any other I've seen?" she asked.

That was surprising. "I am not aware that I am doing anything of the sort, but I trust your judgment," I told her. "In what way?"

"You condescend to him," she said slowly, considering. "Every observation you make about Tyler is about his difference. It's about how he must not understand money, and he can't possibly have gotten someone's joke. You keep assuming he's not as smart or as complete a person as our other clients, and I think it's because he has a spectrum disorder."

I took a moment to consider. "According to societal convention, I have a spectrum disorder," I reminded her.

"Exactly. So you're tougher on him than you would be on someone who doesn't."

"I think you are mistaken," I said.

Ms. Washburn shrugged. "So if we need verifiable evidence, something absolutely objective, how do we get that?"

"An excellent question."

"I try."

I pondered the problem at hand, which was how to verify specifically Richard's feelings toward Tyler. "This is not my area," I said to Ms. Washburn.

She tilted her head to one side, indicating that she was being what Mother would call "coquettish," but usually meant sarcastic. "So you should rely more heavily on my advice," she said, "don't you think?"

"What is your advice?" I asked. "Remind me."

"Let me go talk to Richard. I can figure out if he's leading Tyler to think he's a friend so he can keep getting more ridiculously large tips." She stood up. "I can go right now."

"That is precisely the reason you should not go," I told Ms. Washburn. "Please sit down."

Oddly, she looked hurt. "I don't feel like sitting down," she said. She thought a moment. "Shouldn't you be exercising, Samuel?"

Ms. Washburn was correct; I was behind in my schedule. Every twenty minutes during the working day I walk the perimeter of the

Questions Answered office thirteen times with my arms raised over my head to elevate my heart rate. I was now three minutes behind schedule. I stood and began my routine, but kept an eye on Ms. Washburn in case this was a diversion meant to distract me while she left to talk to Richard Handy.

She did not attempt to leave, but she asked, "*What* is precisely the reason I shouldn't go?"

My voice came a little less easily as I made sure to walk at an accelerated pace. "You have already made up your mind about the question. On the basis of information that is not conclusive, you have decided that Richard is indeed not Tyler's friend. So your questioning would be biased in that direction and therefore any information you gathered would not be completely reliable."

Ms. Washburn considered that, which was admirable on her part. Other people might have become defensive, denying what was obvious because their egos would have been bruised. She put a hand to her chin and stood silently for half a lap around the office.

"I think I could be objective, but I see your point," she said finally. "So what's your solution?"

"Clearly, the only alternative"—I took a deep breath on my third cycle around the office—"is that I should be the one to talk to Richard."

"Aren't you the one who said that asking him if he was Tyler's friend would simply encourage him to lie and the information we got would be useless?" Ms. Washburn said.

"Yes. That is exactly why I will not ask him that question." Then I did not talk for four minutes and twenty-eight seconds as my breath was coming with more effort. Ms. Washburn's eyes fluttered a bit, and she sat at her desk and typed on her computer keyboard.

I believe, however, that I did hear her say something like, "I wish I'd have thought of that." I am not certain whether it was meant to be taken sincerely.

"Remember that Richard has never seen you before," Ms. Washburn said. "So he has no idea you've ever met Tyler Clayton."

We were sitting in her car the next morning, at a closer vantage point to the Quik N EZ store in Somerset than the previous day, because this time we did not have to worry about Tyler appearing and in some way spoiling the mission at hand. His ritual was to come to the convenience store at eleven a.m., and it was now only eight thirty.

"I am aware of those facts," I assured her. "I will make no reference to having been hired by Tyler to answer the question. It would make the interview worthless as a fact-gathering device."

"And it would embarrass poor Tyler to the point of apoplexy," Ms. Washburn suggested.

"He will not be there," I reminded her. "There would be no reason for him to be in any way affected."

Ms. Washburn closed her eyes for a brief moment. "Do you want to rehearse what you're going to say?" she asked when she opened them again.

The question took me back to days in middle school, before my "diagnosis," when Mother did not have a strong sense of what made me different from the other children. She would make me practice, with her playing the role of a classmate, anytime I felt I would like to invite someone to our house to play chess or discuss specific models of fighter jets from the Second World War. The rehearsal rarely helped the cause.

"I don't think that will be necessary," I said now. "I believe I can talk to a young man in a convenience store without having to follow a script." Inwardly, however, I felt that a prepared outline would not have been a bad idea. The problem in doing so for conversations with other people is that they very rarely respond in the way you have prepared ahead of time. It is better not to anticipate an answer if you want to get an honest and useful conversation from the encounter.

Ms. Washburn bit her lip. "Okay then," she said. I did not ask her when it would be okay because I was fairly certain she was not referring to a particular time. "Remember, I'll be watching with the telephoto. If you want me to hear what's going on, just turn on your cell phone and keep it away from Richard's view. I won't say anything and blow your cover."

That was an expression with which I was familiar, so I nodded. "I will be back soon," I said.

"You'd better be."

I got out of the car and closed the door behind me, wondering why Ms. Washburn had said that. I saw no danger in talking to Richard Handy at a convenience store. There was no reason to think I would not be returning to the car in just a few minutes. I decided that Ms. Washburn was attempting to be witty, which is always something of a problem for me to recognize. I did not turn back to ask her to elaborate. The task at hand was more urgent.

Entering the Quik N EZ, I headed directly to the rear of the store, where there were large refrigerated units from which one could extract cold drinks for purchase. Ms. Washburn and I had decided that simply questioning Richard in the store would be suspicious and inconvenient, but buying something would make the conversation seem more natural and would, after all, reward the business for the time I would be monopolizing one of its employees.

I removed a bottle of the spring water I usually buy from the vending machine at the Questions Answered office. I considered getting a diet soda for Ms. Washburn but rejected that notion because the questioning of Richard Handy might take a few minutes, after which the drink might not be at its peak temperature. Ms.

Washburn has told me warm sodas are "a lot like drinking carbonated chemicals," a situation anyone would prefer to avoid.

There was not much business being done in the store at this hour, after most early-morning customers were at work and before the influx of those wanting to buy items during their lunch hour. This was a suburban area, but there were many businesses employing people nearby and surely the Quik N EZ relied on them for the bulk of its sales. So there was only one person ahead of me in line to purchase an item.

But Richard Handy, currently processing the purchase of a lottery ticket at the far right end of the counter, was not the only employee currently working at the store. Another young man, perhaps a student, was standing directly in front of me when I approached and waited for Richard to conclude his business.

"I can take you, sir," the other young man said to me.

"I would prefer to wait," I said.

He squinted at me as if I were very far away and difficult to see. "Huh?"

"I would prefer to wait until your colleague can serve me," I told him. I wondered if that was in some way insulting to the employee who was offering to sell me the bottle of water. "It's not personal," I added.

"You sure? I can ring you up right now." The young man didn't seem insulted, as far as I could tell. He was exuding puzzlement more than anything else.

"I am certain, but thank you for your offer."

There was no one behind me in line, so the employee who was not Richard Handy and I looked at each other as Richard completed the lottery ticket sale, which was quite complicated. The New Jersey Lottery has any number of games available and is affiliated with a number of national lotteries as well, so purchasing a ticket can be quite a complex affair.

The woman buying the ticket finally appeared satisfied with her selection and walked away with her purchase. Then Richard walked back to his spot at the center of the counter. He looked at his colleague, then at me, then back at his colleague. The other young man shrugged.

"He wanted to wait for you," he said.

Richard, up close, was not a very impressive man. He was of average height with flat hair that hung a little over his ears and thin lips that made it difficult to read his expression. "Can I help you?" he asked with what I perceived as a tinge of concern in his voice.

"I believe you can," I said. "I'd like to buy this bottle of spring water." I stepped to the counter and placed the bottle down so I would not have to hand it directly to Richard.

"Okay," he said. He sounded like he was expecting me to say more, and it occurred to me he was wondering why I had made it a point of having him sell me the drink. I did not know how to address that issue, so I did not comment on it.

Instead, I waited until he had scanned the UPC code on the bottle. "I understand you are a friend of Tyler Clayton," I said.

"That's a dollar seventy-five," Richard said. Then he looked up at me. "What?"

But I was distracted. The vending machine at Questions Answered charged only one dollar and twenty-five cents for the same size bottle of the same brand of spring water. And when Les, the man who services the machine, comes once a week to collect the money and restock, he gives me back fifty cents on every bottle, meaning that even while earning a profit, the company selling the water really charges only seventy-five cents. The markup at Quik N EZ was clearly quite inflated.

"How much is that?" I asked. Perhaps I had misheard the amount.

"A dollar seventy-five. Who am I supposed to be friends with?" Richard's eyes were not amused, as they had been when confronted with a customer who wanted to talk only to him.

"That is a very high price," I told him.

"So don't buy the water. I get paid the same whether you do or not. What's going on with you?"

The price of the water, I realized now, was irrelevant. I could deduct it as a business expense. I reached for my wallet and took out my debit card. He noticed that without comment. But I did not hand it to him. "Are you a friend of Tyler Clayton?" I asked again.

"What are you, a cop?" Richard asked.

"I am certainly not a police officer. I am not a private detective, and I do not hold any authority in any security force anywhere in the world." Perhaps that last phrase was an example of overstating the point.

Richard's eyes narrowed. "Then why should I talk to you?" he asked.

It was a good question and one that I had not considered to this point. "Because I am no threat to you or to Tyler and because I have asked you an honest question that deserves an answer. Are you a friend of Tyler Clayton?"

Richard's expression indicated he was considering his options. At least, that was the impression I took from it; reading faces is not my strong suit. He seemed to bite on the insides of his lips for a moment, then looked at me.

"Who's Tyler Clayton?" he asked.

I felt the cellular phone in my pocket vibrate. No doubt Ms. Washburn had sent a text. I did not pull it out to look at it.

"He is a young man about your age," I said. "He comes into this store every day at approximately eleven a.m. to purchase a soda. He talks to you every day and at least once you have gone to his house to play the video games Assassin's Creed and Elder Scrolls, and although he does not play in your group, he is a fellow participant in the role playing game Swords and Sorcerers. That is Tyler Clayton."

"Dude, you play S and S?" The other employee, obviously listening to our conversation while scanning a customer's purchase, laughed derisively.

Tyler's face hardened. "I don't know what you're talking about," he told me. "I've never heard of a Tyler somebody and I don't play those games. So just give me the buck seventy-five or I'll put the water back, okay?"

I could not think of a response. At the same time, a woman carrying a large package of toilet tissue took a position behind me. My time with Richard was concluded.

The debit card purchase would take too long, so reluctantly I pulled two one-dollar bills from my wallet and placed them on the counter. Then I picked up the bottle of water and walked out of the Quik N EZ.

I felt my hands flapping slightly and controlled the impulse by putting my left hand to my face, thumb and middle finger on my temples, stopping on the street, and taking a breath. Then I reached into my pocket to read the text from Ms. Washburn.

It read, You're doing fine. I did not agree with the sentiment.

I had gone into the convenience store with a clear mission and come out with inconclusive evidence. Richard Handy had claimed never to have heard of Tyler Clayton, who had given him a $100 tip the day before. It seemed impossible and worse, I had perhaps given Richard too much information about Tyler, which meant my client might be in for rude treatment or humiliation when he arrived at the store in a little over two hours.

I looked to the car, angry with myself for my poor performance, and saw Ms. Washburn looking at me. Her expression was somewhat urgent, as if there were something she wanted to tell me. I took a step toward the car, but then she pointed to a spot behind me and to my right. I looked in that direction.

The door to the Quik N EZ was open and Richard Handy was outside, walking toward me with his hand raised as if hailing a cab. "Sir," he said, loudly enough to be heard from my position some twenty feet away, "you forgot your change." Approaching me quickly, he held out a quarter.

"That is not necessary," I said when he was within earshot. "Keep it for your trouble."

Richard got closer, then closer still. I have been told that I have an inflated sense of personal space and do not care to have someone be near me, particularly if I do not know that person well. I must have recoiled a bit, although I was not aware of doing so. But Richard said, "Look, I just want to tell you something."

"What is it you need to say?" I asked, trying not to lean too far away from him.

Richard spoke confidentially, almost in a whisper. "I didn't want to admit it in front of Grant, you know?" he said. I assumed he was referring to his colleague at the convenience store counter. "Of course I know Tyler Clayton."

I tried to process that information. "Then you were lying when I asked," I said. It was not an accusation, but an attempt at clarification.

"Yeah," Richard said. "I know the guy. He comes in every day. But he's weird, you know? He buys a soda and he stares at me. Is he gay or something?"

I had no idea what Tyler's sexual identity might be, so I offered no speculation. "He has some personality traits that would make people say he has an autism spectrum disorder," I said. I stumbled a bit on the word *disorder* but it was the best way to express the thought to Richard.

"Why did you come in to ask if I knew him?" Richard asked. His voice, even at a low volume, betrayed some anxiety.

"I did not ask if you knew him," I corrected. "I was aware that he came to this store every day. I asked if you were a friend of his." That was, after all, the reason for my visit to the Somerset Quik N EZ. I did not mention to Richard the appalling spelling his store's name expressed, since I doubted that was his responsibility.

"Why?" Richard had avoided answering the question.

I did not wish to disclose my role in the question. For one thing, I have always maintained anonymity for my clients when discussing a question with anyone but the client or the police. For another, I believed it would be best for Tyler if it were not known he had paid me to answer this question for him.

"Because I have met Tyler and have an interest in knowing if he has friends," I said. That was a very general response, but it might sound to Richard like I had said something valuable.

"Are you jealous?" he asked.

That was confusing. Why would I be jealous? And of whom? Did Richard want me to be jealous? "I don't understand the question," I said.

"Are you, like, in love with this guy and you don't want him to have any friends?" Richard said.

Now I was lost in unfamiliar territory and was coming up short of acceptable responses. "That is definitely not the situation," I said. "I am merely concerned about Tyler's ability to find friends and am trying to verify what he told me, that you were a good friend of his." All of that was true, and I had managed to avoid mentioning I was being paid for my efforts.

Ms. Washburn, who could still hear the conversation through the cellular telephone in my pocket, raised a thumb toward me, telling me I had handled the situation well. She must have known it was awkward for me.

"A good friend?" Richard's face contorted into an expression of something that, if I were reading it correctly, was disgust. "No way,

41

man. Look. I went over to the guy's house once to play some games I didn't have the money to buy myself. Then he starts coming into the store every day and mooning at me like I'm his lost puppy or something. I feel sorry for the big dweeb and this is what I get for it, him sending some truant officer to ask if I'm his friend."

"I am not a truant officer," I said. That was the only thing I could demonstrably refute in the tirade Richard had launched, particularly since I was not familiar with the word *dweeb*. It did not sound like a complimentary term the way Richard said it. This conversation was going in a disappointing direction.

The other counter worker from the Quik N EZ opened the store door and extended his head through it. "Come on, Rich," he said. "I can't cover for you forever."

Richard looked back at him, nodded, and then turned back toward me. "Don't come around here anymore. Okay, man? I don't have anything to tell you and I don't know what your deal is, so just go harass somebody else about the ADHD kid. Okay?"

As he turned to walk back to the store, I felt I had one last chance to clarify the issue and report an answer to my client. "So you are saying you're *not* a friend of Tyler Clayton?" I asked.

This time when Richard turned to face me, his attitude bordered on pity. "*No*," he said. Then he turned back and walked into the convenience store.

Even though I knew he was not within the sound of my voice, I found myself asking aloud, "Does that mean you are not Tyler's friend, or that it wasn't what you were saying?"

FIVE

MY MOTHER SAT IN the reclining chair in the Questions Answered office with her feet raised, sipping on a cup of hot tea I had purchased for her at the small grocery, A Quick Bite, three doors down from our office in the strip mall on Stelton Road. Mother likes to breathe in the steam from the tea, then drink it slowly. She says tea should not be drunk quickly, as that practice would somehow insult the beverage and negate its positive (Mother would say healing) properties.

I believe tea is a drink, one of which I am not fond, and that at best it might help to relax the sinuses. But I also believe Mother is entitled to her beliefs about the liquids she pours into her body.

"I think you're splitting hairs," she said now, after closing her eyes for a moment and thinking about the information I'd just given her. "That means—"

"I know what it means," I said.

Mother nodded. "You asked the boy whether he is a friend of Tyler's, and he said no. You have the answer to Tyler's question. It's not the one he wanted, but it is the correct answer. Why don't you want to give it to him? I've never seen you acting sentimental before." She smiled a tiny bit, and I recognized the look. She thought I was making some sort of breakthrough with my Asperger's Syndrome, and was both hopeful and proud at the same moment. It was going to be difficult to dash her hopes, but she was mistaken.

"I am not being sentimental," I said. "It's not a question of empathy for Tyler. I do understand what it is like to be without age-appropriate friends, and you know that. But this is not about that, and Tyler is not me. This is simply a situation in which I am not certain of the answer and am reluctant to present my client with incomplete data."

Mother looked over at Ms. Washburn's desk. After we'd returned from the Quik N EZ, Ms. Washburn had spent six hours working on research for two other questions our office was answering. She had heard every word of my exchange with Richard Handy, had expressed much the same opinion as Mother was now stating, and after hearing my explanation, had chosen not to discus Tyler's question for the rest of the day. I believe this is called "passive aggression."

"What else do you need to know?" Mother said. She closed her eyes and took another sip of tea, then sighed a bit after she swallowed. "You can't possibly be confused by Richard's answer to your last question. Janet was recording it on her phone and played it for me while you were exercising. He was very clear. He doesn't consider Tyler a friend."

I had spent some time on the telephone—something I do not like to do—with Tyler Clayton's sister, Sandy Clayton Webb, after we had returned to the office. I did not tell her I had obtained a successful answer, but I did get Sandy's perspective on how her brother might react to news that was not what he was hoping to hear.

"Does that mean he's going to hear bad news?" she asked.

"I don't know yet. I do not have enough facts to definitively answer the question." In my mind, that was certainly true. Mother and

Ms. Washburn were questioning my reasoning, but it was, finally, *my* reasoning that Tyler had sought out.

"Well, nobody's happy to find out that someone they consider a friend really isn't," Sandy said after a pause. "But Tyler's a special case, as I'm sure you realize."

In my opinion everyone is a special case, since no two people are exactly alike. What Sandy meant was that Tyler's behavior places him on the autism spectrum, and she was implying that meant he required special treatment. It has long been my contention that the world needs to accept more than modify the behavior of those like myself, but this was not the time to get into a philosophical argument with Sandy while I decided on a course of action.

"I understand that Tyler has a diagnosis on the autism spectrum," I said. "Does his behavior include anger difficulties or depression?"

"Not depression," Sandy said. "Thank goodness we haven't had to deal with that. But he has had anger issues, especially when he was at school. He threw chairs a few times. He never hurt anyone, if that's what you're asking."

"I assure you, I am never asking anything other than what I am asking." That seemed an odd sentence as I heard it out loud, but Sandy did not seem to have an issue with it.

"That's comforting," she said.

"When Tyler was here, he mentioned your brother Mason," I said. It was an avenue I'd wanted to explore since I'd met Sandy the first time, but this was my opportunity to do so without Tyler present. "Does Tyler live with him?"

"Yes," Sandy said. "Mason is not married and doesn't have kids. I was married at the time our mother died, and our father had left many years before. Someone had to take Tyler, and then it couldn't be me, so he went to live with Mason."

"Perhaps I should discuss this matter with him, then," I suggested.

"I wish you wouldn't." Initially I believed that Sandy was asking me to grant her a wish as one would a genie in a fantasy story. Then I realized it was an expression she was using, a way to ask me to avoid talking to Mason Clayton. "Tyler didn't tell Mason he was coming to see you because he thought Mason would tell him not to do it. That's why I dropped him off and picked him up at your office. Tyler spends a lot of his days here, especially when he's working because his job is nearby. Mason works during the day for a company that power washes houses, so we waited for a day when it wasn't raining."

That was perhaps more detail than I had been expecting, so it took me a moment to process all the information. "Is Mason stern or authoritative with Tyler?"

"Do you mean is Tyler afraid of Mason?" Sandy asked. She was astute; that would have been my next question. "I wouldn't use the word *afraid*, really. Tyler wants Mason to approve of everything he does; in a way, I think he wants to be Mason when he grows up."

"Tyler is an adult," I pointed out.

"Physically, yes. But emotionally? He's probably about fifteen years old."

Again, I saw no benefit in explaining to Sandy that the measurements of one's emotional age are devised by and based upon people whose behavior does not place them on the autism spectrum and so therefore are invalid for those of us with Asperger's Syndrome or another form of difference. It would not help answer Tyler's question. The best thing to do, then, was to thank Sandy for her time. I did not request Mason Clayton's phone number or contact information since Sandy seemed reluctant to share them. It would be easy enough for Ms. Washburn to find them tomorrow.

Now I was trying to explain and defend my position in a conversation with my mother. And she had just suggested that Richard Handy had told me in no uncertain terms that he did not consider himself Tyler Clayton's friend.

"The terms were anything but certain," I reminded her. "Richard left it open to my interpretation as to whether he was answering my question, or stating whether he was answering my question."

"I don't think you believe that," Mother reasserted. "I think you just don't want to disappoint the young man who hired you."

I stood up. "I have completed my work for the day," I said. "Shall we go home now?"

But Mother did not extricate herself from the recliner. "What's this really about, Samuel?" she asked.

"I don't understand. This is, as always, about finding an accurate and correct answer to the client's question. Tyler asked whether Richard Handy is his friend."

"And you know that he's not. So why are you delaying the inevitable? Is it that you see too much of yourself in Tyler and you know how much the answer will hurt?"

I shook my head as much in wonder as to communicate a negative answer. "I do not believe myself to be at all similar to Tyler Clayton," I said. "In the neurotypical terminology, his symptoms are not at all like mine. He is less verbal. He is not able to maintain a business as I do. He does not think in logical terms and so his decisions are often driven by projection and emotion rather than by facts."

Mother looked into my eyes for a moment, then stood up slowly, her knees being somewhat stiffened by arthritis. I do sometimes worry about her health; she had a heart issue some years ago.

"Samuel," she said quietly as she began walking slowly to the door, "the Beatles song. The one with all the *yeah-yeah-yeah*s in it."

We reached the door and I opened it for her. I have learned that one opens the door for a lady, particularly for one's mother. I knew she was not simply asking me a random question about the Beatles, but I did not yet understand her point in bringing up the song. "'She Loves You,'" I said, although I was certain Mother knew which song was in question.

"Yes, that one. How would you interpret the lyrics?"

We walked out into the evening and the cooler air was refreshing, but I was paying attention to what I was sure was a ploy by my mother to reiterate her point. "The lyrics are quite straightforward," I said. "It concerns the singer telling a man that a woman he has previously treated badly still loves him."

"But the third party is doing the singing," Mother said. "Right? It's not called 'I Love You.'"

"That's correct, Mother, and you're well aware of it. What is your point?" I opened the car door for her and she got in on the driver's side.

"Do you think the person singing is doing the right thing?" she asked.

I closed her door and walked around to the passenger side as Mother started the car. I got in and sat in the passenger seat. "The right thing?" I asked.

"Yes. Do you think in that case, with a woman who loves a man sending that message through a third party, should the third party have kept the information away from him?"

It had never occurred to me before that such a simple lyric might have contained a moral dilemma. "The decision has been made before the song begins, and we are given very little in the way of detail about the relationship in question," I said. "It is an early song and not one of the more sophisticated lyrics."

"Still." Mother put the transmission into reverse and backed out of the parking space. She changed gears to drive and maneuvered the car toward the parking lot exit. "It's clear the woman in the song asked this other person to deliver a message, and he is doing it. Should he have refused to do so?"

"I don't see why. The woman in the song asked for the message to be delivered."

"And is the man being told *she loves you* better off for the knowledge?" Mother asked. Now her tactic was becoming more transparent.

"It is impossible to say without more information," I said, trying to counter Mother's trap before she could spring it. "It is possible the relationship in question is not a healthy one, or that the recipient of the information might find it uncomfortable."

Mother kept her eyes straight on the road, which is the sensible thing to do while driving. She knows I get very nervous when I ride in a car with someone who does not concentrate on safety behind the wheel.

"So it's better to be kept ignorant of another person's feelings rather than have the opportunity to act on them?" she asked.

I did not see the appeal of continuing this hypothetical. "Mother, we are discussing a song written more than fifty years ago about fictional people. While the situation seems relevant to Tyler Clayton's question on its surface, it is not. Richard Handy did not ask me to tell Tyler he is not a friend."

Mother waited until completing a right turn before answering. "I think he did, but you didn't necessarily understand what he was asking," she said. "You wanted to think Richard was being vague, but he wasn't. You asked if he was a friend of Tyler's and he said no. You know that's true and, having listened to the recording, I know it's true. Why are you hesitating to give Tyler the answer to his question?"

I did not want to readdress my concerns about Richard's statement. I sometimes have difficulty seeing another person's perspective, so I decided to consider Mother's point of view. Her guidance has been extremely valuable in the past.

The same is true of Ms. Washburn, whose interpretation of the events at Quik N EZ were similar to Mother's. I could not dismiss them out of hand.

"I am ashamed of myself for asking the question," I said finally. "I had specifically set out to avoid making it clear to Richard what I'd been sent to find out. I thought he might be cruel to Tyler when Tyler arrived at the convenience store after I left. I felt like I had let my client down. But Tyler's sister Sandy said she has spoken with Tyler after his daily pilgrimage to the store and he had not reported any traumatic event."

"So you know that Richard Handy is not Tyler Clayton's friend," Mother said softly.

"I believe that to be the case, but I am not certain. It seems fairly obvious that Richard was using Tyler for video games and probably for the rather extravagant tips Tyler must leave every day when he appears."

"Why didn't you ask Richard about the money?" Mother asked.

I had wondered about that myself. With a half-day's worth of introspection, I could answer honestly, "I'm not sure. I think it might be because I did not know how to broach the subject without making it sound like Tyler was paying Richard to be his friend."

"How things sound isn't usually a concern of yours."

I nodded. "I know. It is very odd."

"This question has gotten to you personally," Mother said. "I think the best thing to do is go to Tyler tomorrow and answer it. Put the experience behind you and let everyone move on with the next part of their lives."

Other than blinking I never close my eyes in a car, but I did find myself wanting to lean back and rest for a moment. This question had indeed been different than others I'd answered before, although I disagreed with the reasoning Ms. Washburn and my mother were attributing to that difference. I did not see Tyler Clayton as a younger version of myself; indeed, there was little resemblance at all. But his difficulty with social situations and his obvious need for assistance in that area had awakened a side of myself with which I was not entirely familiar. I am not by nature a person who dedicates himself to the needs of others. I answer questions I find interesting and I do so because I am in need of an income and it suits my talents well.

Tyler Clayton's question had been a simple one to answer, but when I considered it objectively, I found myself reluctantly agreeing with Mother and Ms. Washburn—I probably was needlessly extending the process. There was no tangible evidence that Richard Handy was indeed Tyler's friend, yet I had not informed Tyler I had arrived at an answer to his question. That was unlike my usual procedure.

I must have sighed audibly because Mother asked if I was all right. I assured her that I was, because there was nothing noticeably wrong with me physically.

"I believe I will schedule a meeting with Tyler tomorrow," I said. "It's time to answer his question and collect my fee."

"I wouldn't put it exactly like that when you talk to him," Mother advised.

"Don't worry." I sat back in my seat. Mother was steering the car into our driveway.

Once she stopped it and put the transmission into the park mode, Mother looked at me with a sly expression on her face, one I'd seen before but did not consider one of her more recognizable looks. "Was it the Beatles that got you?" she asked.

I couldn't resist. "Yeah, yeah, yeah," I said.

SIX

———

Ms. Washburn arranged the meeting with Tyler Clayton to take place at the Questions Answered office at ten the next morning. Tyler was anxious to hear the answer, she said when she disconnected the call, and wanted to come by as soon as possible. We had not considered traveling to his home because his brother was not aware of our involvement in the question and apparently Tyler preferred that arrangement.

"Are you nervous?" Ms. Washburn asked me.

Why would I be nervous? "I am concluding a business arrangement," I told her. "Tyler contracted with us to answer a question. We are doing so. We never promise to deliver the answer the client hopes to receive."

She nodded but her expression did not signify agreement. Ms. Washburn understands my Asperger's Syndrome better than most people but still does not completely grasp my thought process. In this case, she clearly believed I was being insincere or deluding myself. Neither was true, but Ms. Washburn was merely mistaken.

Tyler arrived with Sandy at ten precisely. It is not unusual in those who present on the autism spectrum to be almost compulsive about time, so I expected nothing else. Tyler's head was vibrating periodically as if he was trying desperately to quell a strong emotion—perhaps anger or fear—trying to dominate his mind.

Sandy also looked tense, but her gaze was almost exclusively trained on her brother.

"What news do you have for us, Mr. Hoenig?" Sandy asked. Tyler appeared to be too overwhelmed to speak first.

Ms. Washburn stepped forward from behind her desk. "We believe we have an answer to your question," she said. "But keep in mind that in this case, the answer can't be definitive because it's not possible to accurately measure how a person feels."

While I appreciated her attempt both to buffer Tyler's feelings and to shield me from having to deliver what he would consider to be bad news, I felt it was necessary to clarify what Ms. Washburn had said.

I was already standing in front of my desk. Sandy sat in the client chair, a small upholstered seat we had placed in front of my desk. The recliner that is Mother's chair was empty, as Tyler was pacing the floor by our desks. So when I spoke, all three of them turned to face me.

"The answer is an accurate one," I said. "Ms. Washburn is correct in saying there is no way to quantify emotion, but it is possible to determine how a person behaves and interpret that accurately. We believe we have done so regarding this question."

Sandy seemed to be choosing between what Ms. Washburn had said and what I said. "I'm sorry, but I don't understand," she said, addressing her comment to neither of us specifically. "Do you have an answer or not?"

"We do," I said. "I was merely trying to indicate how that answer was reached so you can see the validity of the process and—"

"Is Richard my friend or not?" Tyler said, the words coming out of him quickly.

I regarded him carefully. "No," I said. "He is not."

Sandy appeared to deflate. "I was afraid of this," she said, leaning back in her chair. Her expression was either one of sadness or puzzlement; I could not tell. I would ask Ms. Washburn for her opinion after the meeting had ended.

But Tyler's face was not at all difficult to decipher. He was angry.

"You're *wrong*!" he shouted. "You didn't get the right answer! I'm not going to pay you!" He turned and walked very quickly to the office door. He opened it and went outside, presumably back to Sandy's car.

She watched him, then stood up and nodded at Ms. Washburn. "Don't worry," she said, "you'll get the fee."

"That's not really what we're most concerned about," Ms. Washburn told her, although I was certainly wondering if we would be properly paid. "Will Tyler be all right?"

Sandy looked at her strangely as if Ms. Washburn had asked a question that had no answer. "I have absolutely no idea," she said and walked outside after her brother.

Ms. Washburn stood still for a long moment looking at the spot where Sandy had been standing. Having discharged our business, I felt it was time to move on and walked to my desk, where I sat down to work on a question regarding the physical properties of flames by beginning some Internet research.

After shaking her head a few times as if she'd been dazed, Ms. Washburn took her hands off her hips and walked back to her desk. "I'm sorry that didn't go better," she said as she sat down.

I looked over at her. "It went as well as it could have been expected to," I said. "We had a volatile client and the correct answer to his question was the opposite of what he had hoped to hear. It was probably foolish of him to ask it. He should have known the probability was at least fifty percent that he would get a negative result."

"Everybody's not a science experiment, Samuel," Ms. Washburn said. "Emotion isn't something that has no value. Tyler made himself vulnerable to another person, which is something that is clearly very difficult for him to do, and he was rejected. That must be devastating. I hope that the damage isn't so bad he never tries with another person again."

I had not calculated the possible effect the answer to his question might have on Tyler. Frankly, that is not my job when considering a question. Each client is told at the beginning that the outcome is not predictable and the news received at the end of the process might not be what he or she desires. I had made sure to include such language in the Questions Answered contract, a document we require each client to sign before we begin considering a question.

"It would be an extreme reaction if he never tried to make another friend," I pointed out. "If a person can't play the violin the first time he or she attempts to do so, they most often do not avoid making a second try."

Ms. Washburn looked over at me and shook her head. "I think I'm going to take an early lunch," she said. She picked up her purse and walked out of the office.

I looked at the time displayed in the upper right hand corner of my MacPro. It read, "10:24 a.m." That was indeed an early lunch. I wondered if Ms. Washburn's impending divorce was having some unusual effect on her appetite.

Having allowed more than twenty minutes to pass, I stood up to power walk the circumference of the office. Exercise was an important part of my day.

Ms. Washburn returned from her lunch at 11:38 a.m., more than an hour after she had left. We do not own a time clock at Questions Answered, and as her employer I have never considered giving Ms. Washburn less than her full salary per week, but this was an interesting development. She had never been late returning from lunch before. I was in fact a trifle concerned about her absence, since I have lunch with Mother at our house each day at 12:30 p.m. If Ms. Washburn had been much later, she might not have had time to drive me to the house.

"Did you have a pleasant lunch?" I asked when she had settled in at her desk. I have been instructed to ask such questions despite the fact that I knew if something of interest had occurred during Ms. Washburn's break, she would surely tell me about it.

"It was fine," she said in a clipped tone.

I looked in her direction. "Is something wrong, Ms. Washburn?"

She started to reply, seemed to catch herself, and sighed a bit. "No, Samuel, nothing's wrong. I disagreed with some of your diatribe about Tyler before, but I realize that's your way of looking at the world. I just wish you could learn a little more empathy."

Learn empathy? I did not know if such a thing was possible. "How should I have been empathetic?" I asked. Perhaps that was one way a person could learn about such things.

"Of all people, you should know what it's like to be different and hope you have a friend," she replied. "Tyler is hurting right now because we had to tell him the one friend he thought he had was something else entirely. Instead of thinking about how it impacts *us*, consider what it's like to be Tyler at this moment."

I believed that I had already done what she suggested. "Should I not have told him the truth?" I asked Ms. Washburn. "Should I have lied to him as Richard Handy has and let him perpetuate the situation?"

"No. You should have felt the pain that boy felt and tried to assure him that not everyone is like Richard Handy."

I would have responded to that, although I do not know what I would have said, but the telephone on my desk rang. The one situated on Ms. Washburn's desk rang as well, and even after she gave me a quick glance, assuredly to remind me that I can answer the phone too, she picked up the receiver.

"Questions Answered," she said.

I had thought, when I started the business, that the most appropriate way to respond to a phone call would be to say, "Hello." That was how I was taught to answer a telephone. Then I would add, "This is Questions Answered. We will answer any question you might have if we find it interesting. There is a fee schedule. You may leave a message when I finish speaking, or e-mail us at (our e-mail address). Please do not call back." If a person wasn't going to leave a message now it was likely a second call would be equally unproductive.

But I discovered over the first few weeks that merely saying hello led many callers to believe they had reached a personal telephone. There would be a long moment of confusion followed by the inevitable voice asking, "Is this Questions Answered?" I would explain that it was and the potential client and I would have wasted five seconds coming to the point of our business.

That was when Mother suggested that businesses often answer the phone with the name of the business followed by the phrase, "May I help you?" (Actually, most employees of businesses I have called ask, "Can I help you?", which is an unanswerable question. If I am calling your business for the first time I have no way to measure your competence, and therefore cannot determine if you are capable of performing the task I need completed.) I merely say the name of the service and let the client assume we are here to help.

Ms. Washburn listened for a moment and then said, "No, he is here, but—" Then her face lost much of its color and her eyes widened. She took a short involuntary breath and blinked. I was immediately concerned about her health, since she looked much like Mother did when she had a cardiac issue four years ago.

"Are you all right?" I asked.

"Hold on," Ms. Washburn said into the phone when she regained her breath. "I'm going to get Mr. Hoenig." She pushed the hold button on the phone and turned toward me.

"Ms. Washburn," I began, but she held up her right hand to stop me.

"It's the Somerset police," Ms. Washburn said, gesturing toward the phone. "They have Tyler Clayton in custody. He's been arrested."

That confused me. Tyler Clayton had been in my office less than three hours earlier, and while he did have social issues, he hardly seemed ready to run afoul of the police. He did not own a driver's license and therefore would not have been caught in a serious situation with a car. The worst that could have happened would have been a raucous argument and perhaps an embarrassing public scene.

"On what charge?" I asked.

Ms. Washburn hesitated a moment as if wondering how to phrase her response. "They say he shot and killed Richard Handy," she said.

SEVEN

THE CRIME SCENE WAS cordoned off and Det. Milton Hessler was being very clear in his opposition to Ms. Washburn and I entering it, which made me wonder why he had asked us to come here. "You're civilians," he said. "You stay out until the yellow tape comes down."

Detective Hessler had called Questions Answered after he arrested Tyler Clayton because he had spoken to Tyler's sister, Sandy, who had informed him that her brother had been utilizing our services. I had tried to call Sandy but had gotten a voice mail message; no doubt she was dealing with Tyler's arrest and could not respond. Being thorough, Hessler had followed up on every possible angle to the crime, which he described as "as open-and-shut a case as I've ever seen."

That struck me as odd, but as Hessler explained, Tyler had apparently not been very careful about his escape after entering the Quik N EZ and shooting Richard Handy four times with a 9mm handgun. Richard had died instantly, as the gun had been fired at close range and none of the shots had missed him. One had passed through him and shattered the glass on a refrigerated case of dairy products, Hessler said. Milk and blood mixed on the floor.

"We have no interest in seeing the crime scene," I informed Hessler as we stood in a light drizzle outside the convenience store. Ms. Washburn looked surprised but I could not understand why she would find my statement at all unexpected. "We are not answering a question involving the death of Richard Handy. We came here because you asked us to come, presumably because you want to know about Tyler's business with Questions Answered."

"I'm not sure we're going to be able to help you there," Ms. Washburn said, her voice strong and steady. It had been a difficult drive for her, I could tell. She had barely spoken since she got off the phone with Hessler and told me we were to go to the convenience store. She had moved her hands on the steering wheel more often than usual and had bitten her lower lip almost to the point of bleeding. "We keep all client information confidential."

That was technically true, although I have always been careful about sharing data with the authorities when questions have become involved with the business of the police or the government. I do not believe Questions Answered would qualify as a business that could legally maintain confidentiality if an agency filed for an injunction in court and besides, I believe in cooperating with authorities until there is some reason to think corruption might be involved. There was no such suspicion here. But I did not contradict Ms. Washburn directly.

"Tell me what you need from us, detective," I said. "We'll be happy to help if we can."

Hessler took his gaze away from Ms. Washburn and focused it on me. "This Tyler Clayton was a client of yours? What kind of service do you offer?"

I reached into my jacket pocket and pulled out a business card. "This is our agency," I said, and handed the card to Hessler.

He studied it. "Questions Answered?" he said. "So what is it you do?"

That flummoxed me, but it was not the first time someone had reacted to my business name in that manner. "We answer questions," I said slowly.

Hessler seemed to be waiting for more, but since that is what we do, I offered no elaboration. "You answer questions? Isn't that what Wikipedia is for?"

"It's a specialized business that will answer any question within reason," Ms. Washburn interjected. "We aren't able to help if you want to know whether there is life after death. We can't tell you what the future will bring. But if you have a question that can be researched and answered with precision and certainty, we will do that for you." I had heard her say exactly those words to clients a number of times; it was a sales speech she had devised and perfected and she delivered it well.

"Uh-huh," Hessler said. "So what question did you answer for Tyler Clayton?"

Before Ms. Washburn could protest, I answered, "He asked if Richard Handy was truly his friend."

Hessler blinked.

"He paid you money to find out if a guy at the convenience store was his friend?" The detective seemed astonished at the very concept.

"That is correct," I said. "Tyler's behavior is classified as being on the autism spectrum so it is difficult for him to read many social cues. He could not be certain if the young man he knew, with whom he had played video games and talked, was truly a friend. So he made use of our service."

Ms. Washburn looked agitated. "Samuel means that Tyler was trying very hard to be a good friend and wanted to know if there was something he was doing that might have been less than what a good friend would do." Her syntax was somewhat tortured, and her meaning was actually backward—Tyler did not ask if he was a good friend; he asked if Richard was indeed his friend. I did not attempt to correct her statement for Hessler, however. I felt it was the detective's job to interpret the information he received without unrequested perspective.

"That's your business? People just ask you questions and you answer them?" We had covered this particular aspect of the conversation already, and I saw no reason to elaborate. Hessler simply shook his head in wonder, assuming I understood his body language. Deciphering movements, particularly the unconscious ones people make, is a very tricky business for someone like me.

"What has Tyler told you?" I asked him. "Does he admit to shooting Richard Handy?"

Hessler's face seemed to flatten into an expression of irritation. "You want to hear what Tyler has told me?" he asked. Before either Ms. Washburn or I could respond, he said, "I'll show you what Tyler has told me."

He gestured for us to follow him and we walked across the street to one of the four police cruisers parked in front of the Quik N EZ store. He casually tapped on the passenger-side window. It lowered and Hessler gestured toward the back seat.

"Open it a crack," he said.

The officer in the driver's seat nodded and hit the button for the rear window. It lowered about a quarter of its capacity. Ms. Washburn and I looked inside.

In the back seat of the cruiser behind the protective barrier was Tyler Clayton, hands held behind him with handcuffs. He could not flap his hands, as I knew he most likely wished to do. Instead, he was rocking forward and back rapidly, sweating heavily and breathing with some effort although there was no evidence from our perspective that he had been in any way badly handled by the arresting officers or anyone else.

Tyler was saying, "Nnnnnnnnnnnnnnnnnn..."

Ms. Washburn's breath caught audibly. "Tyler," she whispered.

Hessler gestured to the officer in the car with a circular motion and the officer raised the rear car window again. It struck me as interesting that Hessler continued to use the gesture for a manual window crank when virtually every vehicle on the road now has power windows. But that was a discussion for another time, I'm sure Mother would have said.

"That's all he's been saying since we got here," Hessler said. He started to walk away from the car back to the spot where we had been standing previously. In order to hear what he had to say, I followed and Ms. Washburn followed me. "When you met him before, he could talk?"

Both Ms. Washburn and I nodded. "Tyler is not nonverbal," I said. "Or to be more accurate, he was not on the two other occasions we have met him. What happened in the convenience store appears to have affected his ability to form coherent speech."

"Maybe he's just faking it," Hessler suggested.

Ms. Washburn stepped between Hessler and myself. "He's not pretending," she said emphatically. "Whatever he saw in that store really traumatized him. I'd suggest you make sure he sees a really good psychologist, preferably a neuropsychologist, and you get all his previous records, including the ones from his schools. Talk to his sister and his brother. Get experts involved. A man Tyler thought was his friend has been shot and killed and Tyler is being blamed for it. Anyone would be upset by that. For Tyler, it's ten times worse."

Hessler, perhaps reacting to the fact that Ms. Washburn had not spoken much before since we'd arrived, stared at her for a moment. "We'll get him evaluated. Don't worry. But what happened in there is what he did to his 'friend,' so it can't be much of a surprise."

"How can you be sure Tyler was the one who shot Richard Handy?" I asked. "Is there security video in the store?"

"Yes, but we haven't seen it yet and it looks like someone tampered with the cameras. What I can tell you is that when the first officers arrived, Handy was on the floor in front of the dairy display, dead from gunshot wounds. Tyler Clayton was standing over him, making the noise you just heard him making, and he was holding the gun in his right hand."

"That just means someone handed him the gun," Ms. Washburn said. "Did anyone see Tyler actually shoot Richard?"

Hessler gave his head a small tilt and raised his eyebrow, a movement I have studied in social skills training. It most often means that the speaker is largely certain of his statement, but allows for the possibility that he could possibly be mistaken. It is a sophisticated signal and one that takes a great deal of practice to recognize.

"None of the witnesses have actually said they saw him pull the trigger," he admitted. "But there wasn't anyone else in that area of the store and they all heard the gun go off four times. The one other employee and one customer ran back there and saw Tyler Clayton standing over the body holding the smoking gun. Literally."

"That sounds awfully circumstantial to me," Ms. Washburn volunteered.

"I don't prosecute the cases, ma'am," Hessler said. "I just make the arrest. And we've made the arrest because there wasn't anyone else there who could have done it." He nodded in our direction. "Thanks for your help. I'll be in touch because I'm sure there'll be more questions." Then he looked directly at me. "You should be used to that, huh?" Hessler turned and walked back to the police cruiser holding Tyler Clayton.

"That guy is not going on my Christmas card list," Ms. Washburn said as she watched him walk away. That seemed an odd comment, so I turned toward Ms. Washburn, who looked at my face and shook her head. "I don't mean that literally, Samuel. I would have no reason to send Detective Hessler a Christmas card."

"You don't even know if he celebrates the holiday," I pointed out.

She held up her hands defensively. "I get that. Let's move on. What can we do to help Tyler?"

I felt my brow furrow. "Help Tyler?" I asked. "We are under no obligation to help Tyler. His question has been answered. Our business with him is concluded."

Ms. Washburn stared at me with what I can only assume was an expression of shock. "You mean you're just going to walk away and move on to the next question?" she asked.

"Of course. That is what we do. You know that." I looked back at Hessler, who struck the roof of the cruiser twice, a signal that it should be driven away. The officer behind the wheel did so immediately. Hessler walked slowly back into the Quik N EZ.

"Samuel," Ms. Washburn said. "A young man came to us for help and the answer we gave to his question might very well have ruined his life. Don't you think we have some responsibility for that? Shouldn't we be doing our best to find out if he really did kill Richard, and if not, who did?"

I began my walk back to Ms. Washburn's Kia Spectra. She seemed to want to remain at the crime scene but followed me to continue our conversation.

"I do not believe we have any responsibility for what happened here today," I said. "Tyler asked the question. We were extremely clear that the answer would be accurate, but might not be pleasant. We delivered the answer. The actions Tyler took after that are his own responsibility."

Ms. Washburn seemed to have a word stuck in her throat; she coughed a bit. "So you think Tyler really did kill Richard?" she asked.

"I think there is a good deal of evidence that he did, but as you pointed out, it is all circumstantial at this point. But circumstantial evidence is not by definition inaccurate. I am not a judge. I have no reason to question the way Detective Hessler is conducting his investigation."

We arrived at the car and I waited by the passenger door for Ms. Washburn to open her side and then allow me access. But she stood there and looked at me for a long moment.

"That boy has a lot of similarities to you, Samuel," she said in an unfamiliar tone. "You're turning away someone who's like you because you don't want to admit that."

"I am doing nothing of the sort. My job is not to investigate crimes; that is for the police to do. My job is answering questions. I answered Tyler's. Our best move here is to go back to our office and work on the next question."

She shook her head, just slightly. Then she opened the driver's side door and sat down on the seat. Her hand hovered over the control button that would unlock the other doors in the car.

"Ms. Washburn," I said. "May I get in?"

She pushed the button.

I sat down and attached the safety harness. Ms. Washburn started the engine. Before she engaged the transmission, however, she turned to look at me.

"Samuel," she said. "I'm taking from what you said that you don't intend to do any more research on what happened between Tyler and Richard today."

I had said precisely that. "Yes, you have interpreted me correctly." I said.

"Then I assume you have no objections if I do."

Her words took me by surprise, but I had no right to object. It had been Ms. Washburn's husband, soon to be her ex-husband, who had objected to her working at Questions Answered. That had kept her out of the office for three months. Even as she clearly believed me to have some similarities to Tyler Clayton, I did not want her to think there was any connection in her mind between myself and her husband.

"Of course not," I said. "But I am dubious as to your chances of finding anything helpful to Tyler's circumstance."

"Thanks for the vote of confidence."

It took me a moment to comprehend. "I am not casting aspersions on your skills," I told Ms. Washburn. "I believe there is not very much to be found."

She did not turn her head because she was driving, which I appreciated. But I did see her mouth tighten and there was some movement around her eyes. "You're giving up awfully fast, Samuel," Ms. Washburn said.

"I am not giving up because I never began."

The drive to the Questions Answered office took eleven minutes to complete. Ms. Washburn and I did not discuss Tyler Clayton's question or the murder of Richard Handy any further in that time.

When we arrived at the office, however, we found a large man standing outside the locked door. We approached the entrance and he turned toward us.

"Are you the guy who runs this place?" he asked. He had a gruff voice and his face appeared to express something just short of anger.

"I am. Allow me to introduce myself. I am—"

The man reached over and aimed a punch at my face.

Luckily, I am trained as a second-level black belt in tae kwon do, something Mother insisted on when I was in my teens. She thought it would help me develop a sense of discipline and she says now it was meant to introduce me to people my age with "similar interests" who might become friends. That did not happen, but I did acquire some self-defense skills.

I ducked. The man, already starting to breathe heavily, turned to throw another punch even as Ms. Washburn shouted, "Hey!" He did not turn toward her but remained fixed on me as his target, which I preferred. I would not like to see Ms. Washburn hurt in any way.

As he lunged, I put up my hands in a defensive pose but the man's training was poor and his emotion, whatever it might be, was not allowing him to think through an effective strategy. He came at me leaning forward quite pronouncedly so I leaned back as I swept his legs with my left foot. He fell heavily to the pavement.

"What is *wrong* with you?" Ms. Washburn demanded. I did not understand the question, even though it was not aimed at me. Did Ms. Washburn expect the man would lay out a litany of his psychological or emotional troubles simply because she had requested some information? Was it not possible that the man could have made a basic error in judgment or mistaken me for someone else? It was not a given that he had some flaw or medical condition that had precipitated his attack.

Taking another approach, I stood over the man, who was on his back looking up at me, the rage in his face now replaced by what appeared to be exhaustion. For someone who apparently believed he could successfully overcome me physically, he was not in very good condition.

"Allow me to introduce myself," I said. "I am Samuel Hoenig. Who are you?"

He was still breathing rather heavily and sweat had dampened his shirt collar and was rather badly permeating his hairline. It took him six seconds to gather his breath before he spoke.

"I'm Mason Clayton," he said. "What did you do to my brother?"

EIGHT

Mason Clayton had asked me a question, but it was not one I found interesting enough to consider answering it professionally. Still, Ms. Washburn suggested it would be best not to have what she called "a scene" outside our offices, so I helped Mason to his feet and persuaded him to come inside to discuss his rather extravagant intrusion at the entrance to Questions Answered.

He seemed subdued somehow, certainly less explosively angry than when he had initially confronted me. He slumped in the client chair after I advised him that Mother's recliner was not available. He continued to keep his gaze fixed on me and paid Ms. Washburn very little attention except when she spoke. Even then he glanced at her only fleetingly.

"I have done nothing at all to your brother Tyler," I informed him after he repeated his melodramatic question. "He asked me a question and I answered it for him. How he chose to act after receiving that information is not my responsibility. The answer I gave him was the most accurate we could provide. Richard Handy was certainly not truly Tyler's friend."

Mason shook his head as if to clear it. "That's what he asked you? If this guy who's dead was his friend?"

"He was not dead when the question was asked or answered, but yes. Tyler asked if Richard was indeed a friend as Tyler had believed he was. Our research indicated that was not the case, and when I informed Tyler of that fact, he told me I was mistaken, became very upset, and left this office. We knew nothing of his whereabouts or any further developments until Detective Hessler of the Somerset Police called to tell us Richard Handy had been shot and your brother was in custody."

Mason's mouth opened and closed. Then he managed, "You think he shot this guy because he found out they weren't friends?" Again he shook his head. "That can't be right. Tyler's a little off, but he's not that far gone."

"We don't think he shot Richard at all," Ms. Washburn interjected. I looked at her, surprised at the claim she'd made. I had no opinion on Tyler's guilt or innocence, but to say that both Ms. Washburn and I had decided he did not kill Richard Handy was at best inaccurate. "We don't believe Tyler is capable of violence like that."

Mason's left eye widened a bit as he considered that. "He can be violent; I've seen it. But I never thought he'd do something like this."

Instead of informing Mason of my true thoughts, which included the possibility that Tyler had indeed shot Richard Handy in a rage, I decided to eliminate any impossibilities in order to narrow the theories. If I could convince Ms. Washburn that Tyler might indeed have done what the police believed he had, perhaps I could convince her to discontinue any investigation she might be considering.

"Do you know where Tyler might have obtained a firearm?" I asked Mason.

Mason looked at the floor in front of his chair. "Actually, from what I'm told, the gun was mine," he said. "I have a license for it and a carry permit. I keep it in my bedroom but I didn't think Tyler knew where it was. He must have gotten it out and loaded it when I was at work."

"You were power washing someone's house when this happened?" Ms. Washburn said.

Mason's head turned swiftly. "How did you know where I work?" Then he stopped himself and nodded. "Sandy. You've been talking to Sandy along with Tyler, right?"

"We are not at liberty to discuss client information," I told him. Ms Washburn looked at me with something like amusement in her eyes, no doubt because she had said almost the same thing to Hessler and I had contradicted her.

"You don't have to confirm it," Mason said. "If you think that what I do is strictly power washing houses, you've been talking to Sandy, all right."

"Is that not accurate?" I asked. Perhaps all the information Tyler and Mason's sister had given us was suspect.

Mason Clayton's face contracted; he was indicating something, but I could not decipher it. "It's one of the things I do," he said. "We also clean gutters and leaders, we do some roofing—mostly patches—and we will paint and seal foundations to keep water from seeping into your basement. Almost anything involved in home maintenance, we do."

Since I did not actually own a house—it is Mother's name on the deed and she is two years away from paying off the mortgage—water in my basement was not an issue. But I believed that Mason was speaking in the second person only to try to personalize the service he was claiming to provide.

"What were you doing when you got the call from the police?" Ms. Washburn asked. She knows how to make a subject feel that the conversation is about him or her and that she cares. It is a talent I would truly care to cultivate, but I think with Ms. Washburn it is genuine. She actually cares about the people who walk into our offices. I consider them the sources of questions that are interesting or are not.

"I have a three-man crew, and we were installing six windows in a house in Metuchen," Mason said. "When my cell phone rang I almost didn't take the call, but it said it was the police and that made me think of Tyler."

"Has he run afoul of the authorities before?" I asked. Sandy had not mentioned any previous legal entanglements.

Mason waved a hand. "Oh, no. Tyler's a good kid, basically. He's never been arrested or anything. When I saw the cops were calling, I got worried that he might have gotten hurt or something. He doesn't pay attention even when he's crossing the street, like a six-year-old. He's engrossed in the phone, playing those games of his. So I got worried right away that something was wrong and I figured my next stop was the emergency room. Not the police station."

"So you went to the police station in Somerset, saw Tyler, and still got here before us?" My mind was racing. "That doesn't seem possible."

For a moment Mason looked confused. "No. I didn't go to the cops. They told me I couldn't see Tyler for at least a couple of hours. Once I heard about you from Tyler—they let him have a phone call and he called me—I came right here."

"To attack me," I said.

Mason's lips straightened out. "It was supposed to go differently," he said.

"Do you want to ask Samuel a question?" Ms. Washburn said. "Do you want him to find out who killed Richard Handy?"

Mason's facial expression seemed to indicate that he thought Ms. Washburn was delusional. "I don't want anything from either of you," he said. "You talked my brother into shooting that other kid. You're bad news, lady."

Ms. Washburn sat down behind her desk, looking stunned. She must have assumed that this ploy to get me involved in the investigation of Richard Handy's death was flawless. But Mason was not cooperating by being the desperate client she had hoped for.

Still, she was not going to give up without a fight. "I told you, we don't believe that Tyler shot Richard Handy," she said to Mason. "If you think there's a chance he didn't, you should ask the question. Samuel never stops working until a question is answered, and answered correctly."

I wanted to stop this conversation immediately, seeing nothing but problems coming from any research I might do into Richard Handy's death. Clients do not seem to understand the concept of a correct answer versus the one they want, and this question would surely fall into a very emotional area for Mason. Ms. Washburn herself seemed somehow engaged with Tyler Clayton's difficulties much more than any other question we had answered together, and that was confusing.

Before I could reconcile those thoughts, Mason shook his head. "I'm not paying you people a dime," he told Ms. Washburn and, I assume, me. "I don't like the way you handled my brother and now I'm going to have to figure out how to pay for a lawyer. You can forget me asking you a question and giving you money to answer it." He stood up, shaking his head. "I don't know why I came here to begin with." I considered reminding him that his original mission had been to beat me up but decided that would not improve the situation.

"We'll answer for free," Ms. Washburn said before Mason could reach the door. "Just ask the question."

"Ms. Washburn," I began. I had no intention of answering a question for Mason Clayton, and I certainly wasn't going to do so without being paid my usual fee.

She talked over my admonishment. "We can help Tyler's lawyer prove he didn't kill Richard Handy. And you don't have to pay us because Tyler already contracted with us to answer a question. What do you say?"

Ms. Washburn was acting irrationally and that confused me to the point of inactivity. She knew I had no interest in answering a question about Richard's murder. She knew I would not work pro bono for a man who had tried to hit me in the face. And yet she was doing her best to convince Mason Clayton to ask me about the incident in which it was quite likely his brother had killed another man. Besides, Tyler had not given us any money for his question, so we owed him nothing even under Ms. Washburn's logic.

"What's your angle?" Mason asked Ms. Washburn. "Why do you want this so bad?"

"We didn't help Tyler the first time," Ms. Washburn answered. "We answered his question but it made his situation worse. We would like the chance to make it up to him."

I was torn. Since I had met Ms. Washburn I had appreciated her thoughtful support and had attempted to reciprocate by trusting her judgment. She had never actually attempted to make a unilateral decision for Questions Answered before, and had often pointed out that I am the owner of the business and therefore "the one who makes all the decisions," adding, "I'm the employee."

But now she was offering our services—for no payment—when I had clearly stated my opposition to taking on the question even if we were to earn our usual fee. I wanted to tell Mason Clayton that we were not available for the service, that I was not interested in answering the question about Richard Handy's murder, and that, in fact, I expected his brother had probably committed the crime, so the answer would not be the one he was hoping to receive.

Instead, to avoid exhibiting a conflict between the two members of the Questions Answered staff, I remained silent, hoping that Mason would have the good sense to turn down the offer as he had indicated he would. It was difficult for me to know whether my resistance was based on my distaste for the question or whether I simply did not want to prolong any disagreement with Ms. Washburn.

"The cops are investigating," Mason pointed out.

Ms. Washburn nodded. "And they have already arrested your brother. How hard do you think they'll want to search for another killer when they have one in handcuffs who can't even verbally defend himself?"

"Ms. Washburn—" I managed.

"Why would you do better?" Mason was ignoring me entirely and directing his question toward Ms. Washburn.

"Samuel can think like Tyler," she answered. "He too has an autism spectrum disorder, and he uses it to his advantage."

That was, as Mother would say, crossing a line. I do not always inform strangers of my "disorder," and Ms. Washburn had always left that choice to my personal preference until now. I'd never required she ask permission to do so, but she knew how I feel about it.

"Mr. Clayton," I said when my voice had recovered from the stunning pronouncement Ms. Washburn had made. "I do not believe my Asperger's Syndrome is a particular asset in answering this question, and I think the police are best suited to this kind of investigation."

"You're the guy who put Tyler over the edge," he answered, still aiming his gaze at Ms. Washburn. "Don't you feel some responsibility for what happened?"

Before my associate could say we did, I answered, "I do not. Tyler asked a question and I gave him the best answer I could. The fact that it did not please him is not my fault. The truth is not something you can alter to your taste."

Mason nodded toward Ms. Washburn to indicate he was speaking to her now. "Do you think there's a chance Tyler didn't shoot that guy in the convenience store?" He held up a hand in my direction. "I'm asking the lady," he said. I had understood that point and was not going to interrupt. I would express my opinion after Ms. Washburn responded.

"I think there's a good chance, based on what I know about Tyler, that at least he didn't kill Richard with any premeditation. I think either he didn't shoot Richard at all, or he did it on an angry impulse. Either way, considering his developmental disability, the charge against him would be lessened and maybe dropped."

Now Mason turned to face me. "And what about you?"

It was difficult then to know what his question meant. "What about me?" I echoed back at him.

"Yeah. Do you think it's possible Tyler didn't shoot that guy?"

The office telephone rang. I was going to ignore the ringing and let the voice mail function, something I rarely use, receive any message the caller might want to leave. But Ms. Washburn immediately picked up the receiver and said, "Questions Answered. How may we help you?"

She listened for nine seconds, then extended the receiver toward me. "It's Detective Hessler," she said.

"Does he want to speak to Mr. Clayton?" I asked, although the idea that the detective would have looked for Mason at Questions Answered would be an unlikely coincidence.

"No. He wants to talk to you."

I took the telephone receiver from her hand and said into it, "This is Samuel Hoenig."

"Mr. Hoenig, it's Detective Hessler." Surely he should have realized I knew that already. "I have a question for you. How smart is Tyler Clayton?"

I looked over at Mason and placed my hand over the mouthpiece of the telephone. "Has Tyler's IQ ever been measured?" I asked. There is a general belief that people with autism spectrum behaviors have generally higher IQs than the rest of the public; that is not true.

76

It is also not true that we have lower IQs. Individuals respond according to their abilities.

Mason shrugged. "Maybe when he was in school. My parents might have done it when he was diagnosed, but they never told me. Why?"

"I do not have an accurate answer about Tyler's IQ," I told Hessler through the phone. "Why do you ask?"

There was a brief pause on the other end of the line. "Because the guy who shot Richard Handy was smart enough to wear a ski mask and nondescript clothes before spray painting the lenses of two security cameras when he entered the Quik N EZ," Hessler answered. "All I've gotten from the kid is 'nnnnnnnnn,' so I'm asking for your assessment of his intelligence. Would he have thought of that?"

"I don't know yet," I told him, and disconnected the call. Then I turned toward Mason Clayton. "I think there is a strong possibility that your brother did not kill Richard Handy, or if he did, that he was not acting alone. Are you interested in our answering the question?"

"Actually, I think I am."

"Then ask the question."

NINE

"WHAT IS YOUR FIRST move?" Mother asked.

It is my custom to have lunch with my mother every day at twelve thirty p.m. in our house not far from the Questions Answered office. Since much of the day had been spent dealing with Tyler Clayton, the crime scene at the Quik N EZ, and Mason Clayton's visit to our office, I had not eaten lunch at all, but had called Mother on my cellular phone—which I touched in my front pocket every few minutes to confirm its presence—and let her know I would not be able to come home at the usual time.

Now, hungry and charged with a new question to answer, I was having dinner with Mother in our kitchen. She had prepared a steak, well done as I prefer, baked potatoes, and broccoli. I am aware I should eat more vegetables and indeed a wider range of food generally, but menu additions are something of a challenge for me. The concept of "comfort food" is something I take seriously. Tonight, Mother knew I'd had a difficult day and had decided not to introduce anything unfamiliar to our evening meal.

"My first move?" I asked.

"In finding out whether your client shot that other man," Mother said. "How will you go about doing that?"

I chewed carefully as I always do and was careful not to speak with food in my mouth, a disgusting habit I have noticed in others that I will never practice. "I have already taken a few steps in that direction," I told Mother.

"What have you done?" Mother likes to discuss my work with me. I think she is somewhat relieved I am able to operate a business and likes to revel in the fact that it was her idea to turn my research skills into a going concern. Mother is, as with almost all people, not without some ego.

"First, I established that Mason Clayton's favorite Beatles song is 'Fixing A Hole,'" I said.

Mother smiled. She knows I use this technique to learn something about people I have not met before, but I believe she still finds it amusing. I don't understand why; it works quite well a good percentage of the time. "And what does that tell you?" she asked.

"He is dedicated to work, somewhat practical, and perhaps a little afraid of uncontrollable impulses."

She shook her head a little. "You get all that from a song."

"I do, but that was not the most important development. Mason gave me the name and phone number for Tyler's therapist. Tyler had told Ms. Washburn and me that he goes to group therapy with three other people once a week."

Mother looked concerned. "You know a therapist isn't going to discuss a client with you, Samuel. Confidentiality is very important. Dr. Mancuso doesn't even tell *me* anything about his sessions with you."

I nodded. "I am well aware of that, Mother," I said. I took another bite of steak, which was very well prepared (although the potato was a bit dry, but I chose not to mention that to Mother), so it was a gap of thirty-two seconds before I added, "I don't expect the therapist, Dr. Lisa

Shean, to divulge any confidential information. I already know the names of the other people in Tyler's group. But I do believe I can ask questions in a general enough context that some information might be gained. But that, too, is not the most important development."

Mother, who had made a separate smaller steak for herself that was, in my opinion, seriously undercooked, drank some water from her glass while she considered that. "Of course not. What else did you find out?"

"Tyler played Swords and Sorcerers with some people he knew online. He never met any of them, according to both Mason and his sister Sandy. But they might know more about his psychology than either of his siblings or even the people in his group. A young man like Tyler, considerably entrenched on the autism spectrum, might reveal more about himself in a safer fictional environment than in the real world. Ms. Washburn and I will definitely try to find his group online and see if any of them is in the area. They could be valuable sources of background and insight."

Mother's eyes took on a wry quality. "But I'll bet that was not the most important development."

I smiled. This was an inside joke between the two of us. "You know me so well."

"Okay, I give up. What *was* the most important development of the day?"

"I discovered that Richard Handy had a police record." I knew that was unexpected information, so I watched Mother's face. I practice interpreting facial expressions by trying to provoke one in people I know and then storing the visual data when the emotion I am trying to elicit is expressed.

I have seen Mother show most emotions, of course. But in this case, it was not a simple surprise that would be evoked; this was more in the area of a combination. Mother would show some concern, some surprise, and some worry, I would think. Facial configurations that exhibit more than one feeling at the same time are very tricky and therefore valuable to observe.

Mother's face barely registered any reaction at all. It was a great disappointment.

"Well, I would have almost expected that," she said.

"Really?" No doubt my face was betraying more emotion than hers had. Mother had outplayed me again.

"I always know when you're testing me, Samuel," she said. "I'm not terribly surprised about Richard. I think it's because of the way he manipulated poor Tyler. What was he arrested for before?"

My mother rarely fails to amaze me. I shook my head a little in wonder. "Not very serious crimes, but a number of them: trespassing, attempted fraud, burglary, petty theft, intention to distribute a controlled substance."

This time Mother's eyebrows rose. "He was a drug dealer? That's not a serious crime?"

I smiled. The deception had been unintentional, but I did file her expression away. "He was reselling packs of cigarettes he had pocketed at the convenience store," I said. "Tobacco is controlled, even if it is not illegal to sell to someone over the age of nineteen."

Mother looked irritated. "It oughta be illegal," she mumbled. She doesn't like it when I catch her off guard.

"Perhaps, but that is not our concern at this moment." I finished my last bite and stood to bus the dishes off the table. If I do it quickly enough, Mother's knees prevent her from having to stand and clean the kitchen. She allows me to do so, but not always willingly. "Given that he had been involved in some criminal behavior, it is not entirely out of the question that there was a motive for Richard's shooting other than Tyler's disappointment in him."

"Ah!" Mother stood up, a little stiffly. "I see what you're getting at. So what can you do to follow that lead?" She started toward the sink with her plate, which I intercepted as she walked.

"You know the routine," I said. "Pardon me—the *ritual*." When I was younger, Mother referred to my usual order of activities before bed each night as a "ritual" from which I would not deviate. "I am very rigid in my ways and will not allow for any changes."

She put up her hands in a gesture of surrender. "Forgive me," she said and sat back down. Mother is one of the few people I know who understands my sense of humor; Ms. Washburn acknowledges it, but most others seem to believe my Asperger's Syndrome has robbed me of any comic instinct. More often than not, I try to amuse people and receive a reaction of blank stares. "What about Richard's police record?"

"Detective Hessler told me that much but was not interested in saying more," I said. I washed our two plates and put the skillet Mother had used to cook the steaks into the sink to soak for a few minutes. "However, once Richard was no longer a minor, these transgressions became a matter of public record, so they are easier to track down. I believe my first step will be to speak to the owner of the Quik N EZ."

Mother absorbed that, nodding. "Why him first?"

"It will be interesting to find out why the owner of a business who discovers an employee is stealing from him allows that employee to continue to work in the store."

———

"He told me he didn't do it." Mr. Raymond Robinson was a short man, only about five-foot-five by my estimation. But he stood straight with an almost military bearing that increased the illusion of height, which very well might have been his intention.

He was also, rather incongruously given the surroundings and the tasks at hand, wearing a dark gray business suit, which was almost certain to be stained or damaged. We were standing in the Quik N EZ store Mr. Robinson owned and he was about to begin cleaning up the mess left behind when Richard Handy had been shot there.

Ms. Washburn looked up from her notepad. "But you pressed charges against Richard and accused him of stealing cigarettes from behind the counter," she pointed out.

"I dropped the charges later," Mr. Robinson said. "The cops didn't see it that way and went ahead with prosecuting him anyway. He just got fined, didn't do any jail time. I think they were trying to find his 'supplier,' but the supplier was the back of the store counter. Eventually even the judge lost interest and fined Richard four hundred bucks. That was it."

The Quik N EZ was not yet open to the public. The police crime scene tape was mostly removed except in the area where the shooting had taken place, which was not where we had taken up positions. Ms. Washburn had stood—strategically, I thought—with her back to the refrigerated container where milk was normally sold.

It had a good deal of its glass missing but there were still gallons and half-gallons of milk on its shelves. The shattered glass from the contact of the bullet Richard Handy had not completely stopped with his body was more inside the container than outside, although there was some on the floor as well.

"Have the police not yet cleared the area of the shooting?" I asked. I knew the answer but wanted to hear what Mr. Robinson might say about the incident without seeming like we were investigating the crime.

I had simply called the owner of the Quik N EZ, whose name and phone number were on county records registering the business and on a number of licenses (including, ironically, the one allowing the retail outlet to sell cigarettes) and told him I was endeavoring to answer a question about Richard Handy. He asked if I was a police officer or a detective and I had quite honestly said that neither myself nor Ms. Washburn was affiliated with any law enforcement agency.

He had to come to the store anyway to better assess the damage ("The cops wouldn't let me in at all until after dark yesterday") and to meet a representative from his insurance agency who would arrive, he said, in approximately one hour. For now he was answering our questions as if it had become a somewhat wearying but unbreakable habit.

"They said the forensics people might have more tests to do," Mr. Robinson answered. He looked skeptical. "I don't see what the question might be. The kid walked in here with a gun and shot him a bunch of times. How complicated is that?"

"But you weren't here," Ms. Washburn reminded him. "You didn't see it happen, and the security cameras were painted over. As far as we're aware there were no eyewitnesses. How do you know Tyler shot Richard?"

Mr. Robinson looked surprised, as if Ms. Washburn had suggested a scenario he had not considered. "The cops said that's what happened. Why?"

"Well, maybe that's *not* what happened." Ms. Washburn didn't glance toward the crime scene, but she gestured toward it with her right hand. "Maybe someone just wants you to think that's what happened."

"Why would they want that?"

I felt it was best to quell this exchange. Ms. Washburn was reacting emotionally because she didn't want Tyler to have killed Richard. Mr. Robinson, clearly not having considered any alternative scenarios, was simply restating what the police had told him. An escalation of this conversation was not going to serve anyone well.

"It is possible that someone else killed Richard Handy and used the best possible scapegoat, Tyler Clayton, to divert the attention of the police," I said. Before either of them could interrupt me, I added, "We simply don't know enough yet to form a proper theory. Did you know Tyler Clayton, Mr. Robinson?"

He half shrugged. "I knew *about* him. He was this kid who used to come in every day at the same time and buy a drink or something. The guys used to talk about how he would stare at Richard. I guess maybe he had a crush on him or something. You see a lot of stuff in this business."

"We believe that was not the case," I told Mr. Robinson. "Were you aware that Tyler would leave Richard extravagant tips in the jar on your counter? Possibly as much as one hundred dollars a day?"

Mr. Robinson's eyes widened. I could not interpret the emotion behind the expression; it might have been amazement, fear, pain, or disgust. I made a definite note to ask Ms. Washburn for her interpretation as soon as we were out of Mr. Robinson's earshot.

"A hundred dollars?" he asked, probably in wonderment. "Why?"

"That is something else we need to discover before we can offer an informed theory," I said.

Mr. Robinson might not have been a contemplative type, but he was not unintelligent. "What do you need to know in order to form that theory? And what question did you say you were hired to answer?" His eyes narrowed a bit, perhaps in suspicion. Again, I would check with Ms. Washburn later. Since I rarely believe myself to be the proper object of suspicion, it is sometimes difficult for me to imagine that someone would doubt what I say. I very rarely lie.

I chose to respond to Mr. Robinson's first question and hope he would forget his second, which was less simple to address. "Your security cameras were spray painted black before the shooting occurred," I said, acting on information I'd gotten from Detective Hessler. "That seems quite out of character for the Tyler Clayton with whom we are acquainted, and it speaks to a level of premeditation that doesn't seem to jibe with the theory that Tyler killed Richard Handy in an emotional fit, as an impulse. So to answer your question, Mr. Robinson, in order to adequately determine who killed Richard, we would do best with a witness who saw the incident. Failing that, we need some physical evidence pointing to either Tyler or someone other than Tyler. May I examine the crime scene if I promise not to cross the police line?"

It took Mr. Robinson a moment to absorb all I had said. "Sure," he told me. "It's your ass if the cops get mad, not mine." That seemed an odd transaction to contemplate, so I assumed it was an expression that someone—I wasn't sure I could ask either Mother or Ms. Washburn, but perhaps I could bring it up the next time I saw my friend Mike the taxicab driver—would explain to me later.

Ms. Washburn still did not turn her head but asked if I needed her to join me by the refrigerated dairy display. Although she might have noticed something I would not, I reminded myself that Ms. Washburn has some difficulty with unpleasant images of violence. I see them as possible sources of information and do not feel an empathetic tie to the unfortunate victim. Some might see that as a failing; I view it as a strength. I told Ms. Washburn I would simply call out anything she need note, and she nodded.

"I'm gonna clean up behind the counter," Mr. Robinson said. "That's not where the big mess is, but I can't touch anything over there until the cops let me." He walked to a door marked EMPLOYEES ONLY as I focused my attention on the area where Richard Handy died.

The refrigerated container stood approximately six feet high. Its door was completely made of glass except for the frame, which was stainless steel. It stood next to a similar display of soda bottles. The area where I had taken out a bottle of spring water two days before was twelve feet away and at an angle of approximately sixty degrees. I had no instruments to confirm my estimates, but felt they were accurate enough to suffice for the time being.

As I'd noted from across the room, the glass on the milk display door had been partially shattered by a bullet that Hessler had suggested had passed through Richard Handy. Since there was not yet a medical examiner's report, and there was no reason to think I would be allowed to see it when it was generated, I did not know the exact points in the body where the four bullets had penetrated, or which one might have been the prevailing cause of death.

Even at point-blank range it is difficult to shoot a person. I had not asked but I had gotten the impression from Mason Clayton that his brother Tyler was not an accomplished marksman. He certainly had never shot a living human before or the police would have had records about the incident. I was quite secure in my assumption that Tyler's autism spectrum disorder would have kept him out of the military.

What was especially concerning about the crime scene was the blood. There was quite a bit of it on the floor, a little in the milk display container, and none anywhere else. That seemed odd, so I asked Ms. Washburn to make a note of it. I took my cellular phone out of my pocket. I had been keeping my left hand in that pocket to assure myself I was still in contact with the phone anyway but now I could put the technology to good use.

Although Ms. Washburn disdains telephones as devices to take pictures, I was certain she had left her photographic equipment in her car and would certainly not have preferred to use it anyway. That would require her to examine the crime scene itself and she had made clear her desire to avoid doing that if possible. I understood the impulse on an intellectual level but did not from Ms. Washburn's emotional point of view.

My iPhone would suffice. Having practiced a number of times with the control panel I was able to navigate to the camera application quickly. I took various photographs of the scene, noting mentally that I would have to consult with an expert in blood spatter or become one myself. The former was probably less time consuming, but finding such a person not working for the police would be difficult. An expert working for the police would probably not be very forthcoming with information to a civilian.

After viewing the scene from as many angles as I could without breaching the police lines, I stepped back to take it in on a more complete level. Ms. Washburn, to my left and approximately ten feet closer to the exit than I was, called over asking if there was anything of significance she should be writing down.

"The pattern is inconsistent," I answered. "Sections of the area seem either to have been spared any violence at all, which is unlikely, or covered with some sort of protective material that the police might have taken with them. It is definitely not here now."

"What about the security cameras?" Ms. Washburn asked.

"An excellent question, thank you. The one in this area has indeed been covered with a coat of black spray paint. The can that was used must be in police evidence, as it too is no longer on the scene. Can you see the camera near the entrance from where you are standing?"

Ms. Washburn took two steps back and looked up toward the ceiling. I could see the security unit near her, but from the rear and not closely enough to gather any details.

"It's got black paint on it and there's some on the ceiling," she said. "It wasn't very carefully done."

"It couldn't be," I suggested. "Reach your arm up as high as you can."

Ms. Washburn did so, and her arm was still easily four feet from the camera lens. "Was the shooter standing on a box or something when he sprayed these?" she asked. "They're not easily reached at all."

I considered her question. "It seems unlikely. Mr. Robinson, how many people were in the store at the time of the shooting?"

The store owner looked up from his sweeping. "I wasn't here," he repeated.

"I am aware of that, but surely the police gave you something of a report. You had another employee here at the time of the incident."

"Billy. Billy Martinez. He was working the counter with Richard. I haven't spoken to him yet." Mr. Robinson went back to his chore. He seemed to me to be a very uninvolved convenience store owner.

"Do you have contact information for Billy?" Ms. Washburn asked.

"Yeah." Mr. Robinson approached my associate, who took down the information on her cellular phone. He turned back toward the counter, then looked over his shoulder at her. "What are you guys doing here, again?"

"Answering a question," Ms. Washburn assured him. She had learned to say that after only a few days of working with me at Questions Answered.

"Uh-huh." Mr. Robinson went back to work.

I was about to turn away from the crime scene when something small near the police tape caught my attention (some people would have said "caught my eye," but that is a strange expression that brings up unpleasant images in my mind, so I don't use it). I squatted down to get a better view without having to touch the floor or anything else in the area.

"What's this?" I said quietly. I believe I might have heard an actor playing Sherlock Holmes say the same thing under similar circumstances, although a number would also have said, "Hello." I am not British, so the former was more appropriate.

"What's what?" Ms. Washburn asked.

"There appears to be a die on the floor near where Richard was shot," I reported.

"Somebody else died?" Mr. Robinson asked.

"No," Ms. Washburn assured him. "Like in a pair of dice."

Indeed, a multi-sided die, clearly meant for a game other than any I had played, sat on the floor approximately six feet from where I could guess Richard had fallen after being shot. It was a dark shade of green and instead of pips or dots marking its sides it had runes of an unknown nature. I took a photograph of the die, then stood up.

"Mr. Robinson, did the police say they would be back to do further crime scene investigation?" I asked.

"Well, like I said, they told me there might be more forensics tests," he answered.

"But they have gathered all the objects of evidence they intend to take?" I said.

Mr. Robinson shrugged. "Ask them."

I looked on the shelf behind me and picked up a box of plastic sandwich bags with re-sealable tops. "May I purchase this?" I asked Mr. Robinson.

He waved his hand at me. "Just take it," he said. "The sixteen cents I make on it isn't going to be missed."

I thanked him and opened the box, removing one plastic bag. Then I reached into my pocket and took out my handkerchief, which I often use as a buffer between my fingers and any object with which I am unfamiliar, like someone else's doorknob.

Again I squatted on the floor next to the police tape. This time I used the handkerchief to very gently lift the die, which was untouched by the blood and milk mixed on the floor, having landed clear of the scene. I was extremely careful putting it into the bag and sealing it. I walked back to where Ms. Washburn was standing.

"What did you find?" she asked.

I showed her the bag with the die in it. "This. I believe it is used for a game, but I don't know which one."

"Swords and Sorcerers," Ms. Washburn sighed. "Remember, Richard and Tyler both played that one."

I nodded. "Tyler online, and Richard, as I recall, played with people in a local group."

"That's right," Ms. Washburn said. "Some people still play together in the same room, but it's becoming more common for groups to play via Skype or online in some other forum."

I examined the die. The runes were unfamiliar to me, but clearly would have some significance to a dedicated player of the game. I wasn't sure if the item was custom made or would have been mass produced.

"Do you recognize this, Mr. Robinson?" I asked.

The store owner walked to us and examined the item in my hand. "I don't know anything about that," he said. "Is it from a casino or something?"

I shook my head and directed my attention to Ms. Washburn. "It goes against the stereotype for people like me, but I'm afraid I am not an expert on Swords and Sorcerers, and I don't know anyone who is."

Ms. Washburn's eyes closed briefly. I thought she was disappointed in me, especially when she sighed wistfully, then opened her eyes again.

"I'm afraid I do," she said.

TEN

"You found an S and S dice at a place where a guy got shot and you want me to tell you about it?" Simon Taylor, Ms. Washburn's estranged husband, was staring at me incredulously and then at his wife, who had an expression on her face I had not seen before but recognized as contempt.

"Ms. Washburn informs me you are something of an expert on the subject," I explained, not correcting him on the use of the word *dice*. "This item might be significant in answering the question of Richard Handy's murder. If there is anything distinctive or noteworthy about it, it would be extremely valuable to know. Are you able to help?"

Ms. Washburn, it should be noted, suggested consulting her husband only reluctantly. They were in the process of divorcing, which I am told is almost never an amiable activity, and she had been advised by her attorney not to speak to Simon Taylor. All communication, she said, was supposed to go through the lawyer. We had not consulted the lawyer.

After she had mentioned that her husband did in fact play "S and S," as I was told the game should be called, Ms. Washburn had immediately said she did not want to ask him about the die. We were walking away from the Quik N EZ toward her car and she seemed as agitated as I have seen her, even including the moments immediately following an attempt to decapitate her some months earlier.

"We should be able to find someone else who can help," she said as we reached her Kia Spectra. She opened both our doors and we got into the car.

"I have no doubt," I said, looking at the screen of my iPhone. I had texted Mother asking if it would be inappropriate for me to insist on seeing Simon, and she had answered, IT'S NOT INAPPROPRIATE BUT IT IS INSENSITIVE. I decided not to place Ms. Washburn into an uncomfortable position, although it seemed obvious that our question had nothing to do with their marriage or their divorce.

Ms. Washburn started the car and engaged the transmission. We started driving away from the convenience store. "I mean, Simon's just a guy in his thirties who never got over pretending to be a wizard," she said. "He's not the person who invented the game or anything. There have to be people who know more about it than he does."

"Most certainly," I agreed. That speculation was certainly accurate; it was extremely unlikely Simon Taylor was the world's foremost authority on the dice used in Swords and Sorcerers.

"So there's no reason it has to be him," she went on. I was not certain she had heard anything I had said.

"True," I said. "Once we get back to Questions Answered, I can begin to research possible experts on the subject."

"Because I really don't want to have to see him if it's not necessary," Ms. Washburn said.

"Nor should you." The conversation was starting to repeat itself. I was somewhat confused about Ms. Washburn's insistence when I was doing my best to minimize the urgency of seeing Simon Taylor.

I was not even certain that the die was going to be significant in answering the question Mason Clayton had posed.

That reminded me that I had still not heard from Sandy Clayton Webb since Tyler's arrest, and that was odd.

"I'm glad you understand," Ms. Washburn said.

"Of course."

I noticed Ms. Washburn turning right on Easton Avenue in Somerset, the opposite direction one would take heading for the Questions Answered office. "Where are we going?" I asked.

"To see Simon," she sighed.

Sometimes it is difficult for me to understand the "neurotypical."

Standing now in his rather bare apartment in Edison, Simon Taylor peered at me as if deciding something. He put his hand to the stubble on his chin and stroked it as if trying to assess if he needed a shave. "How come every time I hear about my wife working with you, somebody's been murdered?" he asked.

"Ex-wife," Ms. Washburn corrected.

"Not yet, you're not."

Ms. Washburn turned away. I could see her face but Simon could not. It was not a difficult expression to decipher. I looked over at Simon, and his expression was considerably less predictable—he looked surprised.

He was what would be considered a physically attractive man, given societal standards. He stood approximately six feet tall, had dark hair and eyes, and had no visible blemishes or scars. I am not the best judge of aesthetics, so I trusted that Ms. Washburn had found him to be at least reasonably handsome. Beyond that, I knew few details about their marriage, and knew only that Simon had not been pleased with his wife's decision to work at Questions Answered, although she assured me that was not a cause of their impending divorce.

"Our work does not often involve this kind of question," I said. "But in this case, it would be extremely helpful if you could tell me about this die." I felt it best to redirect the conversation back to our purpose in coming here.

Simon looked at the die I was extending in my hand. Then his eyes looked back at the woman who, as he had pointed out, was still his wife. His features softened. "Let me see it," he said, and took the die rather abruptly from my hand. I am not fond of having people touch me, particularly those I have not met before, but I did not have time to react. I believe my hand might have withdrawn a little quickly, but I am not certain.

He examined the item closely inside the bag. If it was determined to be significant to the question of his death, I would make sure Detective Hessler was given the die for the police laboratory to analyze. If it were simply another die from a game of Swords and Sorcerers, there would be no need for that.

"It's not one of the standard dice from the game sets," Simon said. "It's the wrong color and some of these runes are in a font I don't recognize. How serious was the guy who owned this about S and S?"

This was the subject of some debate. Ms. Washburn and I had discussed the die on the way to Simon's apartment, to which she informed me he had moved after she had asked him to move out of their home in Cranford. She was, she said, in the process of trying to sell the house and find a place to live closer to the Questions Answered office.

In the car, she had vacillated about the importance of the die in our attempt to answer the question at hand. "We don't even know if it's Richard's," she'd said. "Tyler plays S and S. The die could be his." It occurred to me that even after she had decided to drive to her husband's home, Ms. Washburn was attempting to find a reason not to do so.

"It is possible," I had admitted. "It is also possible that the die belongs to a third party of whom we are not yet aware. If the killing was related to the game, as the presence of the die might or might not indicate, someone from either Tyler or Richard's Swords and Sorcerers group might be the guilty party, or at least involved. So we don't know about the ownership of the item yet. Perhaps your husband might be able to shed some light on that issue as well."

"Yeah," she sighed. "Maybe he can." Then she drove without speaking for the rest of the trip.

Simon Taylor looked over the twenty-sided die (which I had examined more closely) in his hand. "How serious?" he asked again.

"I am unable to answer that question with any assurance," I said. "We are not sure who might have owned the die."

Simon's lips curled. "Figures." He turned the die around in his hand. "It's not someone who's casual about the game," he said. "Somebody who plays once in a while wouldn't go out of his way to get customized dice made special, even if they had to order them online from a catalog. They'd just use the ones that come in the box."

"Tyler Clayton plays Swords and Sorcerers with people online, not with the other people in the same room," I said. "Would that make a difference?"

Simon nodded. "It could. If he's not the SM, he might not need to have dice at all."

His use of game jargon had confused me. "The SM?" I asked. I had heard the letters used in a different context that seemed to have no significance under these circumstances.

"Sword master," said Ms. Washburn, who had turned back to face her husband and me. "The person who basically runs the game."

"So that person, whomever it might be in Tyler's group, would keep the dice?" I asked.

Again, Simon Taylor nodded, but I noticed he was paying more attention to Ms. Washburn than to me or the item in his hand. "It's even possible to play online using virtual dice, so you wouldn't need the real ones at all."

I turned toward Ms. Washburn. "We have to find out who Richard Handy was playing the game with," I said. "And we need to talk to the members of Tyler's group."

Simon shook his head. "Look—people who play S and S aren't the freaks the media wants you to believe. I can't imagine anybody getting killed over a game."

I understood the problem that people who are different might face when fighting the image of media perceptions. Some members of the public believe everyone with an autism spectrum disorder acts in the same fashion. I believed our encounter with Tyler Clayton, so far, had proved we do not.

"It's entirely possible the game had nothing to do with Richard's death," I said. "It is just an object that was found at the scene. He might have had it in his pocket."

Simon twirled the die in his hand again. "It's got a nice feel to it," he said. "And the runes. That's the part that's weird."

"Why?" Ms. Washburn asked.

"There are a couple I don't recognize, and that shouldn't happen," he said. "Even if the style is different, the shapes should be standard, like the ones I use."

"How are these different?" I asked. The hieroglyphics on the item were meaningless to me, so his assessment would be valuable.

Simon took his time considering. "Well like I said, the font is different. This is more ornate. It's not as readable, but that doesn't seem to have been important to the person who ordered this dice." I suppressed again the urge to correct his misuse of the word. "It's possible this wasn't used in a game, that whoever bought it just wanted it to look cool."

That was a concept I did not completely understand. "If the die was not being used for its intended purpose, what value would its design have among game players?" I asked.

Ms. Washburn smiled slightly. "Simon has an electric guitar he doesn't know how to play because he thinks it looks cool," she said, her expression indicating she might be teasing. "It's how he used to attract girls."

Simon Taylor's face seemed to soften. Until now he had been avoiding eye contact with his wife, looking at her only when her attention was focused elsewhere. Now their eyes met. "Worked once," he said.

Ms. Washburn looked away.

Concerned that the conversation was drifting from the central point, I asked Simon, "Where would someone buy a die like that one?"

"There are places. Mostly online. I can send Janet some links in her e-mail."

I would have thought Ms. Washburn, who had been resistant to contact her estranged husband, would have balked at such a suggestion, but she nodded. "You know where to find me."

"One last question, Mr. Taylor," I said. Simon, who had been smiling as if at a private joke, looked over at me and his expression became more serious. "What is your favorite Beatles song?"

I made a point of not looking at Ms. Washburn after asking the question, and kept my attention fixed on Simon. His eyes narrowed, and then he looked in Ms. Washburn's direction, thinking. "'Here, There and Everywhere,'" he said.

I could not accurately determine anything about his personality from that answer because it was clear he was lying.

But Ms. Washburn, whom Simon was watching, put her hand to her mouth.

It was disturbing to me on a number of levels: First, it was for my business that Ms. Washburn had suggested coming to question her husband, so any potential reconciliation would be at least partially my responsibility. Second, the idea that Ms. Washburn could be so easily influenced by a man whom she had grown to mistrust was somewhat disturbing in our business.

But the thing I found most upsetting was that I had glanced just for a moment to the right, down the hall into Simon's bedroom. I had not intended to absorb any information; Simon had no bearing on the question we were answering other than the technical help he volunteered.

During the half second of my look, however, I had noticed that Simon's bed was not made, his dresser drawers were open, and his socks were strewn about the room and on the rug, not necessarily in pairs.

And there was a blue brassiere hanging out of one of the drawers.

"We have several areas of research to pursue," I told Ms. Washburn when we were back at the Questions Answered office. "When your estranged husband sends you the list of possible sources for the Swords and Sorcerers die, we can determine if that item is unique or something that might have been mass produced, even if just for a limited run that would appeal to certain specialists in the game. That might lead us to someone in Richard's group."

Ms. Washburn sat down at her desk and immediately engaged her computer. She had chosen not to use a MacBook Pro like my own, being more proficient in the Windows operating system, which is not as efficient but offers more compatible software. She immediately began hitting keys on her keyboard.

"What else will we be looking at?" she asked.

I wanted to ask her about the visit to Simon Taylor but was at a loss to determine how that subject should be broached. After having announced quite definitively that she was divorcing Simon and having filed the necessary papers, which were in process, her demeanor in Simon's apartment had been confusing. Once he had begun to make obvious effort to appeal to her, Ms. Washburn had seemed amenable to his attempts, which was counterintuitive. I could ask Mother about the dynamic later, but even talking to her about marriage was somewhat uncomfortable, since my father had left us when I was at such an early age.

Complicating the matter, of course, was the information I had that I assumed Ms. Washburn did not, which was that her husband had certainly entertained in his bedroom a woman who one could only assume was not terribly fastidious about her underwear, and certainly had not been wearing it for at least some of the time she was there. That would probably be pertinent information going forward, but I was not certain whether it was my place to mention it. I couldn't even decide whether to discuss the matter with my mother, who would understand the marital institution better than I but who might find the subject matter disturbing, especially coming from her son.

Indeed, I was not completely sure Simon's behavior would be a problem. Ms. Washburn might simply have been trying to be civil with her ex-husband and had no intention of reconciling. And while they were in the process of divorcing, it was likely any extracurricular affairs he had might be irrelevant.

But it had worried me, and it was now becoming a distraction from the question at hand.

For now, I decided, I would continue to refrain from talking to Ms. Washburn about her marriage or her divorce. Perhaps I would do some online research on the subjects later to better understand the emotions involved.

"Besides the die, our best bets fall into three categories," I said in answer to her question. "We have the two Swords and Sorcerers groups. We can get the names of Tyler's co-players from Sandy or Mason Clayton, or perhaps from the hard drive on Tyler's computer. If Tyler gains his composure to the point where he can speak again he might be very helpful indeed, but we don't know if or when that might happen."

"What are the other two categories?" Ms. Washburn asked.

"Second, there is Richard Handy's Swords and Sorcerers group," I said. "But that will be more difficult to research. We need to find out if Richard had any family members in the area who might be able to shed some light on his acquaintances. A third line of inquiry would be interviewing the other Quik N EZ counter employee, Billy Martinez, whose contact information Mr. Robinson provided. And there is another avenue I had not considered until now."

Ms. Washburn looked up from her screen. "What's that?"

"Tyler Clayton's social skills group."

ELEVEN

SANDY CLAYTON WEBB CALLED back that afternoon at 3:26. She explained that she'd been dealing with Tyler's legal defense and attending his arraignment, during which bail was set at $250,000. Sandy and Mason were attempting to raise the required funds but so far had not been able to do so. She said Tyler was not any more communicative than he had been since Richard's shooting, and "staying in jail isn't helping him do any better."

"What can you tell me about his social skills therapy?" I asked her.

For reasons I could not identify, that seemed to confuse Sandy. "What?" she asked.

I repeated the question. Ms. Washburn, watching from her desk, raised an eyebrow.

"I don't really know that much about Tyler's therapy," Sandy said after a moment. "That's really more Mason's department; he drives Tyler back and forth most weeks. Why are you asking about it?"

"It is a possible area of research," I explained. "It might have some significance in Richard Handy's death."

The silence this time lasted eight seconds. That is a much longer time for a lull in conversation than it might seem. In my own social skills therapy with Dr. Mancuso, I once timed a period of silence at twenty-two seconds, although Mary McWaters, sitting next to me, insisted the interval was at least two minutes. It was not.

"You think Tyler really did shoot that guy at the convenience store?" Sandy sounded shocked. "You think you can find evidence of that by asking Dr. Shean about his group sessions? I thought we hired you to prove that Tyler is innocent."

"Your brother Mason hired us to answer the question of who killed Richard Handy," I reminded her. "I approach the process without any prejudice. The facts lead us to the correct answer, not the desired one."

Ms. Washburn stood up carrying a piece of paper in her hand. She brought it to my desk and set it in front of me.

It read, *You don't always have to tell all the truth.*

"But you seem to be trying to prove that Tyler shot him," Sandy said again. "That's what you think, isn't it?"

"I have not yet formed an opinion," I said, wondering why Ms. Washburn would want me to conceal some facts from a client. How would I decide which ones to withhold? We would have to discuss this at length later, I thought. "I feel it is best to explore every area which might lead us to some more illuminating facts. Can you tell me the names of the other people in Tyler's social skills group?"

Ms. Washburn turned her head sharply and looked at me, brow furrowed. I nodded in her direction; yes, I was aware we already had that information. It was Sandy's reaction that was the important piece of information being sought here.

It was swift and clipped. "I'm not going to violate that confidence," Sandy said. I believed her voice was taking on what Mother would consider a "cold" quality. I was not sure how speech could be measured for temperature and even knowing that was an expression some people used did not help me understand it more fully. I did get the impression that Sandy was not trying as hard to sound friendly as she had before. "Those people didn't ask to be subjected to your questioning, Mr. Hoenig. They have enough problems as it is."

The use of the word *problems* was most significant in my mind. Sandy clearly thought of her brother and others like us as damaged, in some way not as whole as the neurotypical majority. It was stored away in my mind for later. I was not sure knowing that would lead to a swifter or more accurate answer to Mason's question, but at this stage the point was to gather information, not to analyze it.

"Very well," I said. "Can you answer this for me, then: Why would Tyler put one hundred dollars in the tip container when he went to buy a cold drink from Richard Handy, and where would he gain access to that amount of money?"

Sandy's voice was little more than a whisper. "Tyler tipped that guy a hundred dollars?"

"He did, and the casual nature of the gesture indicated that this was probably not the first time it had occurred. I wonder if this was a habit of his. Do you know if he had a bank account he could tap into, and why he might want to bestow that kind of gift on Richard?"

"I have no idea," Sandy replied. "You'll have to ask Mason. I'm sorry, Mr. Hoenig, but I need to go now."

"Can we continue this discussion later?" I asked. Sandy was one of the few sources I had who could tell me about Tyler and his behavior before the shooting. Cutting the conversation short was telling, but it was not helpful to my answering the question.

"I'm afraid not," Sandy answered, which surprised me. When people are impolite, as when they abruptly end a phone conversation, there is usually either a good reason or some indication that the person is angry. Neither was the case this time. "I'd appreciate it if you didn't call me again."

That was odd. "Excuse me?" I said. I have been told that when a comment another person might make confuses me, the best thing to do is to stall a bit, get the time to analyze the situation before responding. If I could think for a moment, I'd be able to determine why Sandy was suddenly asking not to be contacted again. Asking her to repeat her statement was not intended to clarify the request; it was meant to fill a few seconds while I found a proper response.

She disconnected the call.

I have seen motion pictures in which people who have had another person "hang up on them" stared at the telephone receiver or mobile unit in hand as if the phone itself had been rude and confusing. The gesture had always struck me as artificial and irrational. It is not the telephone's fault that someone else has ended the conversation.

Yet I found myself staring at the telephone receiver in my hand.

Ms. Washburn looked over at me. "What?"

"She hung up," I said.

Ms. Washburn's eyes widened. "Really," she said.

"What does it mean?" Perhaps Ms. Washburn would have some insight into that sort of gesture that I would not have otherwise understood.

"There was something she didn't want to tell you."

I placed the receiver back on its cradle. "She could have told me that," I said.

Ms. Washburn shook her head. "She didn't want to tell you that, either."

I do not believe, finally, that there is a significant difference in the thought process based on one's gender. While many standup comedians and even others in conversation seem to believe that women's minds operate differently from those of men (and there has even been some scientific research that examines this supposed phenom-enon), my experience has always been that each individual thinks in a unique fashion. Even people whose behavior will classify them as having an autism spectrum disorder do not behave—and therefore think—in identical styles.

Still, the fact that Ms. Washburn could interpret Sandy's behav-ior without having heard anything but my side of the conversation would indicate there was some inherent understanding between the two. The only similarity I could discern based on my limited knowl-edge of Sandy's personality was that they were both women. Perhaps there was something I was not seeing.

"How do you know that?" I asked Ms. Washburn.

"You think people all act based on your own view of logic, Samuel. My mind is considerably less well structured than yours. I understand the emotional side of things a little better because I'm not blessed with your keen ability to think through every question. So I know when someone is being emotional, because I have acted that way myself."

I'm not sure how, but I did begin to suspect that Ms. Washburn was speaking both of Sandy's behavior on the phone and her own at Simon Taylor's apartment. Something in the back of my mind began to tingle, a nervousness I could not clearly identify. Perhaps this was one of those emotional moments Ms. Washburn was discussing.

(Of course I have emotions. All of us on the autism spectrum do. Part of what so greatly irritates me about the perception the "typical" have of us is that they believe we are robotic, unfeeling entities. The difference is that we feel without necessarily understanding why, and we do not always know how to react to the emotions we have. It is therefore more efficient to keep them hidden because the displays we tend to make are considered inappropriate in the majority's society.)

The memory of that blue brassiere was not currently helping me navigate this conversation.

"Are you thinking of our visit to your husband's apartment?" I asked Ms. Washburn. Perhaps this was how friends showed empathy or at least interest in others' troubles.

Ms. Washburn's face reddened a bit. "Where did that come from?" she asked.

Since the words had come from my lips, the question confused me a bit. I decided to explain my train of thought. "I have observed a difference in your behavior since we were there," I said. "If something is troubling you …" I wasn't sure how to phrase the sentence. " … it would not be inappropriate for you to talk to me about it if that would make you feel better."

Ms. Washburn shook her head. "I'm okay," she said. "Don't worry, Samuel."

"What do you think, then, that I should do about Sandy hanging up on me?"

"Ignore it and move on."

I chose to take her advice, which is almost always wise. "The next order of business, then, should be to contact Tyler's therapist, Dr. Shean," I said. "Would you mind doing that?"

Ms. Washburn gave me a quick look, possibly considering the idea that she should encourage me to make the phone call myself. She knows it is something I dislike doing, but feels I should do some of those things anyway, preparing for a time when she might not be in the office to handle it. She forgets sometimes that I did operate Questions Answered on my own for three months before she arrived to help answer the Question of the Missing Head.

Then, perhaps deciding the ensuing conversation would not be worth it, she picked up the phone and dialed the number she had called up on her screen. She waited a few moments, then clearly was listening to a recorded voice mail prompt. The idea that a caller still needs to be instructed to "wait for the beep and leave a message" is somewhat disturbing.

"This is Janet Washburn of Questions Answered in Piscataway," she said at the appropriate moment. "We have some questions concerning Tyler Clayton, a patient of yours. Please call me as soon as you can. The matter is fairly urgent." She recited the office phone number, thanked the voice mail service, and hung up the phone. She turned toward me. "She wasn't there."

"I gathered that."

My cellular phone rang, and my hand, which had been in my pocket to check on it, pulled it out. The caller was displayed as Mason Clayton, so I accepted the call and assured Mason he had reached me.

"Sandy called me," he said. "She thinks you're trying to get Tyler convicted."

"That is not the case," I assured him. "I am attempting, as you requested, to accurately answer the question of who killed Richard Handy."

"That's what I thought," Mason said. "But Sandy was really upset."

"Women, right?" I said. I have heard that said before. I do not really understand what it means. Ms. Washburn gave me a somewhat amazed look, one which did not seem to be especially approving.

"What?" Mason said.

Clearly I had said something I should have avoided. "Excuse me, Mason," I said. "I do not always know the correct phrasing. What I meant to say was that I am not approaching the question with any prejudice whatsoever. My concern is only to provide the correct answer."

"Sandy wants me to fire you," Mason said. "She thinks you're working against Tyler's best interests."

"What do you want to do?" I asked. I have been dismissed from answering some questions in the past. It is not a pleasant experience, but it's the kind of thing that can't be avoided in business. Usually the client doing so is wrong.

"Well, that depends," Mason answered. "How do you intend to proceed from here?"

Usually I do not discuss methodology with clients. For one thing, I would probably not diverge from a plan even if the client objected and for another, there is no business advantage in revealing how one performs a service if the client can then be persuaded that he or she could do the same thing as effectively. Again, it is unlikely that would be the case, but people are sometimes misled.

In this case, however, I felt it was best to answer Mason's question. If he had moral or ethical objections to my method and wanted me to stop, I could release him from his contract. I would mostly likely continue to research the question, but Mason would not have to pay for my efforts beyond this moment.

"I expect to talk to Tyler's therapist, Dr. Shean, when she calls back," I began. "Assuming that does not happen soon, I will probably go home for the day and watch a baseball game on television before sleeping. Tomorrow I will try to interview Richard Handy's coworker at the Quik N EZ and contact the members of both their Swords and Sorcerers groups. I'll attempt to get Detective Hessler to tell me if the ballistics test on the bullets that killed Richard are from your gun, and also to gain access to the brief security videos taken before the person who shot Richard spray painted the lenses. Beyond that, I do not currently have a plan of attack, but each step along the way will undoubtedly lead to new questions that must be answered so that will mean additional tactics will be devised and executed." I noticed Ms. Washburn was looking curiously at me, writing in her notebook without looking at the page on which she wrote.

Mason seemed to take a moment to absorb what I had told him. "That sounds like a pretty thorough plan," he said. "I don't see any reason to fire you."

"Thank you," I said, although I wasn't sure why.

"Is there anything I can do to help?" he asked.

"Yes. Find the license for the gun and make a copy or scan it and send it to my associate Ms. Washburn. Then please call Dr. Shean and tell her—even in a voice mail message—that you authorize her to talk to me. I will not ask anything that violates her privilege. Are you legally Tyler's guardian?"

"No," Mason said. "He's over eighteen and not in a condition that requires him to be cared for, so there is no guardian."

"That might complicate the dealings with Dr. Shean and a few others, but aside from her, we'll hope no one else knows that." I thought quickly. Mason was asking to help and that is not always the case with clients; many want an answer to appear magically on their doorstep. "Do you have any idea who Tyler was playing Swords and Sorcerers with online?"

"Not really. I could look on his computer, but the cops took his laptop to look for evidence so I don't really have anything." Mason sounded perplexed. "The only one he ever talked about was Margie Cavanagh. She lives in New Brunswick, I think. Somewhere around there. And some kid Adam ... something. He was in Jersey someplace, but I don't know where. All the other people in the group were in other states. Tyler used to have to play late at night because they were in different time zones."

"Were he and Margie friends?" I asked.

Mason hesitated. "As far as I know, they never actually met. Tyler would mention every once in a while that she seemed to be really good at the game. Slaying monsters or something. I didn't really pay attention."

"Did Tyler ever play the game on a computer other than his laptop?"

"No. Wait. I think he did once when his laptop was in the shop for repairs. He used my laptop. Maybe two months ago."

I know a bit about computers, so I suggested that Mason bring his laptop—thankfully Tyler had not played Swords and Sorcerers on a desktop computer, which is harder to transport—to the Questions Answered office the next day, and we made an appointment to meet there at two in the afternoon. Mason said he was not working for the time being as he was uncertain as to Tyler's status and did not think he could concentrate on his job while that was the case.

"Have you secured a legal representative for Tyler yet?" I asked.

"We really can't afford a top-flight criminal defense lawyer," Mason said, expressing some sadness in his voice. "At the moment, I'm working with the Public Defender's office, but we might be able to scrape enough together to hire that guy from TV."

I knew exactly which attorney he meant, because T. Harrington Swain's advertisements were sometimes broadcast during telecasts of New York Yankees baseball games. The ads featured Swain, a somewhat stiff and unconvincing presence, reading from a teleprompter that he would "fight for your rights no matter what you've done," a selling point that might have been considered somewhat accurate given the setup of the American criminal justice system, but which hardly inspired much confidence if the listener was paying careful attention.

Still, giving Mason advice about legal counsel was probably outside my purview in answering his question, so I did not suggest the public defender assigned to the case might be a better option no matter the financial arrangement Mason and Sandy might reach. Instead, I said, "Very well, then. Please keep me informed."

"You do the same," Mason said, and disconnected the call more appropriately than his sister had done before.

I looked at Ms. Washburn. "It's getting late," she said. "Do you want a ride home?" If I am not staying late in my office, Ms. Washburn will provide transportation to Mother's house. If I do stay past her departure, I will call my friend Mike the taxicab driver and he drives me to the house.

I glanced at the time on my computer screen; it was 4:36 p.m. "It's a little early," I said. "Do you have a reason to leave before five?" I was asking not as an employer. Despite the fact that we do not punch a clock at Questions Answered, I was curious as to Ms. Washburn's motivations.

She looked oddly defiant. "I told Simon I would meet him for a drink at five thirty."

That was an odd statement. "Your estranged husband?" I asked. I actually did feel some hairs stand up on the back of my neck. It was uncomfortable.

Ms. Washburn avoided eye contact, something I am familiar enough with that I can spot it easily when someone else is doing it. "Yes," she said quietly.

"Is that advisable?" It seemed to me that if her attorney was against the idea of her seeing Simon on a professional basis, meeting him socially would probably be that much more perilous.

Ms. Washburn's eyes flashed but she continued to look away. "It's a personal matter, Samuel, so let's not discuss it."

That suited me, so I nodded.

"Would you like a ride home?" she asked again.

"No, thank you. I'll call Mike."

Ms. Washburn said good night and left the office.

TWELVE

"She's having second thoughts," Mike said.

The drive from Questions Answered to the home I share with my mother is not a long one, so Mike the taxicab driver had listened to my description of Ms. Washburn's behavior and was offering his viewpoint with only two minutes left in the ride. Mike is one of the few people I can ask about interpersonal relationships, particularly those which I am not comfortable discussing with Mother or Ms. Washburn.

"She is reconsidering her divorce?" I asked.

Mike nodded without taking his eyes from the road. "It's not very unusual. Women especially. They think they can fix the guy or that it was their fault. They're usually wrong—always about fixing the guy—but you can't try to persuade her otherwise, Samuel. She'll do what she'll do."

"But her attorney advised her not to talk to Simon at all," I said. I was not trying to prove Mike wrong, as I trust his judgment; I was instead attempting to understand why Ms. Washburn, usually a very rational woman, would act in such a blatantly emotional and inadvisable fashion.

Mike chuckled a bit under his breath. "Probably one of the reasons she's going," he said.

I had met Mike at Newark Liberty International Airport a few years ago when Mother was visiting her sister, Aunt Jane. I had accompanied her to the airport and had been instructed to find a taxicab to drive me home after her flight had departed. I chose Mike's cab, which he had named Military Transport because he was an Afghanistan veteran not long returned from duty and was not interested in "sitting behind a desk or standing on a sales floor."

It had been an unexpectedly pleasant trip in Mike's cab, so when I discovered that he was based (that is, that his house was) very close to Questions Answered and my home, I asked if he might be called upon to drive me home from work on nights Mother could not do so. Mike had agreed, and even after Ms. Washburn had come to work with me, I would contact him on evenings I worked late to ask for a ride. He had always complied and became a trusted adviser.

"Do you think Ms. Washburn will reconcile with Simon?" I asked now.

He shrugged while keeping both hands on the steering wheel. I know quite a bit about driving although I rarely practice. It makes me feel more secure to pay attention to the person behind the wheel when I am a passenger. I am not able to say whether my attention has the same effect on the driver. "No way of knowing," Mike said. "Janet's a smart girl. Do you think she should get back with her husband?"

"It does not occur to me that I should have an opinion on the subject," I said.

"Except you do, Samuel. Even if you're not admitting it, you don't want her to go back to Simon, and it's bugging you enough that you called me, even when she could have driven you home, just so you could tell me about it." Mike steered the taxicab into Mother's driveway. He stopped the car and shifted into park, then turned to face me. "You care

114

about Janet. You don't want her to get hurt and you know Simon has not been the best husband since time began. So you're rooting for her to get the divorce and move on. Now tell me I'm wrong."

Mike did not, in fact, want me to tell him I believed him to be mistaken. Instead, he was saying he thought it unlikely I could do so honestly. I have learned this particular conversational tactic in social skills training. It was not an easy one to understand, and I am not certain I always recognize it in use even now. This time, however, I knew what he meant.

"I don't know if you are wrong," I told him. "I am concerned about a coworker and hope she does not leave herself open for emotional pain, which is a real condition. It would disrupt her efficiency and be unpleasant for both of us. So it makes perfect sense for me to be concerned about her current direction, doesn't it?"

Mike shook his head but chuckled as he did. "Of course it does, Samuel. But there's something you're not telling me." Mike is an astute observer of people and would no doubt make an excellent addition to Questions Answered if he were inclined to give up driving his taxicab, which he is not.

I told him about my observation at Simon's apartment.

Mike's face turned serious. "Well you know, they are getting a divorce," he said finally. "I don't know if that's a really big deal."

"If Ms. Washburn decides to reconcile with her husband, does it become a big deal?" I asked.

Mike smiled crookedly. "Of course it does, Samuel. Now get the heck out of my cab. I have an actual paying job to get to in New Brunswick." He pointed to the rear passenger door, next to which I was seated.

I opened the door and stepped out. "You know I would pay you for the ride if you would accept the money," I said. I closed the door and stepped toward the front passenger window, which was open.

"Yes, I do. And that's one of the reasons I won't accept the money. You're a friend, Samuel. I don't ever want you to think I'm acting like this with you because you are a regular fare. Clear?"

"Quite so," I said.

"I'll see you soon." He backed out of the driveway while I walked to the back door and entered the house.

Mother was in the kitchen. It was a warm night, so the windows were all open and the ceiling fan was spinning. She looked up and smiled when I entered. But when she saw my facial expression, she asked if something was wrong.

"No," I assured her. "I believe Mike just illuminated part of this question for me."

———————

"I didn't know anything about the guy." Billy Martinez was standing next to the lottery ticket dispenser, the opposite side of the counter at the Quick N EZ than he manned three days earlier when I had come to ask Richard Handy about Tyler Clayton. "He came in every day and bought a soda, then he left some money in the tip jar and left. That's all I know."

He stole a glance at Mr. Robinson, who was overseeing workmen replacing the glass on the dairy display. When Ms. Washburn and I had entered this morning, the police crime scene tape had been removed, the dairy cooler had been emptied, and the floor no longer bore any traces of the violence that had taken place here a few days before. Mr. Robinson, after noting that we were still not police officers but kept coming back to ask questions, had said Detective Hessler (whom Ms. Washburn had called but not spoken to) had given him permission to have the scene cleaned the evening before and the store was now again open for business.

"He left quite a bit of money in the tip jar every day, didn't he?" I asked.

Billy was not attending to a customer at the moment, but frequently looked up the aisle as if hoping one would come and relieve him from the responsibility (completely unofficial) of speaking to me. There were only two customers in the store at the moment—perhaps news of its reopening had not yet spread through the community—and neither of them seemed especially anxious to pay for their purchases.

"I don't know how much money he left," Billy answered. "Richard always took the tips for himself."

Ms. Washburn looked up from her notepad. "That's not the way it's supposed to be, is it?" she asked. "Aren't all the employees supposed to share the tips?"

Billy glanced at her. "Richard didn't keep *all* the tips, just the ones from that guy," he said.

"Tyler Clayton," I clarified.

"Yeah, whoever. He'd come in here staring at Richard like he was in love with him or something, then he'd leave money in the jar and Richard would take it. I figured he was really just coming in for Richard, so he was entitled to the money." Facial expression creates some difficulties for me, as do some vocal tones. I tend not to read emphasis and modulation well. But Billy's explanation was so unconvincing that I did not feel the need to confirm its falseness with Ms. Washburn later.

"He left one hundred dollars every day," I said, although it was not confirmed that this was a daily amount. "Do you truly believe Richard was entitled to that money simply because Tyler considered him a friend?" I believe I sounded skeptical enough to get my point across.

Billy clearly got the point, at any rate. "You think I'm lying?" he asked.

"I do not yet have enough information to form an opinion," I said. "But it is curious."

I traded a glance with Ms. Washburn which we *would* discuss later in her car.

Mr. Robinson walked over from the refrigerated displays. "Have you got enough?" he asked. "I don't want you interfering with my business."

I considered protesting that Mr. Robinson had not expressed any such reservations when we walked in, and that no one else was trying to purchase an item from the store, but Ms. Washburn shook her head slightly. I smiled what Mother calls my "professional smile" and said, "I have only one more question, for both of you."

Ms. Washburn probably thought I was going to ask about Beatles preferences, but at this moment character assessments of Mr. Robinson and Billy Martinez seemed less urgent.

"So ask," Mr. Robinson said.

"Did Tyler Clayton ever change his style of clothing?"

Billy's eyebrows met over the bridge of his nose. "The style of his clothing?" he echoed.

"Yes. Did he vary colors? Change fabrics? Did the climate make a difference?"

Mr. Robinson shrugged. "I'm the owner. I wasn't here every day. I'm just here to deal with ... all this today." It was a variation on his continued insistence that he never saw anything nor heard anything concerned with the killing in his store. He was either lying or the most absentee owner such a business could have had.

Billy Martinez shook his head. "I don't know what you're talking about," he said. "That kid wore the same thing every day, no matter what. Hot, cold, snow, rain. He wore a dark blue hoodie and a pair of jeans. Every day."

"Thank you," I said. "You have been extremely helpful."

Once we were safely away from the possible hearing of either of our interviewees and inside Ms. Washburn's Kia Spectra, she said, "They were lying."

"Yes. About almost everything."

Ms. Washburn started the car and left the parking space we'd used, half a block from the Quik N EZ. "*Almost* everything?" she asked.

"Billy was telling the truth about Tyler's wardrobe. He did indeed wear the same type of clothing every day, probably for years. It is not uncommon among those on the autism spectrum to avoid as many kinds of change as possible."

Ms. Washburn looked like she wanted to give me a wry glance but did not divert her attention from the road, which I appreciated. "I have noticed that," she said. "But you don't wear the same clothes every day."

"I am not Tyler Clayton."

"Why are his clothes important?" she asked.

"Individually, they are not," I said. "Whether he always wore jeans or sweatpants or a tuxedo makes no particular difference to the question we are researching. What is important is that he wore the same thing every day. That means his clothes could be predicted in advance."

Ms. Washburn thought about that for a moment, then spoke after making a left turn. "So whoever painted over the security cameras could know what to wear."

"Precisely. Very good, Ms. Washburn. There was one other point that was relevant, but I think you noticed it when it happened."

Ms. Washburn's eyes narrowed a tiny bit. I curbed my flicker of anxiety, realizing she could still see the road before her. "It was when you said that Tyler left a hundred-dollar bill in the tip jar every day," she said.

"That's right. What do you think was important about it?"

Ms. Washburn shook her head. "Don't school me, Samuel. You know perfectly well what was important. I saw the technique: First you mentioned the hundred-dollar bill the day we were watching. Billy pretended he didn't know about it."

I nodded. "That's right."

"But then you said he did it every day. We didn't know if that was true, but we suspected it. And Billy didn't deny it or even say he didn't know if it was true. He asked if you thought he was lying. That's not the same thing."

"So what does that do for us?" I did not mean to sound as if I were condescending to Ms. Washburn, assuming I was more skilled at researching a question than she. I am merely more experienced, having done this kind of work for years alone in my attic room long before Questions Answered became an ongoing enterprise. But I had the feeling, watching her mouth tighten, that Ms. Washburn thought I was violating her warning not to "school" her.

"Samuel. Stop it."

"I mean no offense," I said.

"I know, but you're treating me like a promising student, not an associate."

"I am exploring possibilities in the question," I said. "Your perspective helps me think of the issues in ways I might not consider. When I ask you about something, it is not because I have an answer in mind; it's because I truly want to know what you think."

That seemed to appease Ms. Washburn, because she smiled slightly and said, "You want to know what Billy's reaction does for us? It confirms what we suspected—that Tyler really did leave a hundred dollars in the tip jar for Richard every day. But it also opens up a number of questions that we need to answer."

"For example?"

Ms. Washburn maneuvered the car into the parking lot of the strip mall where Questions Answered is located. "We need to know where Tyler got that kind of money. That's the big thing. Did he go to the Quik N EZ on Richard's days off? Someone like Tyler probably knew the personnel schedule for the store. Either way, let's say Richard got two days off a week. That's five hundred bucks each week Tyler would put in for tips. A part-time job at an electronics store doesn't afford that kind of money just for throwing around."

It wasn't exactly the way I would have worded the thought, but it helped me to crystallize the concerns I'd been having. "We have not asked Mason Clayton about the money," I said. "We mentioned it to Sandy Clayton Webb before she became hostile to our efforts, and she seemed surprised, possibly shocked, at Tyler's actions."

"I think we need to ask Mason when we see him." Ms. Washburn parked the car near the office door. There are rarely many cars in the strip mall parking lot, as the stores there are not well-known names, part of chains that usually command higher rents in larger venues. It is one of the reasons Questions Answered can afford the rent in our office. We each got out of the car and walked into the office after I unlocked the door.

Once inside Ms. Washburn and I took up our usual positions at our desks. I noted that I had missed a number of chances to exercise, so I checked my incoming e-mail quickly, then stood to start my rounds at the perimeter of the office. The unused space where tables and a counter for the pizzeria had been afforded me enough room to power walk effectively without having to stop often to avoid an obstacle.

Ms. Washburn, accustomed to my routine, did not look up. "Mason Clayton will be here in three hours," she said. "We can't ask him about the money until then. What do you want to concentrate on until then?"

"Do you know how to hack into bank records?" I asked, not really breathing heavily yet on my first of thirteen circuits around the room.

"You know perfectly well that I don't, and even if I did, I wouldn't do it." Ms. Washburn and I disagree on some areas of research. My focus is on results; the process itself does not especially interest me unless it yields answers. Ms. Washburn is convinced that some practices are morally questionable regardless of the good they might bring. I believe that if the question is worth answering and will create a beneficial result, any means necessary to achieve the goal of an answer is legitimate as long as it does no innocent person harm.

Since I know that I would not misuse any bank records I study, there is no particular harm in studying them. I would not remove money from people's accounts or use their information for any purpose other than to answer the question.

Ms. Washburn sees it differently.

"Very well," I said. "I will do that myself when I am finished."

"Samuel," she scolded.

"I do not ask you to violate your moral code," I reminded her. "What I will ask is that you—"

Ms. Washburn gasped and I stopped talking but not exercising, my arms now extended over my head. "What is wrong?" I asked.

"I've been checking on the die you found on the floor in the Quik N EZ," she said. "There aren't many in the world like it."

"That should make it easier to trace," I suggested. "Hardly cause for a gasp."

"There's a reason there aren't many," she went on. "Among gamers it's considered cursed merchandise."

I stopped walking for a moment to think, then resumed my gait. "Cursed?" I said.

"Yes. According to this website, apparently when you see that particular die it means someone is going to be killed soon."

THIRTEEN

"It's ridiculous," said Simon Taylor.

Ms. Washburn had not suggested we call her estranged husband for more information about Swords and Sorcerers, but since he had established himself as our resident expert on the subject, it seemed only logical that we get in touch with him concerning the new information Ms. Washburn had discovered regarding the die I had found at the scene of Richard Handy's murder.

"What makes that more ridiculous than any other superstition?" I asked. I found myself feeling mildly angry with Simon Taylor, although I could not think of a particular offense he had aimed at me. Other than once when on the phone he had said he didn't like me.

The speakerphone option on our office phone was not working perfectly, so there was a one-second delay between the time I finished speaking and the time Simon responded. I was momentarily confused as to whether he was thinking about the question in depth.

"I thought you were going to ask what makes it more ridiculous than anything else in S and S," he said.

"I do not judge people based on their preference in recreational activities," I assured him. I was not certain that had sounded the way I'd intended, but my experience has been negative when I have tried to rectify such perceived situations.

"I appreciate that," Simon answered. "But getting back to your question, the idea of a cursed die is just a little too far for virtually every S and S player I know. We're not delusional and we know perfectly well that this is a fantasy activity. Nobody I've ever met believes in wizards and elves."

"What about Roy McCloskey?" Ms. Washburn asked. Her smile bordered on mischievous.

Simon's voice sounded equally amused. "Roy doesn't count."

I refrained from asking about Roy McCloskey, because it seemed he didn't count. "How would such an item gain that kind of reputation? Is there any evidence that anyone besides Richard Handy has ever died violently while carrying that particular type of die?"

It was Ms. Washburn and not her husband who responded. "According to this website, three other people have been found dead either by suicide or homicide while holding that die, which they call a Tenduline. It is made by one company in Mentor, Ohio, and only on a very limited basis. You really had to look for it to find one, and you couldn't straight order it—you had to request it specifically. Even the price isn't listed, which leads me to believe it's pretty expensive. Richard Handy must have really wanted that item very badly."

"Assuming it was Richard's," I pointed out. "It is still quite possible the die belonged to Tyler or to an as-yet-unknown third party."

"That's true," Ms. Washburn answered. "But I'm betting it was Richard's. It had rolled just to the point where it might be if it was in his hand when he was shot." I had thought Ms. Washburn was not even stealing a glance in the direction of the dairy display when I assessed the crime scene, but she works hard at not letting her emotions get in the way of her performance at Questions Answered. She must have forced herself to look.

"I don't dispute the idea that it is possible," I told her. "I'm suggesting we not jump to conclusions before we have—"

"—a sufficient amount of data. Yes, I know," Ms. Washburn said.

Simon Taylor's voice came through the speakerphone. "I don't want to *intrude*," he said with emphasis, "but is my part of this conversation over?"

Ms. Washburn scowled a bit.

"One last question," I said.

"You say that a lot," Simon interjected. I did not respond to that.

Instead, I simply continued as if he had not spoken. "Is the die itself valuable? Is it possible someone would kill Richard in an attempt to take possession of it?"

This time I think Simon really was thinking his answer through before responding. Ms. Washburn's hand went to her chin and stroked it, a gesture I had seen her husband perform when we were at his apartment.

"I've never heard of any S and S item being so valuable it would be worth killing someone for," he said after a moment. "Some people do get awfully caught up in the game, but if I had to generalize, I'd say most players are about as nonviolent a bunch as you could imagine."

"Thank you," I said. "You have been most helpful."

"You *do* always talk like that, don't you?" Simon asked.

I was about to answer, but Ms. Washburn responded first. "Be nice, Simon."

"Okay, okay. I'll see you later." He disconnected the call.

I looked at Ms. Washburn. "I'm bringing him a couple of things from the house," she said. "It's not a big deal. And we said we weren't going to discuss my marriage, Samuel."

"We agreed we would not discuss your divorce," I pointed out. "Besides, I have said nothing on the subject at all."

Ms. Washburn's eyes rolled in a gesture of either sarcasm or disbelief; I am not certain. "I can barely hear myself think over your not saying anything on the subject," she said.

I did not understand that comment and felt it was best to refocus our attention on the question at hand. "Have any of the websites Simon e-mailed to you given us any additional information on the Tenduline?"

"The only thing I can say for certain about it is that it's very rare," she answered, looking at her screen. "As far as I can tell, there are fewer than twenty of them in the world that are exactly like this one." She looked at the die on the desk in front of her. It was still secured in a plastic sandwich bag. She picked up the bag and looked at the die. "How could this thing cause so much trouble?" she asked.

"We have seen stranger things happen," I reminded her.

"Yeah, but at least I understood those." She stood up. "Do you want a ride home for lunch?" she asked.

I had checked the time on my iPhone one minute before to reassure myself the phone was still in my possession. It was 11:46 a.m. "I am not due until twelve thirty," I said. "Is there a reason you need to leave now?"

"I want to go back to my house and get the things I'll be bringing Simon later," she answered. "Is that a problem?"

I considered the question. It was not a problem for Ms. Washburn to leave at this time. It was not really a problem for me to arrive at my home approximately thirty minutes early for lunch, although it was somewhat disconcerting for me to vary that seriously from my routine. If Ms. Washburn was asking whether there was a problem with her retrieving articles from her home to return to her estranged husband, however, that would be a more complex question.

"Are you going to reconcile with Simon?" I asked.

Ms. Washburn looked as if she had been punched in the stomach with moderate force. She let out a breath quickly, almost a grunt, and her nostrils flared. Her eyes did not have their usual friendly softness to them.

"I thought I made it clear, Samuel. I'm *not* going to discuss my marriage with you."

It was now obvious I had misinterpreted her question about the problem, but it would be irrational to pretend I had not expressed some concern about her private life. Even if we agreed, as Ms. Washburn sometimes suggests, that "it never happened," the fact was that it had happened and there was nothing that could change that reality.

"I misunderstood," I said by way of explanation. "But I am somewhat puzzled by your sudden change of attitude toward Simon."

Ms. Washburn's voice came slowly, as if with effort. She did not raise her voice, which would have been a clear indication that she was angry. Instead, she spoke slowly and in low tones. I was not familiar with that sound from her, which made concentrating difficult. I tried to decode the tone rather than to listen to the words, but I heard them and filed them away for later reference.

A few moments later I realized she had said, "I'm going to leave now." But by the time I had played the message back in my head, Ms. Washburn had walked out the office door. I could see her get into her car and back out of the parking space. I wondered if she meant she was leaving for lunch, or leaving Questions Answered forever.

I did the only thing I could do under the circumstances. I called my mother and asked for a ride home.

FOURTEEN

"THE END OF A marriage isn't ever an easy thing, Samuel." Mother sat across from me at the dining room table. Mother sometimes serves lunch in the dining room, particularly if she is not sure whether Ms. Washburn will be accompanying me. In this case, she had clearly miscalculated. "Janet wants to believe that her marriage wasn't a mistake, that she didn't waste the time she has spent being married to Simon."

That seemed irrational. "But the marriage *was* a mistake," I said, noting the grilled cheese sandwich Mother had prepared was a little more well-done than I might have preferred. It was not seriously overcooked, so I decided not to point out the problem to Mother, who sometimes takes observations about her cooking more personally than they are intended. "If Ms. Washburn is now petitioning for a divorce, clearly she had concluded the marriage is a failure and should be terminated. Why would she want to believe something that is not the truth?"

"Love isn't something you can just quantify and tabulate, Samuel." Mother's eyes caught mine and she looked at the small salad next to my plate. She was signaling that I should not ignore the vegetables. I know that is a rational and reasonable thing to consider, but it is more a chore than I would hope. I took a bite of lettuce and she nodded. "A marriage isn't just a casual acquaintance. People stand up at an altar and promise to stay together forever. You don't give that up lightly."

"More than half of all marriages end in divorce," I pointed out. "I don't want to belabor the obvious, but my father has not been here for as long as I can remember."

Mother's eyes closed for a moment; I was concerned before I'd mentioned my father that I would cause her pain, but I was simply trying to make a coherent point. "I'm sorry if that was insensitive," I told her.

She shook her head. "It's a reasonable point. Your father did not keep his vow. A lot of people don't. That doesn't mean the commitment is less important. Janet is not the kind of person your father was, Samuel. She thinks things through and she doesn't act impulsively. You can be sure when she married Simon she was convinced they would be married for the rest of their lives."

"Do you think she'll come back and work at Questions Answered again?" I asked. That was the aspect of this incident most troubling to me. If Ms. Washburn left again, I believed she would not ever come back. And if that happened because of something I had said rashly, it would be difficult for me to accept. I was not sure I would ever be able to forgive Ms. Washburn.

"Oh, I don't think Janet would quit over a little misunderstanding," Mother said. Since she is usually correct about such matters, I did feel my stomach relax a little. To reward her, I ate more of the salad. "You just have to give her time to get through it."

"Get through what?" I asked after the food was gone from my mouth.

Mother scrutinized me, shook her head a bit, and said, "What do you think is the best lead you have in answering the question?"

I realized it was her way of changing the subject and so assumed that was the appropriate thing to do. There was no point in discussing this with Mother, as her explanation would undoubtedly confuse me more than none. "I think the game group, or at least the greater part of it, is not a promising source of information. Most of them live too far away to be plausible suspects in Richard Handy's death. In addition, finding a motive that makes sense is something of a stretch."

Seeing that we had both finished eating, Mother stood up and began clearing the table, so I did the same because I can perform the task faster. As I took her plate from her hand, Mother seemed to consider protesting and then decided against it. She knows I am determined in such matters to cause the least amount of physical stress on her.

"You're telling me what *isn't* your best avenue of research," she noted. "What *is* the most likely way to go?"

"This is a process of elimination, Mother. The more I can determine in my own mind which leads, as you call them, are invalid, the better I can identify more promising ones. If the only worthwhile person to pursue in Tyler's Swords and Sorcerers group is Margie Cavanagh, we can eliminate a number of other people."

"What about the people Richard Handy would play with?" Mother said. "Obviously all of those people are local."

"I don't know much about them yet," I said. "Ms. Washburn has not been successful in reaching any members of Richard's family on the phone."

"Why are you making Janet do that?" Mother asked, her face suggesting she knew the answer to her question. "Those people must be distraught. Is it that you don't want to deal with the emotion so you're forcing Janet to do it?"

"I don't think *forcing* is the word I would use. Making some phone calls is part of Ms. Washburn's responsibilities, and she knows that."

My cellular phone rang. I reached into my pocket for it and noted the caller was Dr. Shean, Tyler's therapist. Her call must have rung through the Questions Answered office phone. When I leave the office, I now forward the calls to my cellular phone. Until I had purchased the iPhone, all business calls had been forwarded to Ms. Washburn's mobile phone.

I pressed the "accept" button. "Hello, Dr. Shean," I said. "Allow me to introduce myself. I am Samuel Hoenig, the owner of Questions Answered."

There was almost no hesitation on the other end of the line. "Good to meet you, Mr. Hoenig. I am Lisa Shean. You left a message for me?" The last sentence was not a question but Dr. Shean said it as if it were.

"I did. I have some questions regarding a patient of yours, Tyler Clayton. Did his brother Mason inform you I might be calling?"

Mother looked at me defiantly as she began to load our used plates and glasses into the dishwasher. She knew I would not interrupt while on the phone, but she also knew that I would protest if she tried to wash them by hand in the sink. Mother is not frail, but I feel a sense of responsibility and she, after all, does the cooking.

"Yes," Dr. Shean answered. "Mason gave me his permission to discuss Tyler with you, but since Tyler is an adult, Mason's permission is not really all that valid."

"I understand," I said. "Surely he has also told you that Tyler has been arrested under suspicion of murdering a friend and that I am attempting to answer the question of who might have shot Richard Handy. I believe a few key points of information from you might help me complete that task."

"I'll tell you what I can, Mr. Hoenig, but I will not betray any confidential or personal information about Tyler. My privilege pertains even in this case, and you are not representing any law enforcement agency."

That was reasonable, so I nodded. Mother pointed at the phone. "I understand," I told Dr. Shean. "Please let me know if any of these questions would be in violation of that privilege. First, how important was Tyler's perceived friendship with Richard Handy to him?"

"It was very important to Tyler," Dr. Shean said. I waited, but no further statement was forthcoming.

"From what he told you about Richard, was it your opinion that Richard really was a legitimate friend of Tyler's, or that he was in some way manipulating Tyler into believing that was the case?"

Dr. Shean took a moment before responding. "Without going into detail, my perception from a distance was that Richard was not really Tyler's friend."

"I agree," I said. "Did you tell that to Tyler?"

"What was said in therapy is outside the purview of this conversation, Mr. Hoenig."

"Fair enough. How was Tyler perceived by the other members of his therapy group?"

Dr. Shean did not hesitate this time. "I think I just said that anything said in therapy was not appropriate for me to tell you," she answered.

"I am not asking about what was said in session. I'm asking for your opinion."

"My opinion is that Tyler was accepted by the members of the group and there was never any friction evident in sessions. I'm not going to say more than that."

Clearly Dr. Shean did not intend to betray any patient confidences, which was admirable and ethical within the bounds of her profession. It was also a serious inconvenience for someone attempting to answer the question of Richard Handy's shooting.

"I am impressed with your integrity, doctor," I said.

"It's not special," Dr. Shean answered. "If I told you more than this, it would be serious violation of my privilege and I could be brought up on charges or lose my license. I will not do that no matter what your intention, Mr. Hoenig."

"Doctor, I myself have been diagnosed with an autism spectrum disorder," I said, grimacing just a bit on the word *diagnosed* and again on *disorder*, both of which Mother certainly noticed. "I wonder if I might prevail upon you to include me in a group therapy session."

I pictured Dr. Shean's eyes narrowing, although I had no idea what her physical appearance might be like. "I will not include you in Tyler Clayton's group," she said.

"Of course not. Would I be welcome in the group that meets immediately *after* Tyler Clayton's?"

Mother shook her head in wonder.

————

Ms. Washburn called to ask if I needed a ride back to the office as soon as I disconnected with Dr. Shean, who had been persuaded to include me in a group therapy session involving none of the participants in Tyler Clayton's weekly meetings. I accepted the ride, feeling more confident that Ms. Washburn would not have offered it if she were planning on leaving the business forever.

When I mentioned that to her in the car, Ms. Washburn sighed lightly. "Seriously, Samuel," she said. "If you're going to act like a scared puppy every time I leave the office with anything but a smile, you and I are going to have a very long and very tense working relationship."

I focused on the phrase "very long" and sat back in the passenger seat. "Very well," I said. "I will ask no more questions about your marriage or your divorce."

Again came a small sigh, which confused me; had I said something troubling? "I need to apologize to you about that, Samuel," Ms. Washburn said. "I got mad at you because I'm mad with myself and I just misdirected it. My lawyer told me not to even talk to Simon, and then I did because of our new question, and now things are confusing. It wasn't your fault that happened; it was mine. But your asking made me have to think about it, and I didn't want to. So I got annoyed with you. I'm sorry."

Since I had not suggested, nor had I even urged, that Ms. Washburn contact her estranged husband in connection with the question about Richard Handy's death, I did not feel responsibility for the dilemma she reported. But I was not sure why she was apologizing to me when she seemed to be more angry with herself.

"I accept your apology," I said because that was what I had been told was a proper response under such circumstances. "But I think you are, as you have said to me in the past, being 'too hard on yourself.'"

Ms. Washburn made a right turn, one eyebrow raised. "Really," she said when we were again traveling straight ahead.

"Yes. I am told that these types of … entanglements can be very difficult and emotionally draining. Perhaps you are not being cognizant enough of the stress you are experiencing."

"Entanglements?" Ms. Washburn asked.

"Divorce. Mother says it is never an easy thing."

Ms. Washburn approached the strip mall on Stelton Road. "She's right. Samuel, what do you know about your father?"

That seemed an odd *non sequitur*. Still, if Ms. Washburn saw fit to ask, the question must have some significance. "I know very little," I said. "He left when I was four years old. It is my belief, although Mother will not confirm it, that raising a child with my type of behavior pattern was a factor in his departure. When I ask Mother about him—and I have not done so in years—all she will say is that he was a good man who did not know how to cope."

Ms. Washburn considered what I had said and nodded. "Thank you, Samuel," she said. "I know it couldn't have been easy for you to share that."

"You are entitled to a fair answer to a fair question," I told her.

"So are you. I'll try to remember that."

We were back in the Questions Answered office for eight minutes when Mason Clayton and his sister Sandy Clayton Webb arrived in Mason's car, a 2010 Hyundai Santa Fe, an odd name for a vehicle designed in South Korea. They walked into the office, Sandy with arms folded across her chest and Mason with a distraught expression. He cracked his knuckles twice before reaching the office area, opposite the drink machine and the pizza oven.

Ms. Washburn put out her hand in greeting. Sandy did not accept it, and kept her arms folded.

"Really," she said. That did not shed much light on the situation.

I decided to concentrate on the issue at hand. "Mr. Clayton," I said to Mason when they were near enough to hear and be heard, "did you bring the laptop computer?"

"Tyler's started talking again," Mason said.

"That's wonderful," Ms. Washburn said, but her voice betrayed feelings of confusion and concern. Was that just my interpretation? There was no way to know.

"No it's not," Sandy said, her words sounding like they were spat rather than spoken.

"Tyler's been talking to the police," Mason went on as if his sister and Ms. Washburn had not spoken. "And according to Detective Hessler, he has confessed to killing Richard Handy."

FIFTEEN

"I shot Richard. I shot him with the gun."

Tyler Clayton looked agitated.

Arms swinging widely at his sides, he paced the conference room at the Somerset police department headquarters. He was awaiting transfer to Somerset County jail in Somerville, approximately sixteen minutes by car. If the public defender assigned to him was not able to convince the judge in the case that Tyler was not a flight risk or a danger, he would be sent there within the hour, according to Sgt. Thomas Pendleton, who had been at the desk when we had arrived.

Mason and especially Sandy were particularly concerned about this possibility, given Tyler's level of social interaction and his anxiety at dealing with anything outside his routine. I agreed they were correct to be worried—this type of situation would be Tyler's worst nightmare. Naïve, frightened, and barely verbal, he would be terrorized and victimized at even a minimum-security prison, which New Jersey county jails are not.

They had received the news of Tyler's confession through Mason's cellular phone while they were in his sport utility vehicle on the way to Questions Answered, or, Sandy said, they would have gone directly to the Somerset police and cancelled our meeting.

"We can't leave him in the hands of a public defender," Mason said. "I'm calling the guy from TV."

Ms. Washburn winced. "T. Harrington Swain?" she asked. "Do you know any attorneys at all?"

Sandy scowled. "Not *criminal* lawyers," she said. "Divorce lawyers, sure. But a murder charge? What do we look like?" I did not understand how Sandy and Mason's appearance would indicate their previous level of criminal activity, but this did not seem the time to ask.

"I can make some calls," Ms. Washburn offered.

"There's no time." Mason seemed firm in his stance. "We'll call the guy from TV once we're in the car. I want a lawyer in Tyler's corner before we get to the cops."

There was a great deal of disagreement, but we took two vehicles to the police station. I was not interested in testing Mason's driving skills for the first time when he was upset and trying to hire an attorney for his brother via the cell phone in his car. Even with hands-free operation, studies have shown that having a conversation, particularly one on the telephone, while driving leads to increased risk of a vehicular accident. Ms. Washburn and I followed in her Kia Spectra.

"How will we get in to see Tyler?" Ms. Washburn asked. "You and I are not family and we are not part of his defense team. He doesn't even have a defense team yet."

"Police are not always completely rigid on the rules of visitation," I told her. "We can only hope the people in Somerset will see the kind of character Tyler has, that he is not a typical offender, and let anyone who might be helpful in to talk to him."

"Do you think Tyler will want to talk to us?" she said.

"I'll be surprised if he is talking at all, despite what Sandy told us."

Sergeant Pendleton did indeed allow the four of us into the conference room to see Tyler, whose hands were not cuffed. He continued to pace the area in front of the conference table where Ms. Washburn, Mason, Sandy, and I had gathered to confront him.

I was the only one seated.

"I shot Richard," Tyler said. "I shot him. I took the gun and I shot him."

"Why?" Mason asked him, his voice gentle as if attempting to modulate Tyler's mood. "Why did you shoot him?"

"I shot Richard," Tyler repeated. "I took the gun and shot him." His gaze seemed fixed on his sister Sandy.

"The sergeant told us that's all he's been saying," Sandy said. "He hasn't given a reason. He hasn't told them anything about how it happened. He just says he shot this guy and he repeats it no matter what you say to him."

This was probably not going to be an especially useful interrogation if that was the case. "Tyler," I said, "why did you paint the security cameras?"

Tyler stopped pacing and looked at me. His eyes bored into mine like he was trying to find the answer to my question inside my head. He held my gaze for what I believed to be an uncomfortable moment.

"I shot Richard," he said again. "I shot him." He resumed his pacing.

I looked at Ms. Washburn, who appeared very concerned. Oddly, I found myself wondering about her possible reconciliation with her estranged husband rather than Tyler's predicament or Mason's question.

"Tyler," Sandy said, touching her brother on his arm, "tell us what happened."

That seemed counterproductive. Tyler simply stared at her. "I shot Richard." Tyler believed he had already explained exactly what had occurred.

"How many times did you fire?" I asked more loudly.

Sandy gave me a look that was not friendly.

Again, my question seemed to stump Tyler; he stopped his movement and looked this time at the ceiling. He did not repeat his new mantra, instead reverting to his previous sound of, "Nnnnnnnnnnn…"

Sandy flung her hands into the air. "Well *that's* a step backwards!" she exclaimed. "Will you leave so we can get to the bottom of this?"

"If you ask me to do so, I will go outside," I told her. "But I have been getting more useful reactions from Tyler than you have. I am beginning to believe he did not shoot Richard Handy at all."

Sandy opened her mouth to answer but had no time before the conference door opened and a man whose face was vaguely familiar entered the room. He scanned the gathered group with his eyes in less than one second and immediately began barking orders at us.

"Everybody out of the room," said T. Harrington Swain. "I'm here to consult with my client and I don't want anyone coloring his answers."

"I shot Richard," Tyler said. "I took the gun and shot him."

"Let's not broadcast that, son," Swain said to his client. "We have enough of an uphill battle without you giving the other side ammunition against us."

"Mr. Swain!" Sandy sounded offended. But the same words were coming from Mason at the same moment, and if my ear was hearing it accurately, his voice seemed considerably more pleased to see the lawyer. He stood up and offered his hand.

"I'm Mason Clayton," he said. "We spoke on the phone." This seemed information Swain would have already known, but Mason's insistence on telling it to Swain did not seem ill advised. The lawyer smiled and nodded in his direction, then took his hand and shook it.

"Mr. Clayton," he said, "thank you for calling me. I can see why you did."

"I shot Richard," Tyler insisted. "I shot him."

"You might want to stop saying that, Tyler." Swain looked at his client, who continued to pace, then back at Mason by way of Sandy. "What's wrong with him, exactly?"

I did not care for the terminology Swain used in reference to Tyler, but I was not aware of the protocol the Clayton family had for dealing with such issues, so I did not object. In fact, the presence of Ms. Washburn and me had not even been acknowledged yet.

"He has a form of autism," Sandy told the attorney. "He usually does better than this, though."

Swain nodded. "All right." He ignored Tyler's continued pacing, arms constantly in motion, then trained his gaze first on me, then on Ms. Washburn, whom he seemed to find more interesting. He spoke to her. "And who are you? What is your role here?"

I wanted to introduce myself and my associate, but the more professional thing was to listen as Ms. Washburn said, "I'm Janet Washburn. My boss Samuel Hoenig and I were hired by Mason to answer a question." She gestured toward me at the mention of my name.

Swain did not turn in my direction. "And what was that question?" he asked.

Normally it is the policy at Questions Answered not to discuss our clients or their areas of interest with anyone outside the research project. But in this case, Swain's role fell into a gray area; he was involved, although not necessarily in answering the question but in dealing with its consequences—and after all, he had spoken again to Ms. Washburn and not to me.

"Who killed Richard Handy?" she informed him.

"Uh-huh. And what answer did you find?"

This time I felt it was necessary, as the proprietor of Questions Answered, to speak for my company. "We have not yet gathered enough information to answer the question definitively."

Swain nodded curtly and then turned toward Mason and Sandy. "I need you all to leave the room, please. Your presence here is going to make it that much more difficult to get complete truth from my client."

Sandy's eyes narrowed. "*We're* your client," she said. "We're paying the bill. So I think maybe we'll stay in the room while you question him."

"Sandy," Mason admonished.

"No. I don't like the way this guy waltzes in here and tells us what to do. I'll sit here quietly away from Tyler and see how the magician does his job, okay?" She sat down in the chair farthest from Tyler, who was paying no attention to the drama before him and continued to pace, quietly repeating his admission of guilt more to himself than to anyone else in the room.

Swain looked at her, appeared to consider the situation, and nodded. "Very well. But these two should leave." He gestured toward Ms. Washburn and me.

"Mr. Swain …" Ms. Washburn began.

I stood. It was time for me to begin exercise anyway. I considered the dimensions of the room, decided they could not be calculated accurately, and said, "That's fine. It is doubtful you will be able to persuade Tyler to say anything other than that he shot Richard Handy and he used the gun, which is not useful information and is likely not the truth. But our continued presence here will not contribute anything of use to Tyler's defense and we have other avenues to pursue in order to complete our task." I started toward the door.

"Samuel," Ms. Washburn said.

"Yes, thank you, Ms. Washburn, I did forget." I proffered my hand to Swain and said, "Allow me to introduce myself. I am Samuel Hoenig, proprietor of Questions Answered." He took my hand probably more out of habit than thought. I shook his once, let go, and continued to the door.

Ms. Washburn followed, not saying anything else other than good-byes to the other three in the room. I did not see the need, although I am aware that is the social custom. We left the police station and headed toward Ms. Washburn's car.

I will admit, however, that on the way out I turned to Mason and said, "It is a good thing that we had separate cars, isn't it?"

He did not answer.

SIXTEEN

"Richard Handy's parents are divorced," Ms. Washburn said. "His father is in Arizona, and his mother remarried and moved to Delaware. As far as I can tell, neither of them had been in touch with their son for at least a year."

She was driving us toward the home of Dorothy Brewer, a woman who had been part of Richard's Swords and Sorcerers group, according to the aunt she had called just after we'd left the police department. The aunt, whose name was Audrey Seldin, was not close but was the only relative dealing with Richard's funeral. She did not have time to see us, she said. Perhaps in three days, which I thought would be after the question was answered. But Ms. Washburn took Audrey's contact information and stored it in her cellular phone.

"How did you find out about his parents and locate his aunt?" I asked. "You didn't seem to know this before we went inside."

"I flirted a little with the officer who was in charge of the records."

That struck me hard because the admission was so unexpected. I stammered a bit and said, "Ms. Washburn, you are a married woman, at least for the time being."

She laughed. "It was just a little flirting, Samuel. I wasn't going to *do* anything about it. You really do need to get a better sense of this sort of thing."

I had recovered sufficiently, although far from completely, to ask, "When?"

"When do you need to get a better sense?"

"No. When did you … flirt with the officer?"

"You went in first to see Tyler when Mason and Sandy were walking in. I hung back a little bit because I could see how the guy behind the desk was looking at me and I figured I could use it." She did not look at me, but I must have made a sound that indicated my stunned condition. "We needed some help, Samuel. It wasn't a big deal, believe me."

It is true that I do not understand the practice of flirting. It falls into a nebulous territory between mild notice and romantic interest that does not fully make sense. Either a person has some intent or he does not; the blend that is both and neither is very confusing for someone like me. My mother has often intimated that she believes I have some romantic interest in Ms. Washburn, although I do not believe that to be the case. Still, there must be some behavior I exhibit which gives Mother the mistaken impression. I do not see it myself.

"Is it crossing a line to ask how Simon would feel about you doing something like that for your job?" I asked.

Ms. Washburn's crooked smile faded a bit. "That's not relevant," she said.

We did not speak again until we arrived at the home of Dorothy Brewer in a suburban area of Bound Brook, a town on the eastern end of Somerset County, not a long drive from where Richard Handy had lived in Franklin Township. The house was modest, likely a product of the 1980s, and exhibited no frills. It was clean and carefully maintained.

Dorothy told us she was twenty-one years old, although she could have passed for a high school girl. She was small, perhaps five-foot-one, wearing no makeup and sporting eyeglasses she seemed ashamed of, as she removed them as soon as Ms. Washburn and I entered the kitchen, where she asked us to sit on barstools next to a pass through. "The living room is where my folks entertain," she said. "I was just making myself a smoothie. You guys want anything?"

Ms. Washburn, probably cognizant of my rising anxiety level, said, "Could you hold up for a moment? We'd like to ask you a few questions, and it's best if you're not distracted because we need your best answers."

But Dorothy waved a hand. "Oh, don't worry," she said. "I can do both things at once. Fire away."

Ms. Washburn stole a glance in my direction. My face must have appeared grim, but I nodded slightly. "Fine," Ms. Washburn told Dorothy. "Tell us how you knew Richard Handy."

"I played S and S with him." Dorothy poured yogurt into a blender pitcher. She reached into a bowl of fruit on the kitchen counter next to the blender and pulled out a banana, which she started to peel. I wanted to turn away, but I could not bring myself to do so. "That's really all I know."

"How did the group organize itself?" I asked. Dorothy used a knife to cut the banana into slices directly into the blender. My stomach began to churn, and it was very unlikely this would be the end of the exercise. "How does a group of people decide to play a game like this together, assuming you never knew each other before you began?"

Dorothy scooped up some blueberries with her bare hand and literally tossed them into the mixture. I took a deep breath. I prefer to see foods separated, and the idea of these myriad textures being forced together was extremely disturbing. I did my best to focus on the questioning. But Dorothy, in creating her beverage, was not helping, taking time to think of how to answer my question, which I had considered simple.

"We met through the Painted Panel," she said, as if that explained anything.

"The Painted Panel?" Ms. Washburn asked.

"Oh, yeah." Into the blender went seven strawberries Dorothy removed from a plastic bag she found in her freezer, a few steps from the counter. She had not even removed the leaves at the top of each fruit. "It's a comic book store in Somerville that runs some games. That's where we used to play, on Wednesday nights."

Dorothy put the top on the blender receptacle and positioned it on the rotators, about to set the machine in motion. "Before you do that," I asked, "can you tell us about the dynamics of the group?"

"Sure, but I can do this at the same time," she said. And I actually felt nauseated as she reached for the button on the keypad.

"It's the noise," Ms. Washburn interjected. "Just hang on until we can get your answers. You know, I'm recording this for later and we won't be able to hear you." She pointed to her cellular phone, perhaps intimating that it was the recording device. I was as grateful to Ms. Washburn as I have ever been.

"Oh, sure," Dorothy said. "See, there was a flyer up on the wall at the Painted Panel about seven, eight months ago saying they were starting a game and you should sign up if you were interested, and I was, so I did. The three guys did too, and we started a couple of weeks later. Richard was just a player, not the SM."

I recalled that the sword master was the player who actually concocted the storylines and created challenges for the players. Perhaps that was an area to explore. "Who was the SM?" I asked.

"Becky Tanenbaum. She likes telling everybody what to do." She turned back toward the blender. "You guys sure you don't want any?"

"Just one more thing," I said, my voice perhaps sounding a bit more urgent than I intended. Getting out of here before Dorothy pulverized all those ingredients seemed terribly important at the moment.

I'd had the desired effect; Dorothy turned away from the blender and back toward Ms. Washburn and me. "What's that?" she asked.

I gestured to Ms. Washburn, who produced the Tenduline in its plastic sandwich bag from her purse. She held it out toward Dorothy. "Do you know what this is?" she asked.

"Sure. It's an S and S dice." No one seemed interested in getting the word right except me. "So what?"

"Take a closer look," I suggested.

Dorothy leaned in a bit and reached for the bag. "Don't touch, please," Ms. Washburn said. "This might turn out to be evidence."

"In Richard getting shot?" Dorothy was not, apparently, the most quick-minded of women.

"Yes," I said. "Please look at it carefully, but don't touch."

Dorothy's eyes grew wide and she nodded. She looked at the die in Ms. Washburn's hand. "Oh, it's a Tenduline," she said, her voice with a tiny shudder. "They're cursed, you know. Where'd you get it?"

"We found it near where Richard was lying," Ms. Washburn said. "You've never seen it before?"

"No, and I hope I never see one again. Somebody dies whenever— oh my god. You mean you found that right by Richard when he was dead?" Ms. Washburn nodded. "So the curse is true! Get that thing out of here!"

"We just want to understand," I told her. I would have been perfectly happy to leave at that moment just to avoid the sight of the smoothie Dorothy was about to concoct. "That wasn't Richard's die?"

"Of course Richard died! Now take that thing and go!"

"No," Ms. Washburn said, "that's not what—"

But it was too late. Dorothy turned and violently pressed a button on the blender. My eyes couldn't avoid the hideous vision of the fruit and yogurt merging into something that was not smooth and not really a drink, so it was misnamed and deceiving in its function. I felt my neck start to tremble.

"Let's go," I said to Ms. Washburn.

"But—"

"It's fine." I put a hand up to my right eye and turned to the left, where the front door was located. "Thank you, Ms. Brewer!"

"Samuel," Ms. Washburn said, but I was already halfway to the door.

It did no good. I couldn't erase the image of that smoothie and it kept me awake far past my normal bedtime for the next three nights.

———

"Could the Tenduline be Tyler's?" Ms. Washburn asked.

We had spent the ride back to Questions Answered debating my somewhat hasty exit from Dorothy Brewer's home, but I believed that Dorothy had been clear the die was not Richard Handy's, as she had played Swords and Sorcerers with him regularly and had never seen the item before. Ms. Washburn was careful to call Dorothy when we returned to the office, but the young woman did not answer her call, intentionally or not.

"At this moment, all we suspect is that it was not Richard Handy's," I said, finishing an exercise session and sitting at my desk. I had a bottle of spring water from the vending machine, but Ms. Washburn had said she did not want a diet soda. "It is possible that it belongs to Tyler, and it is possible it belongs to the person who killed Richard. It is equally possible, as when Richard answered my question about being Tyler's friend, that Dorothy was simply mistaken."

"Richard Handy was mistaken about whether or not he was Tyler's friend?" Ms. Washburn asked.

I suspect Mother would say I was "pouting." "You know what I meant."

"How do you know for sure that Tyler didn't shoot Richard?" Ms. Washburn asked. "Tyler insists he did."

"Tyler continued to repeat his assertion that he had shot Richard no matter what was being said in the room. But when I asked him specific questions about the crime, he stopped saying he had shot Richard and simply stared. He didn't know the answers."

"That's not much," Ms. Washburn suggested.

"Perhaps not, but it convinces me. Besides, I do not believe Tyler, in a fit of rage over our answer to his question, immediately created a plan to blind the security cameras in the Quik N EZ and stole Mason's gun to shoot his supposed friend," I answered. I began a search on my computer for recent reports of large contraband recovery operations in the Somerset County area. There were no promising results immediately. It did not help that I wasn't sure exactly what I was searching for. "You'll recall that when Tyler left our office, he was adamant in his insistence that Richard was indeed his friend, and that he would prove it to us. What would have changed his view on that subject?"

A Somerset County investigator had taken credit for the recovery of three kilos of cocaine two months earlier, but had then been charged with possession and intent to distribute, indicating he had pretended to find his own supply when it was obvious the authorities were closing in. That was not the contraband I needed.

"It makes sense, but it's all circumstantial," Ms. Washburn pointed out. "It won't stand up in a court of law."

I shrugged, a gesture I had been taught by a classmate in ninth grade. "That is not our problem. We are attempting to answer Mason's question, not to provide a definitive defense for Tyler."

Ms. Washburn snapped her fingers. "That reminds me," she said, and reached for the office phone on her desk. She dialed a number (although the word *dialed* has not really been apropos for decades) and waited a moment. "Mason? This is Janet Washburn from Questions Answered. No, we just wanted to meet with one of Richard Handy's friends. What did Mr. Swain—oh? Well, that's good, isn't it? Yes. I'm glad to hear it."

I searched for contraband grocery items. An initial trial turned up nothing of note. There were some bananas missing in Princeton.

"One question, if it's okay," Ms. Washburn said into the phone. "Tyler's S and S group. Do you have any contact? You were going to bring the laptop computer and then … Yes. Okay, good." She immediately grabbed a pencil off her desk and jotted something down on the blotter I'd insisted she use if she was intent on placing cold cans of diet soda on the desk surface. Ms. Washburn takes notes on the blotter and changes it whenever the blotter is filled. "Great. Yes, thank you." She said good-bye to Mason Clayton—whom I assumed was the person she had called—and replaced the receiver on the phone cradle.

I was scanning my search engine on the seventh page of hits regarding stolen grocery shipments and finding nothing yet that met my criteria. "What did Mason say?" I asked Ms. Washburn.

"Mr. Swain managed to get Tyler out of jail for the time being. He arranged with a bail bondsman for Mason and Sandy, and he argued in a hearing that Tyler's confession, because he wasn't saying anything else, was a symptom of his ASD and therefore was not to be taken as a reliable statement." Ms. Washburn absently chewed on the eraser of the pencil, and I averted my gaze. It's not as bad as watching someone make a smoothie, but it isn't my favorite sight, either.

"I would advise Mason to check and make sure there isn't some prearrangement between Swain and the bondsman," I said. "The interest rates charged, even when the client is not a flight risk, as Tyler is not, can be exorbitant. I hope the Claytons got at least two bids on the bail."

Ms. Washburn sounded slightly irritated. "I didn't ask about that and you know it," she said. "Do you want to hear what *was* said?"

"You sound like an old married couple." I looked up at the voice and saw Mother walking in from the parking lot. "I was in the neighborhood." That is what Mother says whenever she decides to visit my office, although I have told her to feel free to drop in whenever she wants.

Ms. Washburn greeted Mother—they have become friendly—and guided her to her reclining chair. Mother's knees have good days and bad ones, and the way she was walking today indicated this was not one of the good ones. She sat heavily on the recliner and let out what I'm sure she thought was a contented sigh. But I worried that it indicated a level of pain that was increasing lately.

"It sounded like you were talking about Tyler Clayton," she said when she had sat and extended the footrest on the chair. She waved her right hand. "Don't let me stop you. You're working."

I informed Mother of our progress, or at least our activity, since lunch when she had seen me last. She listened attentively. "So Tyler's out on bail for now," she said. "Maybe that will help him get back to speaking."

"He is already speaking," I pointed out. "He is restricting himself to saying only one thing."

Ms. Washburn apparently decided not to argue that point—perhaps Mother's comment about us sounding like a married couple had worried her, although it had simply puzzled me (how can a person *sound* married?)—and pressed on with her recounting of the call with Mason Clayton.

"Yes. Tyler is home now at Mason's house. And according to Mr. Swain, the trial probably won't happen for at least six months, if it happens at all."

"If it happens at all?" Mother sounded concerned, leading me to wonder if I had missed some nuance in the news from Swain. "Does he not expect there to be a trial?"

Ms. Washburn hesitated before answering. "I didn't get much about that, but Mason says so far Mr. Swain is recommending that Tyler let him negotiate a plea bargain."

That would not be an unexpected turn. One of the ways an attorney like Swain retains a reputation for keeping his clients from being convicted is to rarely allow them to stand trial. Swain was simply protecting himself instead of his client. It was clear to me that Tyler had not shot Richard Handy, and I reiterated that stance to Ms. Washburn and Mother.

"*You're* certain, Samuel, but the court is going to need proof." Mother leaned back in the recliner, which made her appear to be preparing to sleep, although I knew it was a tactic designed to keep her knees elevated over her heart. Mother's orthopedist had recommended she stay that way for three hours every day. She normally does so for an hour in the morning and another when she is preparing for bed. This would be the third. "Even if that's not part of answering the question you got from Mason, if you want to keep that boy out of jail, you need to concern yourself with proof."

"You make a good point, Mother. Ms. Washburn, what else did Mason tell you?"

Ms. Washburn sat and looked at me for a moment. "Didn't I just say that? Didn't I just tell you that proof was important, and didn't you tell me it had nothing to do with answering Mason's question, which was our only concern? How come it convinces you when your mother tells you but not when I say it?"

The words were coming at me too quickly. "Which question would you prefer I answer first, Ms. Washburn?" I asked.

Mother chuckled. "Just like an old married couple," she said.

Ms. Washburn shook her head. "Forget it. The only other thing that happened on the phone was that Mason gave me two e-mail addresses, which he said Tyler gave him when he got home. Apparently Tyler is communicating better through the keyboard than through speaking."

That was not unusual for people diagnosed with autism spectrum disorders. For some, the idea of writing or typing out a message is much less stressful than speaking. It is not common among those who until recently would have been diagnosed with Asperger's Syndrome. We are known as "little professors" among those who have a taste for demeaning nicknames, because we tend to impart great amounts of information on specific topics.

"Samuel," Ms. Washburn said, focusing my attention on her once again, "did you hear me?"

"I'm afraid not. Could you repeat what you said, please?"

She did not roll her eyes in exasperation, which is one of the qualities I most appreciate in Ms. Washburn. "I said that Mason gave me contact information for two people in Tyler's S and S group, Adam Pasternak and Margie Cavanagh. He said he wouldn't call them Tyler's friends, but they were people who knew him. Tyler won't say anything more about them. He's not communicating much, especially about Richard's death, Mason said."

"Have you attempted to contact the two players yet?" I asked.

Mother gave me a disapproving look I did not understand.

"You saw me get off the phone with Mason," Ms. Washburn said. "When did you think I had time to get in touch with Adam and Margie?"

"That is a fair point." Sometimes when my mind wanders the passage of time is a less definite thing for me. "Would you do that, please?"

"What should I ask?" Ms. Washburn wanted to know.

"Ask when we can meet with them, and if they would mind coming here."

Ms. Washburn nodded, but looked up. "Why here?" she asked.

"Because our travel time might be limited," I said. "We have a great many people to see."

Ms. Washburn moaned a bit. "You can say that again." Then she looked up at me. "But don't."

Mother chuckled. "An old married couple," she said.

SEVENTEEN

ADAM PASTERNAK WAS A young man of twenty, he told us, who had taken up Swords and Sorcerers because he thought it would be a good way to meet people online. That had turned out to be only partially true, he said.

"I guess when I said I wanted to meet people, I meant I wanted to meet girls," Adam told us. He had been happy to answer Ms. Washburn's e-mail query and had driven to the Questions Answered office immediately upon responding. It seemed that Adam did not have a great deal he needed to do. "As it turned out, the only girl I met was Margie, and she wasn't interested in me. I mean, I've never *really* met her, you know. We just play S and S online. But anytime I tried to e-mail her or anything, she didn't answer."

I looked at Ms. Washburn, behind her desk and taking notes but doing her best to maintain eye contact with Adam. She did not look in my direction, which gave me no particular insight into the nuance of Adam and Margie's relationship. It was too late to ask Mother, who had taken the opportunity to say her farewells and drive home. So I said, "Were you interested romantically in Margie Cavanagh?" It didn't seem to have any relevance to Richard Handy's shooting, but we did not have enough facts to rule out any possibility yet.

Adam looked uncomfortable; even I could see that. He rotated his neck a bit and pulled at the open collar of his t-shirt, which bore an image from a science fiction film franchise. "I don't know," he said. "I mean, she's a girl and she likes RPGs, so it seemed possible, but Margie never gave me a chance to find out."

I looked at Ms. Washburn again. She said quietly, "Role-playing games."

"What about Tyler Clayton?" I asked. "How did he fit in with the group?"

Adam shrugged. "Okay. I never really talked to him except in the game. It's not like we were that social a group. We got together online, went on the mission of the day, and that was pretty much it until the next Wednesday."

"What did you think when you heard Tyler was arrested for murder?" I asked.

"He *was*?" Adam said. He broke into a grin. "That's so *cool*!"

———

Margie Cavanagh had not responded to Ms. Washburn's e-mail yet and it was almost time for us to close the office. We decided to regroup and begin organizing interviews for the next day. Ms. Washburn left, I did some more contraband research, found one interesting possibility I could not confirm, and called Mike for a ride home.

He arrived promptly as always but his demeanor was less gregarious than usual. I felt it was not my place to ask why, but Mike immediately volunteered. "Broke up with my girlfriend," he said. "Found out she was seeing another guy on the side. Made her choose, and she chose the other guy."

"I'm sorry to hear it," I said, because that is what I have been told is the appropriate response to such news. I don't really understand the concept of "breaking up," since people who are not married have no legal or verifiable commitment. Either one can terminate the relationship whenever the mood strikes, but there must be more to it than that because intelligent people like Mike attach a great deal of significance to the end of such a relationship. I might not be able to empathize, but I can respect him enough to recognize that it must be emotionally troubling.

"It's okay, Samuel. I knew it wasn't gonna last from the beginning. It just hurts more when there's somebody else. Makes you feel like you weren't good enough or something."

And that brought my mind back to Billy Martinez. I don't think I heard anything else Mike said on the ride home, but he thanked me for being a good listener when I exited the cab and said he might call me for a ride the next day if he needed to talk some more. I told him I would always be happy to ride in his taxicab and went into the house.

After dinner, since there was no baseball game that night, I told Mother I was going to do some work upstairs and went to my apartment in the attic. There isn't much there, at least less than the space would hold, although the pitched roof somewhat limits the height of furniture I could decide to install if that were my priority.

It was summer, so I turned the air conditioning unit on in my bedroom's lone window. This area of the house was not built with someone occupying the attic in mind.

I am not fond of headphones, as they put undue pressure on either side of my head. Ear buds are dangerous to one's hearing, so I avoid them whenever possible. In the attic, where I know the walls are thick and well-insulated, I play music on a stereo system that was my mother's in the 1980s and 1990s.

It includes a compact disc player, into which I inserted the Beatles album *Abbey Road*. That is among the most complex collections the band created, but so familiar I could listen to it, appreciate the artistry, and think separate thoughts at the same time. That might not be the case with *Sgt. Pepper's Lonely Hearts Club Band* or *Let It Be*. The history of the recording sessions would intrude on my thoughts if those albums were playing.

I do not like to talk to people on the telephone, which is one of the reasons Ms. Washburn so often handles that part of the Questions Answered business. I believe, also, that she prefers to make and receive all the business phone calls because she seems somehow insulted or surprised when I decide to take one myself. So I decided tonight not to call Billy Martinez or Margie Cavanagh.

The only contact information I had for Detective Hessler was his business card, which included only his phone number at the police station. I thought it unlikely he would still be there this late in the evening, and even less likely he would want to share information with a civilian. Perhaps an in-person meeting tomorrow, sometime before three p.m., would be more effective.

Instead, my best course of action for the evening was to revert to my habits before the founding of Questions Answered, only with a more specific focus. Part of the reason Mother suggested I start the business—in addition to her desire to see me leave the house on occasion—was that she knew I would often spend my time doing research on three screens with Retina display connected to an iMac on my desk.

She felt that practice could be successfully monetized, or at least that it would help me focus my skills toward helping others and not simply satisfying my own curiosities. I resisted at first, but as usual, Mother had prevailed. And as was equally typical, she had been proven correct. I not only made some income through Questions Answered, I enjoyed the challenge that answering unexpected questions could bring.

As John Lennon was beginning the vocal on "Come Together," I sat down at my desk to retrace my steps and examine the question from perspectives I had not yet considered, a practice I have found helpful in the past.

First, I researched the name Richard Handy in the Somerset County area. The criminal record (charged with selling contraband) was there, and little else followed it. The only obituary that had been published online or in print listed the name of his aunt, Audrey Seldin, as his only survivor. His parents' names were not listed. Clearly, Richard had not been married and had no children, which was not in any way a surprise.

Tyler Clayton's name, absent his recent arrest for Richard's murder, did not yield anything even that illuminating. He was listed among graduating students at Franklin High School ten years earlier. He had, apparently, taken some courses at Middlesex County College following graduation but had not received the associate's degree that institution offers. He did have a Facebook page, which I accessed through Ms. Washburn's account (with her permission) since I do not participate in social media. But Tyler rarely posted, except to discuss Swords and Sorcerers or video games.

He had three Facebook friends listed. One was his brother Mason, one was his sister Sandy Clayton Webb, and the other was Richard Handy.

Perhaps I had been mistaken in my answer to Tyler's question, I thought as George Harrison was singing "Something." If I had believed that Tyler truly had shot Richard, it might have been possible I'd be feeling partially responsible now. But I knew that wasn't the case, so I pressed on.

Besides, the difference between a Facebook friend and a true compatriot in life is often quite pronounced, I am told. This might have been one more way Richard had tried to convince Tyler he was a friend while simply trying to keep the exorbitant tips coming.

I was convinced that the hundred dollars per day was the key. But I still had no tangible evidence the payment was made more than the one time Ms. Washburn and I witnessed it. Hacking into Tyler's bank account would not be simple, but it would be possible after a large number of steps, not the least of which was determining in which bank he deposited the money he made from his job at the Microchip Mart. It would be a long process and not one I could successfully complete tonight.

I could call Mason Clayton and ask about Tyler's finances, and I might even get a response. But again, making phone calls is not my favorite thing. I am awkward and nervous on a call when I am not very well acquainted with the other party. I tend to choose the wrong word or to forget key questions. I am still somewhat anxious even in face-to-face conversations, but the telephone adds a layer of difficulty in that I cannot use my learned skills of reading another person's facial expression. I was, in short, not going to call Mason tonight.

Instead, I would look into his finances. But first I would compile data on Mason and his sister Sandy Clayton Webb.

Knowing the people for whom one works is not always an imperative in my business. Someone who asks about the comparative gravity of the Empire State Building to the Leaning Tower of Pisa does not invite further investigation (acceleration of an object dropped from any height is a constant, but velocity will vary until terminal velocity is reached because of the density of the atmosphere). But in this case, having some insight into my client and the people involved in the question could prove helpful.

I began with Sandy because she would probably require less time to research. Her personal life was in some ways a matter of public record: Her marriage and divorce were listed in local newspapers, as were the births of her children.

Digging just a bit deeper, I found that Sandra Clayton had graduated from Franklin High School fourteen years earlier, had attended Montclair State University, earning a degree in business administration. There she had met Thomas Webb, shortstop of the Montclair baseball team (which had not compiled a very impressive record) and married him ten years before she and I had met at Questions Answered.

They had two children. Brynna, age seven, was currently a second-grader while her younger brother, Douglas, was attending kindergarten at the Hillcrest School in Franklin Township. Their parents had divorced fourteen months earlier, according to a legal announcement in the *Home News-Tribune*.

Sandy had been working as an industry analyst at Bessemer Trust in Woodbridge before her daughter was born, and returned to work with a smaller firm on a part-time basis two months before her divorce had been finalized. I could only assume she was also receiving alimony and child support from her ex-husband Thomas Webb, who was chief operating officer for an investment firm in Newark. She had not sold the house the couple had bought before the birth of Brynna, and had not missed a mortgage payment or incurred any other blemish on her credit report.

In short, Sandy's information was not terribly interesting.

I did not know Mason's banking information either, but that would not be necessary for the kind of research I intended to do. So I began by running a general search on Mason's name and received over fourteen million hits on Google. By placing quotation marks on either side of the name, however, I could infer to the search engine that those words in that order were necessary to the search, and that cut the results to only 5,600 hits. A much more manageable number.

At that point, Paul McCartney began to sing about "Maxwell's Silver Hammer," a very odd bouncy song about a serial murderer. But since Richard Handy was not killed with a silver hammer (the fictional Maxwell's victims are a woman he knew from a class, the professor who taught the class, and a judge sentencing him for the previous crimes, which makes little narrative sense), the song was merely background music, not a source of information or inspiration.

Even with the possibilities already greatly reduced, it was fairly simple to eliminate a great many of the suggested links the search provided. Some referred to places, others to parts of longer names. Many were simply references to Facebook, suggesting I look for "people named Mason Clayton" on that site, which would be a measure of last resort. By cutting down on the unlikely and clearly useless references, soon the possibilities were reduced to only 307 suggestions and I began examining those more carefully.

Eventually I could determine that Mason Clayton was thirty-seven years old. He was unmarried and had always been so. He had no arrest record at all. The home he occupied was his own, purchased from his mother Eleanor's estate died four years earlier. He had paid his sister Sandy and brother Tyler, the other heirs, $256,000 for the house, on which he had a mortgage currently worth $197,542 from Valley National Bank, information which would make investigating his finances considerably less difficult if that became necessary. Mason had not missed a mortgage payment since buying the house, but recently two payments had been one week late in arriving.

On the surface that did not seem unusual. But online sources also disclosed that Mason Clayton was not an employee of a company that did light construction and power washing of homes and industrial buildings. That was the information Ms. Washburn and I had been led to believe by Sandy and by Mason, but county records filed seven years earlier told a different tale.

At that time, papers filed with the county clerk of Somerset indicated that Mason Clayton was in fact the owner of a power washing and roofing company called Able Home Help, of which he was the only operating officer listed. Instead of being an employee as we had been told, Mason was the proprietor of the company. Either both he and Sandy had deliberately misled Ms. Washburn and myself, or Mason had also lied to his sister and kept his purchase of the business from her.

That was curious, but not worthy of serious concern on its own. Family dynamics, since Mother is the only relative I have ever known on a daily basis, are not my strong suit, but I am aware they are often complicated. Mason wanting to keep his ownership of his business from his sister (and one assumes his mother and brother) was his own affair. It had occurred years before Richard Handy's murder and appeared to have no connection to that incident, which was at the core of the question Mason had asked me to answer.

His business dealings took an ominous turn, however, only three months before Richard's death. At that time, Able Home Help had filed for Chapter XI bankruptcy protection against its creditors, which included suppliers of construction materials, a company providing liability insurance for Mason's employees and clients, and Ms. Annette Cantonara, who apparently had been owed $32,000 by the business for faulty work done at her home, which had been repaired but for which she had paid another contractor to complete.

I looked at the time on my iMac; it was 9:03 p.m. I exhaled; that was not too late to telephone Ms. Washburn. Her voice on the other end of a call does not create any of the anxiety I would have speaking to even an occasional acquaintance. I took my cellular phone from my pocket and called her.

"What's going on, Samuel?" she asked. Ms. Washburn knew if I was calling after business hours, there must have been a development in the question.

I told her what I had discovered about Mason and Able Home Help. Ms. Washburn's voice was slightly strained for reasons I could not discern, but she said, "That's interesting, but I'm not sure it has anything to do with the question we're answering, does it?"

"It does," I said, "when it is noted that there is a second partner listed on the corporation papers for Able Home Help. Tyler Clayton."

EIGHTEEN

"I DON'T UNDERSTAND," Ms. Washburn said as she drove the next morning. "I've had a whole night to think about it and I still don't understand: Why would Mason put Tyler on his corporation papers as a partner and not tell him?"

I too had thought about this overnight. "We can't be sure Tyler didn't know," I said. "Since Richard's death he has not been especially communicative. But the idea that Tyler might need some income later in life, as a trust fund of sorts, might make sense. When we see Mason we will ask."

Ms. Washburn did not look especially satisfied with that explanation, but she did not comment. "How do you want to play this meeting with Detective Hessler?" she asked.

"Play?" I said. It did not occur to me that seeing the detective again would be similar to a game, with winners and losers.

"Yes, Samuel. It's something people say. How should we approach the situation? The detective is a police officer and we're Questions Answered, a private company that has no standing in the criminal justice community. What do you think will be the best tactic to get him to actually tell us something that might be helpful? What do you have planned?"

We were only four minutes from the Somerset police headquarters by my estimation and that of Ms. Washburn's global positioning satellite device. There was no longer much time to discuss strategy. "It never occurred to me that we would need a plan of action," I said. "I intend to ask the detective questions and see what his answers will be."

Ms. Washburn sighed just a little. "This might be a very short meeting," she said.

Indeed, at first it appeared Hessler would not see us at all. Despite Ms. Washburn having called ahead to ask him for a meeting, the detective had not alerted the dispatcher working at the front desk and she almost refused to allow us into the detective's office. When I insisted she page Hessler and ask if we should be allowed in, she finally capitulated and we were eventually led into the bullpen area inside. Hessler, as a lead detective, had one of the larger, more private cubicles.

"Why should I talk to you?" he said, as if asking for a reminder. "What can I possibly gain in this investigation from talking to you?"

"Possibly the correct answer to the question of who killed Richard Handy," I suggested.

"I know who killed Richard Handy. Tyler Clayton killed Richard Handy. He told me that himself."

Ms. Washburn gestured toward the two very functional but not comfortable-looking chairs in front of Hessler's desk. "May we?" she asked. Hessler nodded and we sat down. "Now, detective, certainly you've been smart enough to research Tyler's ASD."

"ASD?" he asked, as she no doubt had anticipated he would.

"Autism spectrum disorder. And since you have looked into it, probably talking to his therapist Dr. Shean, you know that what he keeps repeating over and over again probably has nothing at all to do with the situation or the truth. Not to mention that a person with that kind of disorder is inclined to agree to anything after even moderate interrogation because he wants to give the people asking the questions what they want. So Tyler's confession will get thrown out of court in about two minutes."

"The kid was found holding the murder weapon over the dead body of the victim with nobody else in that area of the store," Hessler reminded us. "I'll take my chances in court."

"Do you want to convict Tyler if he did not murder Richard Handy?" I asked. "Because the overwhelming evidence to this point suggests that he did not."

Hessler pointed his finger like a gun barrel. "Gun. Hand. Body. Confession. What evidence is there that says Clayton didn't pull the trigger?"

"There is the matter of hundred-dollar bills in the tip jar that were only for Richard Handy. There is the premeditation of bringing spray paint for the security cameras, which is inconsistent with Tyler's behaviors, particularly if he were acting irrationally based on the answer I had given him to his question about Richard's friendship. And there is this." I gestured to Ms. Washburn and she produced the Tenduline die in its sandwich bag from her tote. She placed it on Hessler's desk.

"What is that?" Hessler said, reaching for the bag.

"It's evidence we found at the crime scene that apparently your team missed," I said. "If you require a witness, Mr. Robinson the store owner was present when I found it."

"That doesn't tell me what it is, or why I should care," the detective responded.

He was correct about that. I endeavored to correct my error. "It is called a Tenduline. It is a very specific, very unusual die used in the game Swords and Sorcerers, which I'm sure you know was a pastime of Richard's." I did not mention Tyler Clayton's participation in the game because I saw no benefit to giving the detective that knowledge if he had not obtained it for himself.

"And so did Clayton," he said. Detective Hessler was not incompetent by anyone's standards.

"That is true. This is a very rare item, something that must be specifically ordered. There are very few of them in the country. And we found it lying in the area where Richard Handy's body fell. It may have fallen from his hand when he hit the floor."

"So? He could have dropped a harmonica too. That doesn't tell us anything about the way he died."

"Perhaps it does," I said. "This is not the kind of thing a person carries around in his hand casually. Richard had it with him for a reason, and he was holding it at the moment he was shot for a reason."

"Okay, I'll play along," Hessler said. "What's the reason?"

"I don't know. But consider this: When you arrested Tyler Clayton at the store, in what condition did you find his shoes?"

Hessler squinted at me. "His shoes?"

"Were they covered in blood?"

Ms. Washburn grimaced. I did not understand why because I do not have an emotional reaction to the sight of blood.

"Yes," Hessler said. "The soles had blood all over them, and some milk too."

"How about the tops of his shoes? His trouser legs? His shirt? Any blood there?"

Hessler looked at a photograph, probably of Tyler while being booked. "No. The rest of him was clean."

"Don't you think it's odd that a man standing that close to another and shooting him four times would not have been stained with his blood?"

Hessler frowned. Police officers do not care to have their work questioned. To be fair, most people in all professions feel that way.

"I'll grant you it's strange. But it doesn't prove anything," he said. "Nobody else in the store had that kind of spatter on them, either. And somebody for sure shot Richard Handy."

"Very well. May we have access to your evidence lab?"

Hessler stared briefly. "Let me put it this way," he said. "No." Then he paused. "What do you want to look at?"

"The security video from the Quik N EZ," I told him.

Hessler waved his left hand to dismiss the idea. "I've looked at it. You won't be able to see anything. A kid walks in wearing a hood and bending over so his face is hidden. Then a hand comes up and sprays the camera. Three cameras, all the same. You won't see anything."

"I don't expect to see anything," I told him. "I'm curious about what I will be able to hear."

It didn't take long for Hessler to set up a viewing of the security video in the same interrogation room where we had seen Tyler Clayton after his arrest. A monitor mounted on the ceiling provided the picture and sound, which Hessler had a uniformed officer feed through an electronics console outside the room.

"What are we looking for?" he asked.

"We are listening," I said.

Before he could protest, the screen came to life. (It remained an inanimate object, but that expression indicates the recorded image appeared on the screen.) As expected, the image was divided into three sections on the screen: One showing the counter, one showing the entrance to the convenience store, and the third positioned in the back near the dairy display, where Richard Handy was shot.

"Watch the entrance first," Hessler said, although it was obvious that was what we should be doing.

Sure enough, four seconds after the image appeared, a figure approximately Tyler Clayton's height and build, wearing the same loose, dark, hooded sweatshirt he usually sported, along with a Chicago

Cubs baseball cap and a pair of dark sunglasses, walked into the store, seemingly studying the floor. It was difficult to see any facial feature.

The figure walked out of frame in the direction of the camera and immediately after a hand was seen in very large close-up on the screen, followed by something difficult to focus on. "That's the nozzle of the spray can," Hessler said. And his claim was borne out a second later when the screen suddenly went black.

Because neither of the other cameras was trained in the direction of the one near the entrance, the vandal was not visible immediately. Clearly the high angle from the counter camera meant it was mounted near the ceiling from somewhere across the store. I remembered from our visits to the Quik N EZ that it was on the facing wall of the dairy counter, behind a display of magazines.

"He must have snuck under another camera here," Hessler said. There was no footage on that camera that showed anything but Richard Handy and Billy Martinez at the counter. But from somewhere off-screen a voice shouted, "Richard!" and he looked up in the direction of the dairy display.

"That sounds like Clayton's voice," Hessler said. Indeed, it might very well have been Tyler Clayton calling to the assistant manager. I refocused on the screen, thinking about that.

Without a word, Richard looked at Billy, who nodded and took over the cash register on which Richard was working. Richard, in what would be his last mistake, walked away from the counter toward the dairy display. Then the camera facing the cashiers went black too.

"He went for the third camera last," Hessler pointed out. I came close to saying how obvious that statement was, but Ms. Washburn shook her head slightly. That indicated the statement would not be well received. I watched the last monitor.

There, as a voice I did not recognize called out, "Hey!", probably spotting the vandal spraying the last camera (the monitor went black after a huge close-up of a hand), Richard Handy's voice—which I recognized—could be heard saying, "Dude! What?"

And then there were four shots, and screaming began.

"It goes on like that for a while," Hessler said.

I held up a hand to quiet him, and he stopped talking. I was listening very carefully and closed my eyes to better concentrate on the sound. After a few seconds I opened my eyes and said, "There! Did you hear it?"

Hessler and Ms. Washburn looked at me. "Hear *what*?" Hessler said.

"All I heard was a sort of jumble of screaming and general confusion," Ms. Washburn told me. Her description was more useful than Hessler's question.

"Yes. How would you describe the general confusion?" I asked her.

I knew Ms. Washburn well enough to anticipate her answer would be to narrow her eyes and say, "General." But she did not do that. Instead she pursed her lips, trying to come up with the most accurate answer to my question.

"A few moans, possibly Richard in pain," she said. She closed her eyes to better recall the sound. "Someone shouted out to call the police. But under that was a just sort of hum of either activity or speech. I couldn't tell. Does it matter?" Ms. Washburn opened her eyes and looked at me.

I turned toward Hessler. "May we run the last minute or so again?"

He appeared puzzled but picked up the phone on the desk and pushed a button. "Can you replay the last minute?" He replaced the receiver and the three of us, perhaps reflexively, turned our attention to a screen we knew would be completely black.

Through the obvious coat of paint on the lenses came the sounds we had heard before. Ms. Washburn was correct: Richard's groans were audible, certainly, but after six seconds they ceased as he undoubtedly died quickly. There was the sound of woman shouting to call 911 and some general shouting. Someone shouted, "He's got a gun!", which seemed superfluous.

But underneath the identifiable sounds was something considerably lower. Not close enough to any of the three cameras and their directional microphones to be higher in the sound mix was an unmistakably familiar noise.

Tyler Clayton was saying, "Nnnnnnnnnnnnnnn …"

NINETEEN

"It was the volume of the sound that was important, not the content," I said.

We were back in Ms. Washburn's Kia driving to Billy Martinez's home in Franklin Township. Billy knew we were on our way to talk to him on his day off but Ms. Washburn had said he sounded irritable, perhaps nervous meeting us away from the store.

The drive from where we were now would take nine minutes unless an unforeseen amount of traffic were to appear. I have come to trust Ms. Washburn's driving almost as much as Mike the taxicab driver's, so we are able to have a conversation while the car is in motion, assuming no extraordinary maneuvers, like a left turn, were in progress.

"Why was the volume important?" Ms. Washburn asked. "Even when you were explaining it to Detective Hessler I wasn't clear on that. We heard Tyler making that sound he makes when he's upset. Of course he'd be upset if he had just shot Richard or if he'd seen Richard get shot. So his making that sound doesn't really seem all that amazing. Except that it confirms that Tyler was there, so he must have been the person in the dark hoodie."

Despite my knowing Ms. Washburn would not turn her eyes toward me, I held up my index finger to make a point; it's a reflex that doesn't always take context into account. "Volume is important because the microphones on the security cameras are directional. You know what that means."

"Yes," she said, perhaps with an edge of annoyance in her voice, although I could not understand what might have made her feel that way. "I'm a photographer, but I do understand the concept of a directional microphone. It will receive sound only from something in the direction the microphone is pointed. It's not going to pick up peripheral or ambient noise."

"That is exactly correct," I said after she had successfully turned the Spectra. "A directional microphone is like a person with no peripheral vision—it only records what is in front of it. So with those three microphones all pointed in different directions—one toward the counter, but from a high angle; one at the front door from directly opposite, again bolted to the ceiling; and the last pointed at the area where Richard was shot, mounted on the side wall rather than directly opposite the refrigerated counter—the sound we should have gotten would be from close to those three locations."

"So that's what we got," Ms. Washburn said. "So what?"

"I believe you know the significance," I said. I did not want Ms. Washburn to think I had a low opinion of her intelligence. "You are not considering the sound we heard from Tyler."

"It was the 'nnnnnnn' sound. We've heard it a number of times now."

"Yes," I agreed. "But assume for a moment that Tyler *did* shoot Richard Handy in front of the dairy display. That camera is the one mounted most closely to its subject; it is actually less than ten feet from where the shooting took place."

Ms. Washburn considered that fact for a moment and then nodded her head enthusiastically, which worried me a bit as she drove. "So Tyler's voice should have been louder. When we were watching the painted-over security videos, we should have heard Tyler more clearly than anyone else if he really was the shooter."

I smiled. "Precisely."

"So this proves that Tyler didn't kill Richard Handy."

"You heard Detective Hessler," I reminded her. "He was not convinced."

Ms. Washburn's mouth curled a bit. "Yeah, he seemed to think that Tyler could have shot Richard, run to some other spot in the store and then started freaking out. He doesn't really seem to have a firm grasp of what Tyler is up against on a daily basis."

"Most 'typical' people do not," I said. "We need to bring more specific data to the discussion if the detective is going to be moved to look in a direction other than the one he is pursuing now.

"In addition, Tyler was found standing over the body of Richard Handy, so it is significant that as the recording goes on, the vocalization he is making gets louder. He is being moved into position. The detective was not open to that suggestion immediately."

"In other words, he's taking the easy way out." Ms. Washburn had navigated us into Franklin Township. Another three minutes and we would be at Billy Martinez's front door.

I shook my head, more for my own benefit than hers. "Detective Hessler is not an incompetent police investigator," I told her. "He is going to investigate all the possibilities, but given the system in which he works, he is not able to go to the county prosecutor and say Tyler's charges should be dropped based on an incoherent soundtrack to a vandalized security video. What our revelation has accomplished is that the detective will now concentrate on Tyler's case *and* the possibility that he is not the person responsible for

Richard Handy's death. But that is not our responsibility; our job is to answer Mason's question."

"He wants to know who killed Richard, and we have pretty convincing proof that it was not Tyler," Ms. Washburn said. "If we find out that someone else did it and we can prove that, the detective's job will be done just as we are answering the question." She pulled the car into a space across from a split-level suburban house with blue vinyl siding and a brick facing on its front stairs.

"That will be the ancillary effect, yes," I agreed. We got out of the car and walked to Billy Martinez's front door.

Billy, dressed in jeans and a Metallica t-shirt, did not exactly greet us at the door so much as he allowed us to enter. As Ms. Washburn had reported, he did not seem happy to talk to us, and ushered us toward the basement stairs as soon as we were inside.

"This is where my room is," he said. "My mom's upstairs and she doesn't need to hear more about what went on at the store. She wants me to quit the job as it is."

We descended the stairs into the area that was indeed Billy's room. It was essentially a finished basement with small casement windows on either side wall and fluorescent fixtures installed in a dropped ceiling. There was a rug on the floor that clearly had some water damage and a television on a stand opposite the sofa that no doubt folded out when Billy slept at night.

"You don't make that much working in the Quik N EZ," he added, although we had not commented. "I don't know where she gets that idea." He was sweating. It was not exceedingly warm in the room.

Something about money was making Billy nervous; that was the only reasonable explanation. When trying to answer a question by talking to someone who is not eager to share information, it is sometimes necessary to amplify that person's weakness. It is not pleasant, but it can be effective.

"How much do you make at the Quik N EZ?" I asked. Ms. Washburn, perhaps taken slightly by surprise, turned to look at my face.

"I'm only part-time," Billy said. "If they don't give me thirty hours a week, they don't have to pay benefits or anything, so I'm usually at five hours a day, four days a week or eight hours a day three days a week."

"And you earn the state's minimum wage?" I said, following up. Billy looked slightly pained by the question. I avoided Ms. Washburn's glance. She is sensitive in such areas and sometimes her negative opinion can cause me to soften my resolve. That is one of the rare areas in which Ms. Washburn is occasionally not helpful.

Billy nodded. I was aware that at that time the minimum wage in New Jersey was under nine dollars per hour. Even after the maximum number of hours Billy might be assigned, he would earn an annual salary well under the poverty line as defined by the United States government.

"So why, then, did you always let Richard Handy take the hundred-dollar tips Tyler Clayton would leave for him every day?" From my right I heard Ms. Washburn let out her breath; perhaps now she understood what this tactic had been designed to accomplish.

I found that somehow reassuring. I prefer Ms. Washburn not to think of me negatively.

"I told you before, that was Richard's business," Billy said, but he did not establish eye contact when he said it. "The weird kid had a thing for him or something, and he gave Rich money to like him, I guess. Rich pretended to be the kid's friend and he got those big tips every day."

"Every day?" Ms. Washburn asked. It was time to establish that fact definitively. I appreciated her help.

"Every day Rich and I were working there," Billy said. "I can't say anything about the days I wasn't there, but if Rich was working, the kid was there and so was the Benjamin." He was referring to the image of Benjamin Franklin printed on the one-hundred-dollar bill.

"Were you never tempted to take one?" I asked.

Billy shrugged. "The first few times Rich grabbed it out of the jar so fast I didn't even see how big the bill was. You know, the action in that place gets pretty serious that time of day, so I'm usually concentrating on what I'm doing. I don't have time to look at what the other guy is up to."

I nodded. I was attempting to act the role of the interrogator who understands the witness's dilemma, the one commonly referred to as the "good cop." In this scenario there was no "bad cop," as Ms. Washburn would not be attempting to threaten or intimidate Billy into giving us stronger answers or a confession to any crime.

"Of course," I said. "Your work would require you to pay close attention to the customer in front of you and the cash register you were operating. Richard would be seen more through peripheral vision than directly observed."

Billy, looking confused, simply looked at me.

But his eyes frequently darted toward a door to his right, carved into a false wall built for storage or simply to make the room seem more like living space. It was possible the home's heating system was housed behind that door. Billy, though, was looking at it nervously, as if something dangerous might pop out and eat him if he were not careful. I had that fear as a young child, but I did some research on the structure of my bedroom closet and concluded that no evil creature could possibly gain access without Mother's knowledge or permission.

In this case, I wondered whether there was someone behind the door whom Billy did not want Ms. Washburn and me to see.

The glances were telling in more ways than one—closer examination of the knob on the door in question indicated that it had no lock. That clarified Billy's anxiety; there was no way to keep us away from whatever secret lay behind the door except through distraction, and they way he looked at the door was not helping his cause.

The best thing was to keep him talking and not let on I'd determined there was a reason to investigate behind the door in question. "So if the oversized tips Tyler gave Richard were in the jar to your left and you were simply serving the customers in front of you, there was no reason you would be looking in that direction?" That was not so much a question as a recap, but it did engender a response.

"That's right," Billy exhaled.

"But you said that was just when the big tips began," Ms. Washburn reminded him. Her statement made Billy's head swivel toward her quickly and his expression of relief was overcome with a replacement that was closer to panic. "What about later? When did you first see that it was a hundred-dollar bill every day?"

"I dunno." Billy shrugged. "It went on for a long time, so I guess I took a better look one day. Maybe I didn't have a customer at that moment or something."

"Didn't it strike you as odd?" Perhaps Ms. Washburn was playing the "bad cop" after all.

"Sure, but everything about that kid was odd." His quick glances at the door to my immediate left were not decreasing; if anything he was looking at it more often and more urgently.

There was no point in prolonging the moment. "I'm sorry," I said, walking toward the door. "But I must ask if I may use your restroom."

Ms. Washburn, fully aware that I would never barge into a strange restroom unless I had no possible alternative, covered her mouth. Billy raised his hand, almost pointing at the door as if to protest, but I gave him no time to speak. I grasped the knob on the door and turned it.

The door swung open and I looked inside very carefully, but not slowly. "Oh, my mistake," I said.

"Bathroom's upstairs," Billy managed. He pointed up to the ceiling in the event that I could not discern where "upstairs" might be.

"It's not necessary," I said. "I just needed to wash my hands."

"Wash your—"

"Come along, Ms. Washburn," I said. "I believe we have occupied enough of Billy's time today."

Ms. Washburn's face registered some surprise but not enough for Billy to notice. He actually looked relieved, no doubt glad to have these two prying people out of his house as quickly as possible. He saw us upstairs, reminded us to be quiet once on the ground floor, then ushered us to the front door and did everything but slam it behind us with glee.

We were not even in the car before Ms. Washburn asked, "What was in the other room?"

"Nothing," I said.

Ms. Washburn settled into the driver's seat looking disappointed. "That's too bad."

I sat down on the passenger's side and closed the door, checking to make sure it had definitely engaged the latch. "Not really," I said. "It was the *way* there was nothing that makes it significant."

Ms. Washburn rotated the key and engaged the ignition but turned to me before activating the transmission. "Significant? You think the nothing was important?"

"It might very well be crucial to our answering this question. But I will have to do some additional research before I can be certain, so please do not ask until I can confirm my suspicions."

She thought that over and nodded. Ms. Washburn knows the way my mind works and does not question the things that she believes help me achieve maximum efficiency. "Anything I can do to help?" she asked.

"Yes. I believe you should get in touch with Mr. Robinson of the Quik N EZ and ask him if we might see his most recent inventory figures."

Ms. Washburn began driving back to the Questions Answered office. "Any item in particular?"

"Cigarettes," I said.

TWENTY

"Do you have any recent copies of *Rolling Stone* or *Yankees Magazine*?"

The receptionist looked what Mother would call "askance" at me from behind the window and took a moment. "The only magazines we have out there are the ones you can see."

She was a large woman in every way and had a weary air to her that is unusual in my experience. Dr. Mancuso's receptionist Joanie is very pleasant, even if the affability does not always seem completely sincere. Joanie tries. This woman, whose name I did not know, was not trying.

There was nothing to do but sit back down in one of the uncomfortable chrome-and-fabric chairs lining the room. The coffee table just beyond my feet held copies of *O The Oprah Magazine, Golf Digest, Psychology Today,* and (rather incongruously) *Cycle World,* a magazine for motorcycle enthusiasts. No doubt Sherlock Holmes would have been able to piece together a complete biography and psychological profile of Dr. Shean just from those titles, but unfortunately I do not share the fictional detective's powers of deduction.

I was aware that seven minutes remained before the current group therapy session taking place inside Dr. Shean's private office would end. There was nothing to do but consider the question I was solving or to look up at the television, which was projecting an afternoon talk show with the sound muted so that only a person well versed in lip reading would be able to gain any insights from the programming.

It had occurred to me that I might alert Dr. Mancuso of my visit to Dr. Shean's office, but I had not done so after mentioning my intention to Ms. Washburn and hearing her advice that such a call was not necessary. But I was still concerned, given that therapy sessions reveal some emotional information about the subjects but almost nothing about the therapist, that Dr. Mancuso might discover I had visited another psychologist and mistakenly assume I was unsatisfied with his services. I'm not always certain that I need to attend therapy sessions, but that is not the fault of the doctor himself.

This moment afforded me time to ponder the information I had gathered about Richard Handy's shooting and to conclude that we had made some progress toward answering the question, but not yet enough to support any theory regarding it. Richard had definitely been shot at the time and place the police had noted, but the evidence was mounting that Tyler Clayton was not the shooter. Unfortunately, none of that evidence was definitive. I believed Tyler had not shot Richard, but I could not prove it and therefore had to leave the question open even in my own mind.

The information gathered from Margie Cavanagh and Billy Martinez had been diverse but not inconsistent. Margie believed the die in our possession to be cursed. That was of course nonsense, but it did indicate a thought pattern that might be useful. Billy, although he had no knowledge of Swords and Sorcerers, did have some insight into Richard Handy's psyche and had determined that Richard would not believe in such theories of magic and sorcery. He was practical, and he had probably been involved in some illegal activities during his employment at the Quik N EZ, the extent of which was not yet clear.

The inner door opened and from inside the office I heard Dr. Shean say, "Very good session, guys. Remember what I gave you to think about for next week."

I watched the doorway closely. Through it walked four people. Three of them, ranging in approximate age from nineteen to twenty-eight, watched their own feet as they walked. I knew not to expect Tyler Clayton, as Mason had told me that since the arrest, Dr. Shean had been seeing Tyler privately. So the fourth person exiting I had to assume was Dr. Shean. She was about forty-three or forty-four, dressed more formally than the three younger people in a suit with a skirt and her hair up in what Ms. Washburn would later tell me (based on my description) was a French twist. It did not look especially Gallic, but that is far from my best area of expertise.

The young man who exited first was shaking his head as he walked but he did not appear to be disagreeing with the idea of remembering what he should think about to prepare for the next session; it was something of a self-stimming action, much like my hand flapping when I was younger. He was vocalizing but did not form words. It was possible he did not have the ability to speak but might have been able to communicate, as Tyler now did, through written or typed messages. He carried a tablet computer whose screen he studied raptly.

The young woman after him, who must have been Molly Brandt based on what Tyler had told us about his therapy group, was dressed in jeans and a blue denim work shirt. She wore one red cotton sock and another that was white striped with orange. Her hair was clean but uncombed. She was making up for the first young man's lack of verbal communication by talking without a pause as she walked.

"It's not about the Book of Leviticus," she said. "It's about the Book of David. Nobody sees that. There's a general disconnect on the subject, but I can prove it because I've read both books. I'm an atheist and

I've read both books. Not many people who are devout believers have read both books, but I have. It's about the Book of David."

The young man walking out immediately before Dr. Shean raised his head from looking at the carpet. He was not speaking to himself and he was not murmuring in tones only he could understand. But he clearly had some behaviors that would place him on the autism spectrum in the eyes of those who think in such terms.

I do not dispute that some of us identified in that way act in an unusual manner. What I dispute is that the "usual" manner is by definition a rational or better one. Heroes in books, films, television, and drama behave in ways that are not usual. They are not considered "odd" or as having a "disorder" because of their actions.

This young man, the oldest of the three, placed his fingers up next to his cheeks and rubbed them on his face. He nodded in understanding or satisfaction and repeated the gesture. Again, there was a nod. When he saw me looking at him, he stopped but did not look embarrassed. As he passed where I was standing, he simply looked a foot to my left (pretending to look at me without having to do so) and said, "It's what I do. I have autism."

"I know," I said. "So do I." The definition has shifted enough that I am not sure that is technically true, but the argument could certainly be made for it.

That caught his attention and he looked at me for a very brief moment. "Really. I wouldn't have known."

"I'd like to talk to you about Tyler Clayton," I said.

The young man's eyes looked back down at his feet. "You a cop?"

"No."

"Then let's talk. There's a Starbucks on the corner."

"I don't drink coffee," I said.

"Neither do I. But you can buy a bottle of water there and they have couches." He walked past me and to the office door, the matter apparently being settled.

The three members of Tyler's group left and Dr. Shean approached me. "You must be Mr. Hoenig," she said. Three adults in the waiting room—two men and a woman—stood up as the doctor approached, so I assumed they were the members of the group I had contracted with Dr. Shean to attend.

"Yes, I am," I said.

"May I shake your hand?" she asked. It was wise of her to get the information first; too many people make an assumption and irritate or frighten those of us who do not follow the norms.

"I prefer not, but I hope that does not offend you," I said.

Dr. Shean smiled very professionally. "Not at all. I'm glad I asked." The three other people walked by the doctor and down the corridor toward her inner office where the session would take place. "Won't you come in and join us?" Dr. Shean asked.

"I think not. But thank you, Dr. Shean. I will see to it that you are compensated for the session." I started for the door.

The psychologist called toward me. "I don't understand," she said. "You specifically asked for this group and this time. What is it you have to do that is more important than this?"

"I need to go to Starbucks to buy a bottle of water," I said and left.

———

The young man from Tyler's group was seated in an overstuffed easy chair in a corner of the Starbucks that was indeed on the corner of the street on which Dr. Shean's office was located. He had purchased a bottle of water and a slice of pound cake, which he was eating rather carefully, making sure each crumb was caught on the paper plate in front of him. He looked up when I walked in.

"I thought I'd have to wait longer," he said. "Didn't you have a session with Dr. Shean?"

I had purchased a bottle of water but no other food and sat down on a loveseat next to the man. There was no other person on the loveseat, which is called that not because people fall in love on such furniture but because it is small enough that it can be assumed those who use it would prefer to be near one another.

"I did," I said. That was true. I had never intended to keep the appointment, but it had been established. "But I decided this was more important. Allow me to introduce myself. I am Samuel Hoenig and I am the proprietor of a business called Questions Answered."

The young man's face did not change in any way. He continued not to look in my direction, but to be fastidious about the pound cake he was eating slowly. "So you're trying to find out what happened with Tyler? Tyler is in jail for shooting a guy."

I shook my head. "No. He is not in jail. He posted bail and is now living at home awaiting trial, which could be as much as a year from now. I am trying to answer the question of who killed Richard Handy, the person Tyler is accused of shooting."

I took a sip from my bottle of water and waited. There was, as I had anticipated, no reaction from my companion. "What is your name?" I asked.

He looked up and into my eyes. His social skills training was very good. He did not hold out his hand to shake, which indicated to me that he still had a serious aversion to being touched. I was, as Ms. Washburn would say, fine with that.

"I'm Jim O'Malley," he said. "I'm very glad to meet you, Samuel."

He probably was not all that glad, but I understood he'd been taught to react that way to a new acquaintance. I nodded without proffering my own hand. "Thank you. What can you tell me about Tyler Clayton?"

Jim, having completed the prescribed ritual, reverted to his previous behavior. He was taking a very long time to eat the pound cake. "I'm not sure I want to tell you anything. Are you working to help Tyler, or to send him to jail for life?"

"Neither. I am working to answer the question. The correct answer might help him or hurt him, but it is still the correct answer. I am not able to change that, and I am not attempting to color the research in order to acquire one outcome or the other."

I crossed one leg over the other. This was meant as a gesture of relaxation, to indicate to Jim that I was comfortable in his presence (although I was not, as I did not know him well enough at all for that) and to signal that he should drop his guard and give me the information I required. This approach does not always yield accurate results, but it can be helpful at times.

Jim accepted the information I had given him without an outward reaction. "Interesting," he said. "So you would prefer that I keep my opinions out of my answers?" It was a legitimate question.

"Except when I specifically ask for opinion, yes. For example: Do you think, based on your acquaintance with Tyler, that he could be a violent person?"

Jim took a sip from his water, set the bottle on the table, and replaced the cap carefully. "I think anyone could be a violent person under the proper circumstances."

"True. But do you think Tyler is more apt to resort to violence than most people?"

Jim took a deep breath, probably to give himself time to think. It is something I do when presented with a situation or question I had not previously considered. "I don't have the proper data on how many people act violently overall," he said. "But I think what you're asking is whether I have seen Tyler behave violently or threaten to do so. I have not."

"Excellent," I said. It is advisable to praise the subject whenever possible, to provide positive feedback in an effort to encourage the person you interview to offer more such information. "Has Tyler mentioned Richard Handy in therapy?"

Jim's eyebrows lowered. "I don't think it would be ethical to discuss anything that was said in a therapy session, Samuel," he said.

"No. I suppose not. May I ask if you have heard the name Richard Handy before today without specifying context?"

He nodded. "Yes. You may ask."

It was an answer I would have given to a question worded that way. Perhaps the best way to approach Jim was to assume he would react similarly to the way I would under similar circumstances. "Have you heard the name Richard Handy before this conversation?" I asked. It was necessary to change the wording of the question because it was possible Jim had heard the name today, but before I had mentioned it.

Again there was a pause. He collected the last of the pound cake crumbs from his plate with intense concentration using a fork and ate them. "Yes, I have."

"Was Tyler the one who mentioned him?" I asked. If Jim had seen a newspaper or television news account of the murder, he would have heard Richard's name but it would have no particular significance to my research.

Jim nodded.

"Very good indeed. When Tyler mentioned Richard's name, what was his mood? I am asking for your assessment: Did Tyler seem angry at Richard, or did he have some other reason to talk about him?"

"I wasn't paying much attention," Jim said. "I was trying to think of the next thing I would say." Again, I understood that impulse completely.

"One last thing," I said. "Jim, do you have any idea where Tyler would have gotten enough money to tip a convenience store clerk one hundred dollars at least five times a week?"

There was no sign of surprise or concern from Jim. In fact, he snorted a small laugh. "I have no clue. You'd have to ask Molly."

"Molly Brandt?" I asked. "The young woman in your therapy group?"

Jim nodded again and raised his eyes to meet mine, which I assumed signified some importance. "She is Tyler's girlfriend," he said.

TWENTY-ONE

"Tyler has a girlfriend?" Mason Clayton seemed both surprised and oddly pleased at the suggestion. "Are you sure?"

We sat in the living room of Mason's house, a relatively small four-bedroom Cape Cod that had been furnished years before from the look of the pieces on display. I could assume only that much of the contents of the house, along with the building itself, had been inherited from Mason, Sandy, and Tyler's parents.

"No, I am not sure," I said. Ms. Washburn winced a tiny bit. Perhaps I should have taken into account Mason's pleasure at hearing what Jim had told me and softened the blow. "I am merely reporting what I have been told without having had time to research the point to an objective conclusion."

"Samuel means we haven't been able to ask Molly about it yet," Ms. Washburn said. "Can we ask Tyler?"

After Jim O'Malley had left the Starbucks following a brief conclusion to our conversation, Ms. Washburn had met me there and we had agreed it was best to talk to Mason and Tyler again, if that was possible. Ms. Washburn had called Mason, who reported they were free and suggested we drive to their home in Franklin Township and discuss what we had found out so far.

In the car, I had to admit to Ms. Washburn that this wasn't very much.

"This question has been a very confusing one," I said. "We began with the idea that Richard either was or was not Tyler's friend, since that was what we had been commissioned to answer. And I still believe we rushed to an answer. We did not have definitive proof to give to Tyler."

"Does that matter at this point?" she asked, watching the road. "We've determined that Tyler didn't shoot Richard, so does the answer to Tyler's question really have any impact on what we're doing now?"

I am usually fairly adept at committing my thoughts to words, but even that was becoming elusive now. "I think it might be, but I don't know why," I said. "Are you going to stop the divorce proceedings?"

Ms. Washburn's eyes widened and her grip on the steering wheel visibly tightened. "Samuel!" she barked. "Where did that come from?"

Clearly, she was not asking where my words had originated; as with all such things, they were the verbalization of a thought. What Ms. Washburn must have meant, I decided, was that I had changed topics of conversation too quickly. It would not be the first time.

"Please excuse me," I said. "The thought has been claiming my attention for some time and I thought it best to express it so we could go back to concentrating on the question. I did not mean to offend you, Ms. Washburn."

She relaxed noticeably, loosening her grip and trying to smile. "There are times I really wish you would call me Janet," she said.

"If it is important to you, I will try to change my pattern."

Ms. Washburn laughed lightly and shook her head a little. "It's not necessary. I know you're more comfortable this way. In answer to your question, Samuel, I don't know what's going on with my marriage right now. Simon and I have been talking without yelling at each other and that's good, but we're still the same people we were before and I don't know if that's going to change."

It was extremely unlikely they would become different people, but I was certain Ms. Washburn knew that, so I asked instead, "When do you think you will know? About the divorce."

"I don't know, Samuel. I'm sorry. I know uncertainty bothers you."

That was true, but in this case I felt divided by my knowledge of Simon Taylor's having had at least one other woman in his home while he was separated from his wife. If I told Ms. Washburn I could hurt her and overstep my boundaries as her employer. If I did not and she chose not to tell me of her decision-making process, she could easily make a serious mistake because she would not have vital information. It was a frustrating conundrum, but for the moment I decided Ms. Washburn's emotions should take precedence over my own. "I will survive ... Janet," I said.

She wrinkled her nose. "Go back to Ms. Washburn," she said. "It doesn't sound natural the other way. Now about the question. What about the S and S die? I can't figure out why it's important that Richard had it in his hand, or at least on his body, when he was shot, but I get the feeling it is."

"You are correct up to a point," I told her. "I think Richard had the Tenduline with him at all times, that it was a talisman for him as it would be for many role-playing gamers. He went to great trouble to obtain it, which would indicate it held a lot of significance for him."

"So then it's not important that he had it with him," Ms. Washburn said.

"No, but as you pointed out, the Tenduline was discovered away from Richard's body but close enough that we can be fairly sure it was Richard who was holding it. So the importance lies in the fact that it was not in his pocket or somewhere he might keep it normally. It was probably in his hand when he died and fell out when he hit the floor."

"Do you think the person who shot him wanted the die?" Ms. Washburn asked. "Then why not pick it up after the shooting?"

"Precisely why I think theft was not the motive," I answered. "No, I think the die next to Richard's body delivered another type of message entirely. I think it was a warning."

Ms. Washburn thought that over. "A warning to whom?" she asked.

"To Tyler."

Now in Mason's living room, with the sounds of Tyler's movements audible from a room upstairs, Ms. Washburn had asked whether an interview with Mason's brother would be possible. "I don't think he'll talk to you," Mason answered.

"Why not?" she asked.

But the answer was forthcoming. Tyler's footsteps—indeed more like stomping—could be heard on the stairs to our left. Before he was visible, however, his vocalization of "nnnnnnn" preceded him into the room.

"That's why not," Mason said.

Tyler walked into the room, saw us, and started to shake violently. Clearly Ms. Washburn and I did not hold especially pleasant memories for him. It was technically understandable, but not logical. We were simply the bearers of news he had disliked.

I had no idea how to placate him to a point that he could communicate with us. I have experienced moments during which I was too agitated to speak coherently. But I have not had the kind of difficulty Tyler had clearly been living with since Richard Handy was shot. Seeing Ms. Washburn and me seemed to exacerbate the problem.

Luckily, she has some experience dealing with those of us with autism spectrum behaviors. "It's okay, Tyler," she said. "We're not here to do anything but help. Can you tell us how we can help you?"

"Nnnnnnnnnnnnn…"

"Okay," Ms. Washburn continued, not acknowledging any special difficulty with Tyler's speech. "We can't do it that way, so maybe there's another way. Can you write for us on that pad there?" She pointed to a legal pad that had been left on the table in the adjacent dining room. No doubt Mason had been trying to work out either Tyler's best course of defense or how he would pay Swain to provide it.

But Tyler shook his head violently; no, there would be no writing. His hands went to the sides of his head and vibrated with frustration. It was a feeling I could recognize.

"Wait," Mason said quietly. "What about the iPad?" He walked to a cabinet nearby and extracted the tablet computer from a drawer. Mason brought the tablet to Tyler and extended his hand. "Want to talk on that for a while?"

Strikingly, Tyler stopped his frantic motion and looked at the iPad. He reached his hand out and took it from his brother. He immediately sat on a bench in front of a piano that did not look like it had been played in some time and began tapping the screen with a great air of purpose.

When he stopped, he turned the iPad toward Ms. Washburn. I moved to her side to see the message he had typed.

It read, *I shot Richard. I shot him with the gun.*

Mason shrugged. "We've been getting that a lot." Then he turned to his brother. "Tyler, is Molly your girlfriend? Why didn't you tell me?" Even in the light of Tyler's impending trial for murder, this seemed to be the priority for Mason.

Tyler stared at him, then pointed at the iPad again. He was focusing on the issue and insisting he had shot Richard Handy.

"No, you didn't," I told Tyler. "You didn't shoot Richard. You were on the other side of the store when that happened. So tell me, why are you taking the blame for a terrible crime you didn't commit?"

Tyler stared at me for three seconds, the longest he had ever made eye contact in my experience. Then he pointed at the iPad again as if to reinforce the message he had keyed in.

I shook my head. "That is not the truth. Please do not insult my intelligence."

"Samuel," Ms. Washburn said softly. Mason Clayton looked at me as if I had slapped his brother's face.

I have spent enough time being talked about while present in a room with other people. I have known what it is like to be given "special treatment" that was sincerely intended to "soften the blow" of my "disability" but ended up simply solving the short-term problem and doing nothing to help me develop useful skills. Mother never treated me like someone with an affliction, but doctors, teachers, administrators, and even some personnel at the college I attended would choose to follow their own instincts without ever challenging mine. The progress I have made has been largely attributable to Mother, Dr. Mancuso, and myself. And Dr. Mancuso insists that I have done most of the hard work on my own.

So when I did not coddle Tyler Clayton it was not out of cruelty, although his feelings were not my paramount concern. I needed the answers to questions if I could answer the one I had been commissioned to research. Tyler held some if not all of them. Getting through his defenses, including those that others were encouraging, was imperative.

I pointed again to the iPad. "Please. Tell me why you are taking the blame."

Tyler took the tablet and began using it again. When he turned the screen back toward me this time, it read, *I was angry because Richard was not my friend. I shot him.*

I repeated shaking my head. "You did not. Your voice is too far away from the directional microphones recording sound when

Richard was shot. You were not close enough to have done it. What were you doing?"

Ms. Washburn and Mason seemed mesmerized, although concern showed on their faces. I imagine they did not know whether they should intervene, but for the first time since coming home from jail, Tyler's answers were more than the simple repetition of his confession.

Angrily he grabbed the iPad from its position and started typing again. Perhaps this time his emotion getting the best of him, which was what I was hoping would happen. If Tyler did not have the time to censor himself, it was more possible to get accurate information.

This time when he turned it back, it read, *I didn't see who shot him.*

"Show that to your brother," I suggested, even as Ms. Washburn was craning her neck over my shoulder to see it.

Mason walked toward Tyler, who did as I had said. Upon seeing the words, his eyes watered a bit and he seemed to reach toward Tyler, who backed away instinctively. Mason held up his hands to show he knew better than to try to hug his brother.

"Where were you?" I asked. "What were you doing?"

Tyler's mouth twitched. He looked at the iPad, put a determined look on his face, and then looked intently at the floor. "I ... I went to the counter," he said.

That was a breakthrough, certainly, but I didn't have time for Tyler's personal progress at this moment. "But you weren't close enough to the security camera on that side to be heard more clearly," I said, mostly explaining the discrepancy to myself.

"Yeah." Tyler wasn't going to start reciting soliloquies anytime soon. His work to begin speaking spontaneously again would be a long one and require a good deal of work, but he had taken a very large step in the past minute.

The best strategy, then, was to word questions in a way that would require the least effort on Tyler's part to answer. "Were you looking the other way when the shots were fired?" I asked.

Tyler nodded.

"Were there any other customers in the store at the time?"

Tyler nodded and held up his fingers: Two.

"Did you know them?"

He shook his head.

I was operating completely on speculation at this point, and that was not going to be a fruitful avenue of questioning. I could not determine how to construct a question that could be answered in one syllable on the subject, so I pointed to the iPad again and said to Tyler, "How did you end up with the gun in your hand standing over Richard Handy's body?"

His eyes narrowed with effort. He touched areas on the screen again, this time taking longer than he had before. This was going to be a longer message, I assumed.

But my hopes were not borne out. *I don't know* was what Tyler had typed on the screen.

That led to one conclusion but it was not one I could pursue at this moment. "Thank you, Tyler," I said. I started for the door, hearing Ms. Washburn make our socially conventional farewells to Mason and promising he would hear from us soon. I noted that she did not make the same assurance to Tyler, but she did say good-bye to him on the way to the door.

Once we were outside, she spoke to me quietly but urgently. "You know something now, don't you?" she asked.

I had always known some things, so I extrapolated her question as one asking if Tyler's information had been helpful in the research of Mason's question. I nodded.

"Care to share?" Ms. Washburn asked.

I had nothing to share, as I do not carry chewing gum or any other such treat with me, so I stopped on the sidewalk in front of Mason Clayton's house. "Share?"

"The conclusion you have reached," Ms. Washburn said. "Sorry for not being precise in the way I asked. What did you learn from Tyler just now?"

"I did not learn much but I was able to confirm some suspicions I have had for some time," I said.

We reached Ms. Washburn's Kia and settled into our traditional seats. She started the engine. "Such as?" she asked. That I understood.

"There was someone else in the store whom Tyler knew, someone he is trying to protect with his story," I said. "He knows how he ended up holding the murder weapon but he is not explaining, despite the fact that it could exonerate him."

Ms. Washburn began to drive back to Questions Answered. "How do you know that?"

"Detective Hessler said there was one other patron in the Quik N EZ when the shooting occurred," I reminded her. "Tyler admits there were two. Whoever actually shot Richard Handy managed somehow to escape the scene before anyone could see. But Tyler knew who it was and decided the only way to protect the other person was to pick up the gun and take the blame for the murder."

"So who was it?" Ms. Washburn asked.

"An excellent question," I said. "Something we will have to ask Molly Brandt. May I have the GPS unit, please?"

TWENTY-TWO

MOLLY BRANDT WAS THE young woman I'd seen leaving Dr. Shean's office and seemed an unlikely candidate to be Tyler Clayton's girlfriend, only because she never seemed to talk to anyone except Hawkeye Pierce, Trapper John McIntyre, and B.J. Hunnicutt.

Although she had been obviously concerned with biblical verse when I'd seen her outside the therapist's office, that did not seem to be Molly's primary special interest, which was helpful, as I am not well schooled on the subject. Instead, today she seemed to be especially intrigued with the television program *M*A*S*H*, which was something of a phenomenon in the 1970s and '80s.

"Hawkeye came from Maine and fell in love with Carlye Breslin when he was in his surgical residency in Boston," she informed us without being prompted. "When she arrived at the four-oh-seven-seventh, Hawkeye said his heart started beating again."

We were seated in the very tidy family room of the home owned by Molly's parents, Jack and Evelyn Brandt. Evelyn sat on a sofa nearby, hands folded in her lap, her face just a little tense at what her daughter might do or say. I have seen that kind of anxiety before. Molly did not seem to notice it.

Ms. Washburn had parked the car on the side of the road and telephoned Evelyn when I'd suggested we divert our route to include a trip to Molly's home. Evelyn had informed her that Jack was away on business at the moment, but agreed to the visit, although she had warned Ms. Washburn that Molly would probably not be of much help. She rarely had conversations, Evelyn said. Molly preferred to lecture.

"But Carlye was married and didn't want to cheat on her husband," Molly went on. Ms. Washburn, in a recliner she had chosen not to recline, was taking notes, although I could not determine exactly what might be useful to us in answering Mason's question.

"That is true," I answered. "But she and Hawkeye did renew their romance and Carlye resolved to ask her husband for a divorce." I avoided looking at Ms. Washburn when I mentioned the dissolution of a marriage and when Molly had brought up a cheating spouse.

Molly looked at me for the first time. Ms. Washburn and Evelyn also seemed somewhat surprised by my contribution to the conversation. I went through what Mother would have undoubtedly described as a "*M*A*S*H* phase" during my high school years.

"But Carlye didn't want to compete with Hawkeye's work, so she applied for a transfer," Molly pointed out. "Hawkeye could not change who he was, even for the woman he loved."

That last phrase referred to a comment the character made in a much later episode, but an encyclopedic knowledge of the subject was to be expected in such an area. I know a great deal about the New York Yankees and the Beatles because those subjects have piqued my interest, so I absorb a good deal more about them than I would about something in which I am not as completely engaged.

Because I understood the concept of a special interest in a topic, I could try to relate her fascination with the information I wanted to obtain. "Is that what happened between you and Tyler Clayton?" I asked.

Molly looked at me, seeming less stunned than surprised. "Hawkeye and Carlye were in a Mobile Army Surgical Hospital in Korea decades before I was born," she said. "At the time of their affair, they were under the command of Colonel Sherman Potter and the spiritual guidance of Father Francis Mulcahy."

"They were also fictional," I noted. "I am asking about you and Tyler Clayton, two people who are real."

"A lot of people think Hawkeye was in love with Major Margaret Houlihan, but I believe Carlye was his true match," Molly volunteered. It was not a response to my question or to my remark about Tyler and her, but I wondered whether there was a message Molly was trying to deliver.

"Why do you think he did not love Margaret?" I asked, eschewing the crude nickname "Hot Lips" that the character was given in the novel, film, and television series. "Did you see something about the way he acted with her that was different than his manner with Carlye?"

"He told Carlye he loved her," Molly said without hesitation. "He never said that to Margaret."

Ms. Washburn, who had been watching intently, said, "How did Hawkeye know Margaret?" I understood that she was asking about Molly and Tyler, but that was not going to be an effective strategy in this context. Molly might be speaking in metaphor, but she would answer any questions about her special interest in a literal sense.

Indeed, she looked positively contemptuous when she said, "She was assigned to the four-oh-seven-seventh when he got there."

"Of course," Ms. Washburn said. "Sorry."

Molly's mother was squinting at her daughter and me as if he were speaking a language she did not understand. "Why are we talking about *M*A*S*H*?" she asked. "Molly, Mr. Hoenig has questions for you. Please answer them." Sometimes parents are anxious to have their children with behaviors on the spectrum show off that they can act without those "quirks." But it is often more effective to indulge the idiosyncrasies and work with the personality.

"When *M*A*S*H* aired its final episode in 1983, it attracted the largest viewing audience in broadcast television history with the exception of some special events like the Super Bowl," Molly said. She was drifting further from the conversation. Evelyn grimaced but did not respond.

I decided the metaphor would be most helpful. Where talking bluntly would be the more useful tactic with Tyler, Molly needed to communicate in her own fashion, which appeared to be through her own agenda and specialized information. "What did Father Mulcahy think about the fact that Hawkeye and Carlye were not married to each other, and she was in fact married to someone else?" I asked.

"It didn't matter that they weren't married because she was really his true love," Molly said. It was not an answer to my question, but it gave me information that was going to be helpful. But I wanted to know one thing more.

"Did Father Mulcahy think Hawkeye should be in love with Margaret?"

"He knew who Hawkeye really loved," Molly said definitively.

"Thank you, Molly," I said. I stood and Ms. Washburn followed my lead. We began to walk to the door. Ms. Washburn turned to face Evelyn, who was leading us out as Molly retained her seat.

"Does Molly have any other special interests?" Ms. Washburn asked.

Evelyn's eyes went up to indicate she was trying to remember. "Certain books of the bible," she said. "But also New Jersey Transit train schedules and Beyoncé," she said.

"'Let's be careful out there,'" Molly said as we left.

"Right," her mother said, nodding. "And *Hill Street Blues*."

"It's late," Ms. Washburn said. "I'm going home. You?"

"I believe I'll call Mike," I said. "There is some computer research I want to do."

Ms. Washburn had not asked me to interpret the conversation I'd had with Molly Brandt during our ride back to Questions Answered. So it was not a surprise when she turned before reaching the door and asked, "What was all that about Hawkeye and Father Mulcahy?"

"I believe Molly might have been Tyler's girlfriend, or at least believed she was, at some point," I said. "But Molly thinks another woman came between them and distracted Tyler to the point that he left her for the other woman. I don't know whether that is the truth or not, but it appears to be what Molly believes."

Ms. Washburn turned a little bit more toward me with a thoughtful look on her face. "Why did you ask about the priest?"

"Molly is interested in some books of the bible," I answered. "She might have spoken to a religious leader about the difficulty with Tyler," I said. "When you were bringing the car to the front of the house, I asked Evelyn if there is a minister or priest in whom Molly might confide. She did not know of one, saying Molly is interested in the bible as a book but is not at all religious."

"Do you think that's true?"

"Again, I think it's what Evelyn believes is true. The facts are not yet clear."

"That's confusing," Ms. Washburn said.

"Yes." I find so many things confusing that it has almost become the norm for me; I don't often even note it anymore. "I hope you have a good night, Ms. Washburn." I say that as she leaves each evening; it is the accepted salutation for that occasion.

"You too, Samuel." With that, Ms. Washburn left the office. Less than one minute later I saw her car leave the parking lot.

I decided to begin my research with a continuation of the previous work I had done on some contraband items confiscated in the past month. But I was only about four screens into the searches when the bells attached to the office door (left over from San Remo's Pizzeria) jangled and I looked up.

Sandy Clayton Webb walked in wearing a tan trench coat and blue jeans. She was holding the coat tightly around herself, which would have been more understandable if this were February.

"Has it begun to rain?" I asked, forgetting the necessity of social ritual in such cases. (It is never clear in such a question as to *what* has begun to rain, but no one questions that usage.)

Sandy, in the midst of striding purposefully into the office, stopped abruptly and stood still in the middle of the room. "No. Why?"

There was no point in explaining my reasoning. "I thought I heard something," I said. "How can I help you, Ms. Webb?" I gestured toward the client chair, but Sandy sat in Mother's recliner. I did not correct her.

"Please, it's Sandy," she said. "I'm just here to get a progress report."

Since her demeanor since Tyler's arrest had been almost adversarial toward Questions Answered (Ms. Washburn had told me), it was unusual for Sandy to make that request. It was more distressing because she was technically not a client of the agency. "I have already told your brother Mason all that is currently relevant toward answering his question," I said.

"I haven't heard from Mason. What can you tell me?" Sandy sat leaning forward with her elbows on her thighs and her hands supporting her chin.

In such cases, it is sometimes a useful distraction to ask a question of one's own. "Is there a reason you are not in touch with your brother?" I said.

"It's a family matter." Sandy's veneer of joviality vanished. "Now would you please give me a progress report?"

There was no longer a reason to couch my answers in niceties; I have never had much success with such a strategy anyway. "I'm afraid I can't," I said. "My client is Mason Clayton. He asked the question at hand. Without my client's permission, I am unable to divulge any information we have discovered in regard to that question."

"Really." Sandy stood but did not turn to walk to the door as I had anticipated. Instead she took two steps toward my desk and put her palms down on it, leaning uncomfortably toward me. It was not so much intimidating a gesture as it contemptuous. "Have you received your fee from my brother yet, Mr. Hoenig?"

We had not required our usual retainer of one-half the agency's fee from Mason in advance because of the pending nature of the original question Tyler had asked, for which we had also waived the retainer at Ms. Washburn's insistence.

"I believe that is a matter of some privacy between myself and my client," I told Sandy.

"Well, I'm betting you haven't gotten a dime out of Mason," she responded, her voice dropping to a raspy growl. "And you should consider this: You're not going to get paid. Answer the question, don't answer the question. Mason won't give you the money he owes you. Want to know why?" She did not wait for a response to her question. "Because he doesn't have it. Mason's business went bankrupt and he's trying to find a way to avoid paying his creditors."

I had known of the financial problems with which Able Home Help had been grappling. In fact, I had planned on asking Sandy about Tyler's name being listed as a partner in the business, but she had begun abruptly with her questioning about Mason's payment. "I am aware of the Chapter XI proceedings," I said.

"So why are you still working for him?" Sandy asked.

"He is a client and has shown no cause for me to stop working for him," I answered truthfully. I had required nothing of Mason so he had not fallen short in any way. "Are you aware that Tyler is listed as a partner in Mason's business?"

Sandy blinked three times, an indication that the information I'd just given her was a surprise. But she answered, "Of course." If Ms. Washburn had been here, I was sure she would have informed me that Sandy was likely lying. I made that my assumption.

"I assume most of Tyler's income, his savings, his finances generally, come from Able Home Help. Is that correct?" It was best to ask while Sandy was stunned; she would have less capacity to think of untrue answers.

"Yes. Tyler gets almost everything except his walking-around money from Mason," she said. She stood up straight, abandoning her position leaning on my desk. She appeared to be thinking. "The electronics store job was just for his personal expenses, like a sandwich or comic books or something."

"So how do you explain the fact that Tyler was leaving one-hundred-dollar tips in the jar at the Quik N EZ for Richard Handy virtually every day?" I asked. "Where would he get five hundred dollars a week just for that?"

Sandy coughed. "I have to go." Without another word, she left.

Immediately I called Mike the taxicab driver. "Are you close to my office?" I asked.

"I'm two blocks away," he answered. "I stay close this time of night. Do you need a ride?"

"No. But come here quickly. I need you to follow someone."

TWENTY-THREE

"I DON'T MIND DRIVING you home, Samuel, and you know that." My mother sat behind the steering wheel, driving at the speed limit, which in this case was thirty-five miles per hour. We were headed back to our home, two-point-eight miles from the Questions Answered offices. On occasion when there was no ride available, I have walked home, and it is not difficult. I would have done so tonight, but there was work to be done and I did not know when to expect to receive a visitor at the house. "My point is that you can drive yourself and should start thinking about doing that. You're making money now. You should buy a car."

This was an ongoing conversation. Mother and Ms. Washburn had apparently discussed the subject at some length, as each had broached the subject of my driving more regularly. I own a valid driver's license, which I maintain, but I have not driven in four years. It makes me unusually nervous to have that much responsibility at my disposal, so I avoid the practice.

"Normally, I would have asked Mike for a ride," I told Mother. "But as you know, he is doing something very important for me at this moment."

"I don't understand that one," she answered. "You just said he was following someone."

"You'll see very soon."

I believe I saw the hint of a smile on Mother's face. She likes to believe that I am more intelligent and capable than I actually am. I have given up trying to convince her otherwise. She said nothing for the rest of the short drive.

We were clearing the table after dinner when Mike the taxicab driver knocked at our back door, which is located in the kitchen. When Mike drives me home, he parks in the driveway, which is closer to the back of the house, so he uses it as his entrance, with our permission. I let him in and he sat at the table, accepting Mother's offer of some cold water but declining any leftover roast beef we might have.

"Maybe now I'll find out exactly what you were up to all this time," Mother told him as she handed him the glass.

It had been only fifty-three minutes since I had phoned Mike with a request to follow Sandy Clayton Webb from the Questions Answered office and report back on where she had gone and what she had done, but concepts of time are not objective. So I did not comment on Mother's remark.

"I was following this woman around in her car, but Samuel never told me why," Mike answered her. They both looked to me so I assumed they wanted an explanation.

"The woman is named Sandy Clayton Webb," I told Mike. "She is the sister of Tyler Clayton and Mason Clayton, the man who asked me who shot Richard Handy at the Quik N EZ convenience store in Somerset."

I thought that was sufficient, but neither Mike nor Mother said anything for eight seconds (which is actually quite a long gap in a conversation) after I spoke.

"Why did you need me to follow her?" Mike asked. "Do you think she killed this Handy guy?"

I shook my head. "If Sandy had been present in the convenience store at the time of the shooting, she either would have been visible before the security cameras were disabled or there would have been audio of Tyler speaking to her as she entered. I do not believe Sandy was there, or that she could have shot Richard Handy."

"So why are you suspicious of her?" Mother asked. "And don't tell me you're not, because you wouldn't have had poor Mike here gallivanting around central New Jersey when he should be home after a long day."

"Actually, I'm working until eleven tonight," Mike said. Mother looked concerned, but he waved a hand. "Taking a friend's shift for him."

"Please," I said to Mike before more small talk could be offered, "tell me what Sandy did after she left Questions Answered." Mother began to ask another question, but I held up a finger, indicating I would answer after Mike did. Which I was sure he would do as soon as he finished drinking the glass of water.

He nodded, realizing I had been waiting for the information. "Sorry. Sandy drove out of your parking lot just as I got there. She didn't ride around; her route was very direct. She drove to an address in Franklin."

"What was the address?" I asked.

Mike glanced at a small notebook he carries in the pocket of his denim work shirt. He looked at my face after reading the address and told me what it was; I think he wanted to see my reaction.

I would probably not have been able to read my own expression if I'd had a mirror, but I was feeling something like a small amount of validation. It was one of the places I'd suspected Sandy might go.

"That is Billy Martinez's address," I said.

"Billy Martinez!" Ms. Washburn had barely made it into the office the next morning when I'd told her the results of Mike's surveillance the night before.

"Yes. Mike reported that Sandy went to the front door of Billy's home, rang the doorbell and was admitted by someone Mike could not see. It could have either been Billy or one of his parents, I suppose."

"What would Sandy want with Billy Martinez?" Ms. Washburn asked, removing her jacket and sitting behind her desk. She hung the jacket on the back of her chair despite my having offered to install a coat rack in the office. Ms. Washburn says it helps her to feel like we're doing something urgent when she can pull the jacket off the back of her chair as we leave to do research. I don't entirely understand the concept, but I accept it helps feed some emotional need of Ms. Washburn's.

"That is indeed an interesting question," I said. "Mike told us Sandy stayed inside for approximately ten minutes, then got into her car and drove directly to her residence in Somerset, went inside and didn't come back out. He said that, in violation of all New Jersey traffic regulations, Sandy was talking to someone through her cellular phone during her trip home. Mike drove to my house to report. But he couldn't possibly know the intent or content of the meeting."

"I was asking for your opinion," Ms. Washburn said. She got up from her desk and walked to the vending machine. Every morning she gets a bottle of green tea when she arrives, although diet soda is her preference the rest of the day. She claims it is "too early" to drink a soda before eleven a.m., which I am unable to understand. "I didn't think Mike had answered the question for us all by himself."

I considered what she had said. "My opinion is that there is a connection between Sandy, Billy Martinez, and an unknown third party that involves some contraband merchandise being sold illegally, possibly through the Quik N EZ. And it is becoming increasingly clear that is the reason Richard Handy was killed."

Ms. Washburn took a moment to absorb the information while sitting back down at her desk. "I get the connection between Sandy and Billy Martinez, because she immediately went to see him—and we didn't even know they'd ever met—after you talked last night. And I get the unknown third party from the phone call on Sandy's way home, although that could be you stretching a little bit because for all we know she was calling her dry cleaner. But the contraband merchandise? Stolen merchandise? Is that from Richard's little skirmish over the cigarettes he was stealing from the convenience store a while back?"

"Yes," I said. I had activated a software program I'd been working on that would run deep Internet searches in the background while I was working on other areas and inform me when a relevant match was found. So far there had been nothing, but what we were looking for was fairly obscure and had very narrow parameters. "I suggest we talk again to Mr. Robinson, the owner of the Quik N EZ. He is not often present on the store premises. Did you get his contact information?"

Eighty-five minutes later Ms. Washburn and I were in the office of Raymond J. Robinson on the eighth floor of a building he owned in Bridgewater Township. The view, which mostly featured Route 22 running east to west, was unspectacular, but the corner office and the expensive furnishings (including a photograph of Mr. Robinson with a past president of the United States) were clearly meant to impress. It was, plainly, not the image that would have been conjured after seeing Mr. Robinson sweeping the floor of his convenience store in Somerset (even in a business suit), and I mentioned that to him as we sat down in chairs upholstered with leather.

"If you want to be successful in business, you have to know what your employees are doing," Mr. Robinson said. "If you don't do it yourself even for a short time, you won't know. I take a week every once in a while and go work at one of my businesses. I have my assistant call and say an older gentleman needs a job and is coming in to work. Some of the managers balk at it. They don't like having the boss tell them who to hire. They treat me with a vengeance like it's my fault—which it actually is, but they don't know that—and that tells me what the job is like and what the manager is like. It's invaluable."

"That's very interesting," Ms. Washburn said. I have noticed that people often say exactly that when something is not the least bit interesting at all, but it was not the case in this instance. "You just happened to be working at the Quik N EZ the week Richard Handy was shot?"

Mr. Robinson dropped his brows and held up his hands. "Oh no," he said. "I wasn't working there this week. You just saw me at the store because of that horrible incident. I was looking after my employees and my property."

"How many businesses do you own?" Ms. Washburn asked. This was meant to ingratiate herself with the subject—we had already gained this information through a simple search before leaving our office.

Mr. Robinson leaned back in his chair, thinking. "Besides the Quik N EZ chain, with those eleven stores, I own three frozen yogurt franchises, a small electronics chain that I'm about to close, two dance studios, and four food trucks in Manhattan." He seemed especially proud of that last item, perhaps because the trucks were located in New York. Some New Jerseyans suffer from an inferiority complex concerning the city to the north and east.

"Why didn't you tell us about all your other businesses when we met before?" Ms. Washburn asked. The question was valid and intelligent.

"You didn't ask," Mr. Robinson said. His answer did not live up to the question.

But I was not inclined to spend time building a rapport with Mr. Robinson; I was more interested in getting to the heart of the matter quickly so I could exercise upon my return to the office and then get home in time for lunch. "Mr. Robinson, with all your effort to remain aware of the inner workings of your businesses, is it not odd that a black market was operating through your convenience store and you were unaware of it?"

Mr. Robinson stopped leaning back in his chair. Ms. Washburn, who was accustomed to my style of questioning, did not look at all surprised, but our subject appeared stung by my words.

"What exactly do you mean, a black market operating through my convenience store?" he demanded.

It was an odd comment, since none of the words I'd used was at all obscure. I assumed Mr. Robinson was simply trying to delay having to answer me by asking a question to which he obviously already knew the answer. So I did not answer, simply letting him process the statement.

"You're saying someone was selling illegal merchandise under my manager's nose?" he said, apparently thinking changing the words would somehow also alter their meaning. In this case, that was not going to happen.

"We never met the manager," Ms. Washburn noted. "May we talk to him or her?"

"You'd have to talk pretty loud," Mr. Robinson answered with an odd look on his face. "The manager at that particular location was Richard Handy."

That was news to us, and it shouldn't have been. I looked at Ms. Washburn reflexively. Her eyes widened.

"We were told Richard was the assistant manager," I said.

"It was a symbolic thing. I had just promoted him."

"Richard was only twenty-two years old," I said. "He was the store manager?" Left unsaid was the fact that Richard Handy had also been implicated by the police in a previous incident of illegal sales, in that case of cigarettes he had embezzled from the Quik N EZ stock.

"He was an ambitious kid and he knew the store backwards and forwards," Mr. Robinson said. "When the previous manager quit, he was the logical choice. I believe in promoting from within."

That was an admirable business plan, perhaps, but it had no relevance to the conversation. "So you had no idea someone was involved in selling some sort of contraband items through your convenience store?" I said, trying to redirect Mr. Robinson to the topic at hand.

He looked startled. "Of course not," he said. "You don't know what was being sold?"

"I have a few ideas," I said. It was an attempt at being evasive, or at least appearing to be speaking from a stronger empirical position than I was capable of doing at the moment. "But I am not able to list items definitively."

But Mr. Robinson's eyes narrowed. He had not been fooled. "What evidence do you have?" he asked.

"I prefer not to name specific individuals," I said. The expression to "name names" is simply redundant. "But I can say that I am aware of where some stock was being kept, and at least two of the people we believe to have been involved."

"This is serious, Mr. Hoenig," the entrepreneur said. "If you have some proof that this sort of illegal activity was being perpetrated in my business by my employees, I will have to take actions against those people and make sure it can't happen again. Now what can you tell me?"

I stood up. Ms. Washburn, who no doubt found the move unexpected, took a moment to follow. "I'm afraid I've told you everything I can at this moment," I said. "But you can rest assured that as soon as I know more, I will be sure to let you know."

"I don't think that's good enough," Mr. Robinson answered, not standing nor proffering his hand to shake (which was something of a relief to me, actually). "I'm going to need names and I'm going to need facts, not innuendoes. Now please sit down and tell me what I need to know."

I shook my head and started toward the door. "I think we have already taken enough of your valuable time, Mr. Robinson," I said as I opened it. "We will certainly be in touch."

Before he could respond, clearly not used to the idea that people would not simply do as he instructed, Ms. Washburn and I left Mr. Robinson's office and walked into the hallway toward the elevator.

"Did that actually accomplish anything?" Ms. Washburn asked me quietly, better to avoid the ears of the well-dressed receptionist.

"In fact," I said, whispering because my voice modulation is at best uncertain, "it accomplished quite a bit. I believe we can now be fairly sure that Mr. Robinson knew about the operation going on at the Quik N EZ. It would be interesting to see if we can trace similar situations to his other retail locations."

We entered the elevator, but kept our volume low even after the doors closed. "I didn't see it," Ms. Washburn said. "When did you get all that information?"

"It was fairly clear once we discovered that Mr. Robinson wasn't a simple small businessman with one convenience store. Men like that don't let too much happen at their businesses without them knowing about it. But that is just conjecture."

"Then what's not conjecture?" Ms. Washburn asked. The elevator doors opened and we headed out of the building toward the parking lot.

"We just told a wealthy entrepreneur that one of his businesses was the front for an operation that was certainly stealing from him and putting his entire livelihood at risk to investigation by any number of local, state, and possibly federal agencies." I tried to smell the air, because I am told it has a pleasant odor when the trees and flowers are blooming. In this parking lot, there was not a noticeable scent.

"Yes, that's what we did," Ms. Washburn said. "So?"

"So what would you expect would be the first thing that man would say when he heard all that?" I asked her.

She continued to walk, almost reaching her car, keys in her hair. She pushed the button on her key to release the door locks. "You'd think the first thing would be that we should call the police and let them know what we found," she said.

"Precisely. Did Mr. Robinson ever even mention the word *police*?"

Ms. Washburn opened the driver's side door. "Never," she said. "So what do we do?"

"I think the only logical thing is to tell the police."

TWENTY-FOUR

DETECTIVE MILTON HESSLER STOOD behind his desk with an expression on his face I could read only as incredulity. Or impatience. Those two are actually somewhat difficult to differentiate.

"You had evidence of a black market operation working out of a murder scene and you kept it to yourself?" he demanded.

"We are here to tell you about it right now," I explained. "And our evidence is not completely empirical, detective."

"Empirical?"

"Verifiable," Ms. Washburn explained. "Something you could use as evidence."

Hessler nodded in understanding. "All you've got right now is a guess?"

It wasn't the word I would use, but he was essentially correct. "Perhaps an educated guess," I said. "I have been searching for the kind of contraband that would have been in sufficient quantity to merit this kind of operation, and perhaps the murder of Richard Handy. But so far I have found only small recoveries. Is there a way you could search the list of merchandise seized by the State Police or local authorities?"

"Yes, there is," Hessler said. "And I will definitely do that. Thank you for your help." He began to scan some papers on his desk, probably in a theatrical gesture of dismissal.

"Wait," Ms. Washburn said before I could signal her to hold back. "You're not going to tell us what you find out?"

Hessler looked up, now pretending to be mildly surprised. "Why should I?" he asked. "You're civilians. I appreciate the tip you've given me. Now it's time for you to go on home and let the police do their job." He went back to the papers on his desk, which I felt was overplaying his role just a bit.

"That's not fair," Ms. Washburn protested.

"Oh, it's entirely fair. You've played your role in the investigation, as a good citizen should, and brought information to the attention of the proper authorities. I'm the proper authority. You can trust that I will follow up on that information and take whatever action is appropriate depending on where it leads. Again, thank you."

Hessler was not at all an incompetent detective. I had little doubt that if there were some large seizure of contraband merchandise, he would find it faster than I could, given his official resources. And there was every probability that he would arrive at an accurate solution to his problem. But it did not necessarily mean I would be able to answer Mason Clayton's question, and that was my priority.

"I am withholding some of the information I have," I told the detective while Ms. Washburn's face reddened.

They both stared at me. "What did you say?" Hessler asked.

I did not repeat my declaration, as I had no doubt he had heard what I'd said. Instead, I told him, "If you would like to share the information you discover based on what we have already told you— information you did not already have—I can be persuaded to tell you the rest." I folded my arms because I have been taught that can be a gesture of immovability.

No doubt Hessler saw the look on my face and my body language. Ms. Washburn was badly stifling a smile, but luckily the detective was looking at me and not her. I did not find the situation amusing, which helped me maintain my expression.

"What have you got?" he asked.

"When you agree to share information," I insisted.

"You're aware that I could charge you with withholding evidence and interfering with a police investigation," Hessler said. I assumed he meant the sentence as a question, although it was not structured as one.

"I am aware," I said. "I suppose you would have to arraign us, then explain to a judge why you are unwilling to share information with a local business and imprison a man with a neurological disorder in the process."

There are times when the public perception of Asperger's Syndrome is useful.

Hessler curled his lip but he did not actually sneer. His expression, if I was reading it correctly, was less one of a man being defied and more one of a man realizing he should take the easy path.

"Okay, I'll tell you what the seizure search turns up," he said, dropping his hands onto his desk and sitting down. "Now you tell me what other information you have."

I nodded my agreement. "There is a closet in the basement of Billy Martinez's home that has been used as a storage area for the stolen merchandise, probably cartons of cigarettes," I said. "I saw the marks of the stacked cartons on the wall, which had suffered some minor water damage. If you obtain a search warrant, you will probably find some traces of tobacco and possibly other evidence, assuming that the thieves were operating with more than one product."

Hessler took a note on a pad in front of him, then looked up at me. "That's it?" he asked.

"It is. I've already told you about Raymond Robinson's unusual response to my revelation of the black market operation in his store. I assume he has not called you regarding that."

"That's right." Hessler responded as if I had asked a question. "But there's something else you are not telling me." He was a better observer of people than I had originally believed.

"Yes, there is," I said. "But it would be a breach of my professional ethics to tell you one part of the information I have." Mentioning the name of Sandy Clayton Webb would violate the Questions Answered policy of betraying a client's name without permission. Admittedly, Sandy was not a client of the agency, but her brother Mason was, and my strong impression was that he would not have wanted us to give his sister's name to the police if it was at all avoidable. For the time being, it was avoidable.

"Your professional ethics?" Hessler scoffed. "You run a business out of a pizzeria that answers questions people are too busy to Google themselves. What professional ethics does that industry have?" I believe he was being sarcastic, although I am not always correct about that particular tone of voice. Mother says I should have learned it by living in New Jersey all these years. That, too, might be sarcasm.

"All professions have ethics," I told him. "Not all are codified. If I am to protect my client's rights, anonymity is going to be necessary."

Hessler scowled at me. "I can't say I'm crazy about this." Again, I had to overlook the use of the word *crazy*, which does not truly fit in that expression.

"I don't doubt it, and I understand. If my client releases me from my non-disclosure agreement, I will be happy to share the information with you. And if it becomes dangerous to anyone for me to withhold the information, I promise to come forward. Is that sufficient?"

"No, but I'm not going to press charges," Hessler said. "Now go do what you do. I have an investigation to run." He waved a hand toward the station entrance, so Ms. Washburn and I headed in that direction.

Ms. Washburn suggested she drive me home for lunch, and as Mother had insisted, I invited Ms. Washburn to join us. She hesitated a moment, then accepted, which I did not expect.

Mother, never unprepared for such circumstances, had tuna salad sandwiches for herself and Ms. Washburn. I had my usual turkey sandwich. It was also a sign of Mother's comfort level with Ms. Washburn that we could eat in the kitchen rather than the dining room. It intimated a certain familiarity reserved for very few other than ourselves.

We brought Mother up to date on the research into Mason's question, which was the only one Questions Answered was currently contracted to answer. She listened carefully, attentively. Mother finds my work fascinating and is often more impressed than she should be with the answers Ms. Washburn and I manage to find.

"So did Detective Hessler give you any useful information?" she asked after Ms. Washburn mentioned our recent visit to the Somerset police department.

"No," I answered, "but he did promise to let us know what he discovers about the black market merchandise Billy Martinez was selling through the Quik N EZ. And I expect the detective is a man of his word, since he was so reluctant to give it. A person willing to go back on a promise makes a lot of promises."

Ms. Washburn looked thoughtfully past my right shoulder toward the kitchen door. "Something's been bothering me about this whole question for a while now, and I think I just figured out what it is." She sharpened her focus and looked at me. "Why did Tyler go to the Quik N EZ?"

That seemed an oddly simple question to be pondering for very long. I thought I would answer, "To get to the other side," but the joke probably would not have been appropriate under the circumstances. I often think some things are funny when others do not agree. "What do you mean?" I asked. "It seems obvious that Tyler frequented the Quik N EZ because he believed Richard Handy was his friend and he doesn't have many friends."

"Not lately. The first time. Why did Tyler go to that convenience store the first time, when he met Richard and decided he might be a friend?"

"It's a convenience store," Mother said, clearly having some difficulty grasping Ms. Washburn's meaning. "Why wouldn't he have just gone in to get a soda or something?"

"Tyler lives with his brother Mason in Franklin Township," Ms. Washburn said. "The Quik N EZ is in Somerset, at least a few minutes' drive from his house. He must have passed three or four other convenience stores every day on his way to that one. Why did he go there the first time?"

"Is it near his work?" Mother asked. "Samuel said the boy has a part-time job at an electronics store."

"The Microchip Mart," I said. "And from the address Mason gave us to talk to the owner of the store"—who had told us Tyler was a model employee and nothing else—"that store is in Franklin, not walking distance to the Quik N EZ." I turned to face Ms. Washburn. "I think you're right. We have overlooked something quite obvious that we should have considered much sooner."

"What do you think?" she asked. "Why would Tyler walk that far to go to a convenience store when he could have gone to any number of others?"

Sometimes when I think I put my hands on either side of my head next to my eyes. People who do not know that it is a pose that helps me concentrate sometimes think I have a headache or am upset. Neither of those things was the case.

223

Now, I was doing just that because Ms. Washburn had asked a question that required my considering hypotheticals, something I am loath to do. It is difficult for me to think about things that are not verified by facts or measureable factors. But the question had been asked, and it was relevant to our research.

"I think it means that you might have just taken a very large step toward our answering this question," I said. "Just one other thing: We need to call Tyler's manager at the Microchip Mart."

"Why?" Ms. Washburn asked. "He already told us Tyler is a wonderful employee."

"Yes, and still Tyler's hours are decreasing. So we need to ask him who owns the store."

"Why?"

"Because Mr. Robinson said he has a small electronics chain he's about to close."

TWENTY-FIVE

When I called Mason and asked him to bring Tyler and Sandy to the Questions Answered office, I did not inform him that we were also inviting Molly and Evelyn Brandt. That was perhaps an unfair tactic, but one that was necessary. I wanted both Ms. Washburn and myself to gauge the reactions of Tyler and Molly when each realized the other was present in the room.

Ten minutes before they were due to arrive, I asked Ms. Washburn (who had called the Microchip Mart and left a voice mail for the manager) if she thought it would be inappropriate for me to complete an exercise session with so little time to spare. She believed there was no harm in it "even if they see you walking around the room with your arms in the air for a minute or two; it'll catch them off-guard." So I began my routine, circumnavigating the office and raising my arms to increase my heart rate. I find this to be an excellent way to clear the mind.

"What about the Swords and Sorcerers die?" I asked Ms. Washburn as I completed my first lap. "Have you asked your estranged husband about my theory?"

"The idea that Richard was holding the Tenduline when he was shot and dropped it as a warning to Tyler? No, I didn't consult Simon on that. He's not the best at analysis. He's better for raw data." She looked away as she spoke, then seemed to force herself to face me again, but by that moment I had stopped looking at her.

So close to answering the question, this was not the time for me to concern myself with Ms. Washburn's marriage. It was unusual and puzzling that it occupied my mind at all. Ms. Washburn was remarkably able to separate her private life from her work at Questions Answered. Indeed, the only time I had met Simon Taylor was in connection to Mason Clayton's question. We had spoken on the phone more than once—which had not been a pleasant experience—but Ms. Washburn's life outside the office was entirely her own affair. I had no connection to it and normally would not have even thought about it. Why was my mind wandering to that topic now?

"Samuel," Ms. Washburn said, breaking my train of thought, "it looks like Molly and Evelyn have arrived." She pointed toward the door.

I looked up. Approaching the entrance, clearly visible through the plate glass window, were Evelyn Brandt and her daughter, Molly. I frowned. "I thought we'd asked them to come later," I said.

"I did when I called," answered Ms. Washburn. "I guess they hit all the lights." That suggestion did not make sense, as a person hitting a traffic light with her car would be delayed rather than accelerated, but I did not question it. I was disappointed that Tyler Clayton would be here after Molly. My plan would have to be adjusted.

The bells on the entrance pealed as they entered. I saw Ms. Washburn stand up, so I did the same and walked toward the two visitors to welcome them. This, I have been taught, is a way to make newcomers feel more at ease. And right now, I wanted Evelyn and Molly especially to be comfortable with the surroundings.

"Welcome to Questions Answered," Ms. Washburn said. "Thanks for coming on such short notice."

"We could have taken the train to Edison from Bound Brook," Molly informed us. "But that would have required changing trains in Newark, so driving was faster."

Evelyn looked slightly pained. "Sorry," she said.

"There is no need to apologize," I told her. It was true; her daughter's autism spectrum behavior was not her fault, nor was it at all offensive in this case. "We are glad you could come to help us with this question."

"The same would have been true if we'd taken the train from Bound Brook to New Brunswick, Metuchen, or Metropark, all of which are near this address," Molly said. "But then we would have had to ask you for a ride from the train station because none of those are close enough to your office for us to walk."

"That is true, Molly," I said. "Won't you please sit down?"

Ms. Washburn and I had added to our usual complement of seats with some folding chairs I had found in the pizzeria kitchen when I took over the space for Questions Answered. At Ms. Washburn's suggestion (and with my enthusiastic agreement), they had been cleaned with disinfectant wipes. I gestured toward the chairs. Evelyn immediately took one but Molly stood.

"Come sit, Molly," she urged, but her daughter did not acknowledge that anything was said.

"We could have taken the number one-hundred-fourteen bus and that would have been faster and less expensive, but it would have dropped us off too far from here," Molly continued.

"Molly," Evelyn said with an edge of tension in her voice.

Molly, apparently sensing her mother's anxiety or simply because she was acquainted with that tone of voice, took one of the other seats Ms. Washburn had arranged in front of our desks.

"What can we do to help, Mr. Hoenig?" Evelyn asked.

As if by way of answering, the bells on the front door rang again, and we—with the exception of Molly—looked toward the office entrance. In walked Mason Clayton looking haggard and tired. The ordeal of his brother's incarceration coupled with his own financial difficulties (which apparently he was attempting to keep to himself) had begun to take a toll on him.

Behind him was Tyler.

Hands moving rapidly at his sides, eyes darting from the ceiling to the floor with little time spent in between, Tyler seemed more agitated even than when we'd seen him in the interrogation room at Somerset police headquarters. No doubt the events of the past few days had damaged any progress he had made in social skills or fine motor training. He was, in the terms of the "typical" world, "regressing."

"Thank you for coming," Ms. Washburn said to them as they entered. "Is Sandy meeting us here?" Their sister clearly was not following the two men into the room.

"Sandy's not coming," Mason said. "Sorry about that, but there just wasn't time for her to rearrange her day."

That was not an unexpected development but it was a slightly disappointing one. Sandy Clayton Webb seemed to be at the center of much of the activity to be discussed, so her absence would limit the amount of information that could be gathered today.

But I was watching Molly and Tyler as closely as I could given their relative distance from each other. Molly was facing away from the entrance and Tyler had not yet spoken. (Indeed, I was not sure if he would say anything at all.) Molly was not yet aware that he had entered the room.

As Tyler followed Mason toward our small conference area, his attention was anywhere but on the people gathered in the office. He seemed, as before, fascinated with the pizza oven, which I could understand—they are a very unusual feature, one that most people do not get to see up close on a regular basis.

Then he noticed Molly was there. "Uh-oh," Tyler said too loudly.

Molly's reaction to Tyler's voice was considerably more dramatic. She broke into a wide smile and spun to face him. "Hawkeye!" she shouted and lunged at Tyler, catching him in an enthusiastic hug. Tyler looked startled, then uncomfortable.

"Carlye," he said quietly. He was not smiling.

Molly's mother Evelyn dropped her mouth open in astonishment. "Carlye?" she asked.

Mason, eyes wide, smiled slightly at the sight of his brother being hugged tightly by a young woman Mason had probably never seen before. "Tyler," he said, "do you want to introduce us?"

"No."

"Molly," Molly said. "I'm Molly. I'm Tyler's girlfriend."

Mason, to his credit, did not look surprised now. He extended his hand and said, "It's nice to meet you, Molly." But Molly was not releasing Tyler from her embrace.

He seemed uncomfortable, standing with his arms at his side, head occasionally vibrating with tension. "I shot Richard," he said to no one in particular. "I took the gun and I shot him."

Evelyn's face registered fear.

"No, you didn't," Molly assured Tyler. "You couldn't shoot anybody. You're my Hawkeye."

Mason looked at Ms. Washburn, who said, "It's a thing about the TV show *M*A*S*H*. They identify with two of the characters."

"No," Tyler managed.

"We don't really think we're at the four-oh-seven-seventh," Molly said. "It's a game, like Swords and Sorcerers."

"I shot Richard."

Evelyn stood up. "Is that true? Did Tyler shoot someone?"

"No," Molly crooned.

"We believe Tyler did not shoot Richard Handy," I assured Evelyn. "We are in the process of answering the question for Mason." I gestured toward Tyler's brother to identify him, as he and Evelyn had not been met before. "Allow me to introduce Mason Clayton."

Evelyn, at least, did accept Mason's hand and stood up to take it. "Evelyn Brandt," she said. "Molly and Tyler are in the same therapy group. I've seen you pick Tyler up sometimes."

"I remember," Mason said. I do not know if he was being truthful.

Tyler said, "Let go of me now, Molly." Molly did not seem the least bit upset by his bluntness, which I have been told can be construed as impolite. She released the embrace but hooked her right arm through Tyler's left and stared up at him, grinning. He did not move his arm to indicate she should let go, but did not seem to participate in the gesture at all.

"Mr. Hoenig, why are we here?" Mason turned and asked me. "Is there some breakthrough you have to report?"

"Not yet," I admitted. "I have some things to ask all of you, and I'm hoping that will get us very close to answering your question, Mason."

Ms. Washburn turned on a voice recorder she keeps on her desk but also got out her notebook and pen. Mason and Evelyn sat in the two folding chairs while Tyler remained almost immobile in his spot and Molly cheerfully held onto his arm and never took her eyes off his face.

"Tyler, Molly says she is your girlfriend," I began. "Is that accurate?"

Tyler's eyes rolled backward and up. "Nnnnnnn ... "

I had not expected Tyler to retreat into nonverbal behavior so quickly. "Tyler," Ms. Washburn said in a tone I recognized. "You don't have to worry. Molly will like you no matter what you say." I did not see how she could be sure of that, but I trusted Ms. Washburn's instincts in such matters.

"That's right," Molly said. "Hawkeye and Carlye love each other even though they can't be together when she asks for a transfer. But I am your girlfriend."

Mason stood and got very close to Tyler so his younger brother could not avert his eyes. "Tyler. Mr. Hoenig is trying to help. Tell him what he needs to know."

"I shot Richard."

"No, you didn't, but that's not what we're asking you now. Is Molly your girlfriend?"

Tyler's mouth widened as if in a grimace of pain. He opened it but no sound was emitted for six seconds. It was like a muscular cramp had overtaken his speech. I have had moments when emotion has made it difficult for me to articulate myself, but this was much more dramatic and severe than anything I have ever experienced.

Finally Tyler managed, while fixing his gaze at a point some three feet over my head, to say, "Yes."

Molly grinned at him. "See?" she said without averting her eyes.

I knew the next question would be especially stressful, so I wrote it out on a legal pad and handed it to Ms. Washburn. She read it and after a brief hesitation, asked Tyler, "Are you trying to protect Molly by saying you shot Richard?"

What I had written was, *You didn't shoot Richard. Did Molly?* I believed I knew the answer, but Tyler's heightened emotional state would make the answer more fraught with difficulty. I knew Ms. Washburn would be able to word it more palatably.

Again, Tyler struggled to speak and found the effort too overwhelming. Molly, as her mother watched open-mouthed, stepped in to rescue her boyfriend. "Yes, he's protecting me," she said.

This time I knew I could ask the question myself. "But you didn't shoot Richard Handy, did you?" I asked Molly.

She laughed. "No. That's silly. Carlye is a nurse. They don't shoot people, not even in a war."

"Did you see who shot Richard?" I asked Molly. "Were you at the Quik N EZ when he died?"

She seemed distracted, staring into Tyler's face. "No," she repeated. "I left almost as soon as I got there. Maybe two minutes."

"Molly!" Evelyn exclaimed. "You were there? You couldn't have been there. I always know where you are, don't I?"

"I said I was going to see Tyler," her daughter answered. "I went to see Tyler." She hugged his arm a little tighter. Then she grinned. "I dressed like him too." She turned toward Tyler. "Why did you ask me to do that?"

"Nnnnnnnnnnn…"

Mason, still close to his brother, put his hands on Tyler's triceps. "Look at me, buddy," he said. "Tell me who shot that guy in the convenience store."

Tyler grunted but did not respond verbally. Mason turned toward Molly. "Do you know?" he asked.

She seemed to refocus from a thought she had been having—something to which I can easily relate—and shook her head. "At the Quik N EZ? I just painted the cameras, then I left," she said.

"You what?" Evelyn looked stricken, face white and eyes wide.

Molly was apparently unfazed by or insensitive to her mother's panic. "Tyler said I should dress up in a hoodie and spray paint the cameras in the store," she said, as if explaining that she had gone to the movies that afternoon. "So I did, but then he made me leave. No talking, nothing, just go. And that's what I did."

Ms. Washburn looked concerned and walked to Molly to make eye contact. "That was you on the security video? You spray painted the lenses of the cameras so nobody would see when Richard was shot?"

Molly was about to answer, then stopped short. "Someone got shot?" she asked.

TWENTY-SIX

TYLER CLAYTON WAS NO longer capable of conversing, even less so than he had been when he entered the Questions Answered office. He had not completely reverted to his "nnnnnnn" vocalizing, but he sat in Mother's cushioned armchair and stared ahead. Mason said he believed the stress was proving too much for his younger brother, but I believed the cause was considerably more complex than that, although certainly Tyler was feeling pressure.

He could tell us nothing, not even when Ms. Washburn offered him a legal pad or the use of her computer keyboard. He held his arms tight, as if hugging himself. Molly Brandt seemed offended by Tyler's disinterest in having *her* hug him instead, and pouted for three minutes and sixteen seconds.

During that time, I asked Mason about the Tenduline, and showed him an image Ms. Washburn had taken of it before we'd surrendered the die to Detective Hessler. He said it was unfamiliar to him and Tyler was not communicating. I was irritated with my own stupidity at not anticipating his reaction. I should have showed him the Tenduline first.

"It's one of the things for S and S, isn't it?" Mason asked.

"Yes, it's cursed," Molly volunteered. All heads (except Tyler's) turned toward her.

"You play Swords and Sorcerers, Molly?" Ms. Washburn asked.

Molly laughed, although the question did not seem at all amusing to anyone else. "No. But Tyler told me about it, and once he did I looked up all I could find. The Tenduline is an ancient gaming piece that was cursed by an evil sorcerer hundreds of years ago when he lost a wager using it. His name was Androsken the Wicked, and he instilled the Tenduline with a power to predict when there would a violent death. If you see it, something bad is going to happen."

"Oh my," Evelyn said under her breath.

"Is that what happened?" Molly asked in a light tone. "Somebody died after they saw the Tenduline? That would explain it."

"No, it would not," I responded. "There is no such thing as a cursed gaming die. Richard Handy was shot by another person for reasons considerably more human."

"But the … Tenduline? That's significant?" Mason asked.

"It was found at the scene of the murder," I told him. "I believe it was there as an intended message."

"A warning from the killer?" Mason said.

I shook my head. "A warning from the victim. I believe Richard Handy was trying to send a message to someone else who was there when he was shot, a warning that the person who killed him could easily do so again, and that the circumstances led him to believe there would be more violence. If the killer or killers believe someone is close to exposing them, there could be great danger for the person Richard was trying to warn."

"Who is that?" Evelyn said, looking worriedly at Molly.

"Tyler," I told them.

We did not establish any further useful information during the meeting, which was disappointing. Mason, concerned for his brother's safety and his present uncommunicative condition, led Tyler out of the office and into his Sport Utility Vehicle only a few minutes later. Evelyn, overwhelmed with information she had not known before, said something about trying to make an emergency appointment with Dr. Shean and took Molly, who was protesting that she should be able to go with Tyler, out of the building.

"So you think Richard was trying to warn Tyler that someone might try to kill him?" Ms. Washburn asked when the others had gone.

"That is the theory under which I am currently operating, yes. I don't believe that Richard, as he saw that he was in desperate danger and knowing he probably would not survive even a few seconds, immediately thought of the Tenduline and decided to hold it for luck. It is much more likely he saw the danger to the witness who actually knew something about the killing and the reason behind it, and was trying to send a message of warning."

"But Tyler hasn't said a word about the shooting. The only thing he says is that he's the one who killed Richard, and we're pretty sure that's not true, aren't we?"

I sat down behind my desk and considered Ms. Washburn. She in an invaluable part of the Questions Answered staff because she understands parts of questions that are difficult for me and because she understands how I think. But Mother says that it's easy to see the solutions to someone else's problem but very difficult to see the solutions to your own. So Ms. Washburn is very capable when dealing with the things I need assistance with, and not when she is dealing with her own issues, particularly with her husband and the difficulties in their marriage. I felt that strain was not really impeding her work with me, but that she was sometimes distracted to the point that she would fail to notice some details she would normally spot.

"We are certain that Tyler did not kill Richard," I said. "The fact that the evidence is not supported with anything we can see on a chart or a video surveillance tape does not diminish the fact that there is indeed evidence."

She sat down in Mother's chair, facing me. This is something Ms. Washburn does when she wants to discuss the intricacies of a question. As long as Mother is not present, it is a perfectly acceptable thing to do.

"Is it worthwhile to look for evidence that we *can* show conclusively?" she asked. It was not an attempt to disagree; it was an honest question.

"I think not," I said. "Our burden of proof is not the same as that of a court of law. We have no need to show a judge or jury our evidence; we need only to prove without doubt that the answer to the question is correct, and that will be enough to report to our client."

Ms. Washburn frowned. I knew she wanted me to help Tyler avoid imprisonment or if possible trial for the murder of Richard Handy, but that was not what Questions Answered had been hired to do, and she was aware of that. Ms. Washburn forms some emotional ties to clients that I almost always do not. I had no obligation to help Tyler Clayton; my job was to conclusively answer the question his brother had asked. Still, the fact that he had not killed Richard Handy indicated answering the question would be of benefit to Tyler.

Wisely, Ms. Washburn avoided making an emotional plea. "Shouldn't we at least call Detective Hessler and inform him that we know who painted the security cameras at the Quik N EZ?" she asked.

"Actually, yes, we should," I said. "I hesitate to implicate Molly Brandt in criminal activity, but I think her behavior would probably be seen as too sensitive and difficult by a prosecutor, not worth the time since Molly was not involved in the shooting. Besides, I believe the detective might be less reticent with us if we volunteer help for him. Would you call him, please?"

But Ms. Washburn shook her head. "You do it," she said.

I felt my brow wrinkle. "Why?" I asked.

"Because I'm not always going to be here to do it, and you need to develop the skill."

That brought up thoughts I would have preferred to avoid, but I was reasonably sure Ms. Washburn was not suggesting she would leave Questions Answered anytime soon. She tended to act annoyed when I expressed any concern about that issue. "Is this the time for me to work on such an issue?" I asked.

"Yes. Call. You're closer to the phone, anyway." She pointed to the landline we each have on our desks.

There would be no movement of her position, so I made an involuntary sound in the back of my throat and picked up the receiver. I had Detective Hessler's phone number listed under contacts on my MacBook Pro, so I accessed and dialed it. Hessler's voice mail answered after four rings.

"This is Samuel Hoenig, proprietor of Questions Answered," I said after the inevitable tone. "I have some information to share regarding Richard Handy's murder." Then I reminded the detective of my phone number at the office and disconnected the call. I looked at Ms. Washburn. "Was that satisfactory?" I asked.

"It was perfect. See how easy it is?"

"No."

Hessler returned the call only two minutes later. He had no doubt been on another call or had been screening his incoming messages. "What's the information you have to give me?" he asked as soon as he had identified himself.

Ms. Washburn had insisted I answer this call as well, and since the Caller ID had shown Hessler's number, I had not resisted. "I have some new information on the person who painted over the security camera lenses before Richard Handy was shot," I said. "Can you tell me if you have any data regarding the recent seizures of contraband merchandise in Somerset County?"

"I thought you were calling to tell *me* something," Hessler answered. "Why do I have to give you information first?"

"Because you had promised you would do so when you had the information, and I calculate you would have received it quite some time ago now, but you didn't call," I said. "Are you planning to live up to your end of the bargain?"

"You're not going to get anywhere impersonating my ex-wife," Hessler said.

"I have never met your ex-wife."

There was a pause of three seconds. "Fine. I have some data on the seizures, and I'll give it to you immediately after you tell me about the security cameras."

This was not the kind of negotiation I had anticipated, but I looked at Ms. Washburn and she nodded her head to proceed. No doubt she felt we could trust the detective, that he was simply testing us with his insistence that we offer our help first.

"Very well, detective. The person who painted the camera lenses was not Tyler Clayton. In fact, it was Molly Brandt, who is Tyler's girlfriend but who had already left the convenience store before the shooting occurred."

I could hear the sound of fingers on a keyboard; no doubt Hessler was taking notes as he asked for a spelling on Molly's name. This surprised me, as I would have thought Hessler had already spoken to Dr. Shean. Perhaps she would not give him the names of people in Tyler's group, either.

"How do you know that?" he asked me.

"Molly told me she did it," I said. "She has an autism spectrum disorder and believed she was simply engaging in a prank."

"What made her think to spray paint security cameras?" Hessler asked.

"Tyler asked her to do so."

Ms. Washburn grimaced. Since she has an agenda and I do not in solving questions, she no doubt felt that this disclosure had weakened Tyler's case. And perhaps it had. But it was true and it was relevant to Hessler's case. Withholding it would not have been the right thing to do.

"So Tyler Clayton was in on the shooting at the convenience store?"

"He was present; you've known that since the beginning. Tyler did indeed ask Molly to spray paint the cameras. We don't yet know if he was aware there would be a shooting after that or if someone had told him something else."

"It's an awful lot of coincidences," Hessler said. "You're asking me to believe this kid showed up at the convenience store with a grudge against Richard Handy, asked his girlfriend—who we didn't even know about—to paint over the security cameras, and was found with the gun in his hand over Handy's body, but he didn't shoot Richard Handy."

Ms. Washburn, who could hear the detective on the speakerphone, frowned.

"I am not asking you to believe anything, detective," I said. "I am stating the facts as we know them and pointing out the ones for which we do not yet have evidence. Molly says she painted the cameras and there is no reason to disbelieve her so far. She says Tyler asked her to do so. Again, there is no evidence that is not true. But we have proof on the audio tracks of the security cameras that indicates Tyler was not positioned properly to be the shooter. And although Tyler is not communicating verbally, it is clear that he has been covering the tracks of someone else who probably was much closer to the killing than he."

"Who?" Kessler asked.

"That is the question," I said, quoting Shakespeare's *Hamlet*, although neither Hessler or Ms. Washburn appeared to notice. "Any number of people could have been involved, but there is not a clear track yet. Can you send Ms. Washburn a digital copy of the audio we heard from the security camera recordings?"

The detective hesitated. "Why?"

"Because it might help to answer the question." I had assumed that was clear.

"I believe Samuel would like to review the sound and find out if there are any further conclusions he can reach now that we know more," Ms. Washburn explained for me. Apparently I had not been as direct as I had intended. I nodded thanks to her.

"All right," Hessler grumbled. "I'll e-mail it over, but I'm not crazy about giving that kind of evidence to a civilian."

"There is no reason to be concerned," I assured the detective. "You will still have the original source material and can make as many copies as you like. Now, please tell us what the search of seizure information might have yielded."

Ms. Washburn walked to my desk and positioned herself closer to my desk telephone so she could better hear the reply. I noticed she had started wearing the wedding ring on her left hand again. That might have some significance. Should I mention what I had observed at Simon's apartment? Morality was such a confusing concept.

"Oh, fine." Hessler sounded as if he were being harassed, rather than carrying out an agreement we had already forged. "There wasn't a huge haul of anything like what you're looking for anywhere, but we did pull in three separate shipments in two days. Cigarettes, chewing tobacco, and one other thing—handguns."

"Handguns are not sold at convenience stores," I said to myself.

"No, they're not. And that's what makes this especially interesting. Now, what do you know about this operation?"

"There is not much I can verify yet," I told the detective. "There were watermarks in the basement of Billy Martinez that would indicate the presence of what I would imagine were cartons of cigarettes. I did not see anything that would indicate weapons had been stored there, although that does not rule out the possibility."

"Martinez is the one who works at the Quik N EZ?" Hessler asked.

"Yes. You'll recall I suggested you obtain a warrant for his home to search for signs of tobacco."

"Yes, and the county prosecutor reminded me that tobacco is a legal substance and its presence in someone's basement would not indicate a criminal act. Thanks for that one, Hoenig."

"Nonetheless, Billy Martinez was present in the store when Richard Handy was killed, but it is unlikely he was the shooter because the footage shows him at the counter only a second or two before the shots ring out and he would not have been able to get to the dairy display that quickly." My mind was racing at the inclusion of firearms among the items sold illegally through the convenience store. There had to be some information in that fact that would lead to an answer to Mason's question.

"Take a look at the security footage, or at least a listen to it, and get back to me," Hessler said. "Let me know what you hear and don't wait to verify anything. Just call me as soon as you listen to it."

I looked over at Ms. Washburn, who had returned to her desk and was looking at her computer screen. She looked up at me and nodded. "It's here," she said.

"I will do that, detective," I said, and disconnected the call. I did not say "good-bye." Police officers on television and in motion pictures are often pictured as overlooking the normal niceties of social convention when a case is about to be solved. Of course that usually involves danger to at least one of the major characters, but this was reality so I did not concern myself with that convention.

Ms. Washburn looked up briefly from her screen. "I'll have that audio up in a second," she said.

"No rush," I told her. "I have it memorized. Right now, I think the most important thing to do is call Mason Clayton."

She appeared startled. "Why?"

"Because Mother was right to wonder why Tyler would have started going to the Quik N EZ. That is the key to this question."

"I'll get him right away," said Ms. Washburn, reaching for the telephone.

"No need," I said. "I'll do it."

TWENTY-SEVEN

Ms. Washburn and I arrived at Sandy Clayton Webb's Franklin Township home at 2:26 p.m., having arranged a meeting for 2:30. That, Ms. Washburn and Sandy had agreed, would leave some time before her children arrived home on the school bus. We did not expect the meeting to last long.

Mason Clayton had been helpful when I'd called him. He had confirmed, as I'd suspected, that Tyler had not been drawing upon any Able Home Help funds to pay the $100 tips he would leave for Richard Handy every day at the Quik N EZ. Mason had no idea where Tyler might be acquiring so much cash, particularly since his job at the Microchip Mart had been cutting back on his hours for three months before the shooting incident had taken place.

Sandy opened the door immediately when Ms. Washburn pressed the button for the bell, as if she had been waiting in the front window watching us approach. She smiled when she greeted us with an expression that seemed practiced but not without emotion. I simply could not determine which emotion was being expressed.

"You said on the phone you have new information," she said, ushering us into her very tidy living room. "What have you found out?"

"Why did you give Tyler one hundred dollars per day to put into the tip jar at the Quik N EZ?" I asked. Clearly some rule of social discourse had been violated because both Sandy and Ms. Washburn appeared somewhat surprised by my question, and I had expected only Sandy's expression to change.

"I beg your pardon?" Sandy croaked. She did not ask us to sit down.

"The key is that Tyler ever knew Richard Handy at all," I said. "He lives with your brother Mason in Franklin Township. It is three-point-four miles from Mason's home to the Quik N EZ in Somerset. But the convenience store is only a seven-block walk from here and it's much faster if someone is driving you. So we can assume that your brother Tyler knew Richard Handy through visits to the Quik N EZ that started here at your house. Isn't that correct?"

Sandy's eyes were trying very hard to look intimidating but the effect was considerably less so than she might have hoped. "So what?" she said. "So Tyler comes over here sometimes and he walks to the convenience store. How does that lead to me giving him all kinds of money to put in the tip jar?"

"That was the question we had to answer." Ms. Washburn, having recovered from her reaction to what I can only assume was an abrupt change of tone on my part, stood tall. "So we called Mason and asked him about the finances of Able Home Help."

Sandy's lip curled. "He's going bankrupt," she said.

"Interesting you should say that," I answered. "When we first met less than a week ago, you said Mason worked for a company that power washes homes. You did not mention that the company also did home contracting, or that Mason owned the business. And you failed to say that Tyler owns part of the company too."

"I'll ask again: so what?"

Ms. Washburn took a step toward Sandy to better make her point. "*So*, that means you were concealing some information about Mason's finances. And when we asked him why you might want to do that, he said you might have been covering up the fact that you'd loaned Able Home Help some fifty thousand dollars to stay in business, only three months ago. Did that slip your mind?"

"I didn't want to embarrass Mason by saying his sister had to bail him out of a business that should be thriving except for his bad management," Sandy said. She also stood tall and seemed to feel she was in direct competition with Ms. Washburn. She did not alter her gaze.

"Where'd you get the money?" Ms. Washburn asked. "You were looking for work and were coming off a divorce. Your husband didn't pay you nearly that much in alimony or child support. Where did the fifty grand come from?"

There was a certain interest in watching the two women contest each other. Since Ms. Washburn was asking the questions I would have offered, but doing so with a considerably more combative attitude than I probably could have mustered, I stood back and waited to see how the scene would resolve itself.

"I had some savings. I'm really starting to get tired of this. You come in here accusing me of … something, and you have no proof. So I loaned Mason some money. What's that got to do with Tyler and these crazy tips he's handing out? And even if I had given him the money for those, what's the problem? It's not illegal to over tip, is it?"

Ms. Washburn seemed to hesitate, so I answered without changing my position in the room. The body language and physical dynamics were interesting to study, so I tried not to disturb them.

"No, it is not," I said. "But if the tips were meant to help finance an operation that was selling merchandise that was not listed on the books of the Quik N EZ, and if some of those items included firearms, that would certainly be illegal, and might even be considered a federal crime. So Detective Hessler has alerted the Federal Bureau of Investigation, and we are here to see if you can extricate yourself from that investigation by telling us what actually happened, and how it led to Richard Handy being murdered."

Sandy's eyes were very wide now and her neck muscles barely moved. She was still looking in Ms. Washburn's direction and seemed incapable of turning her head. Her teeth did not clench, but her jaw was very tight as she spoke.

"I don't know what you're talking about," she said.

"Yes, you do," Ms. Washburn answered. "Someone was selling cigarettes and handguns and other items through the Quik N EZ and they weren't listing those items on the books. It's illegal to sell guns at that kind of store in New Jersey anyway. You have income you can't explain, enough to give Mason fifty thousand dollars and still live in this house despite the fact that you only have one income now that your husband is gone and you've been looking for work. Somehow Tyler had enough money to tip his supposed friend Richard at least five hundred dollars a week. He didn't get that from his job and he didn't get it from Mason. The only person left who could have supplied that money was you."

Sandy sat down on a loveseat near where she had been standing. In fact, she seemed to collapse without thinking of her position and simply landed on the loveseat. She did not cry. She did not even breathe heavily. But she slumped in the cushions and seemed to be very tired very suddenly. The back of her left hand went to her eyes.

"I don't know what you're talking about," she repeated.

Ms. Washburn, to my surprise, sat down next to Sandy on the loveseat and lowered her tone to a sympathetic level. "Look, I understand how difficult it can be to get divorced. You were secure and now you're scared and you feel like everything is coming down on your head. You're all by yourself and you have kids to raise. That's overwhelming. So when you hear there's a possibility to make some very attractive money helping to sell things that would have been sold anyway, you would have to think about it, wouldn't you?"

"I don't know what you're talking about." The voice was barely audible.

"Sure you do." Ms. Washburn was almost crooning; she sounded like Mother did when I was a boy and needed encouragement to explain my sudden bursts of anger or sadness. "You're embarrassed and scared because of what you did, but you can make it a little better by telling us how it happened. You'll feel better." Yes, that was the tone.

Now Sandy could not really speak. She did not vocalize like her brother Tyler, but she shook her head and choked back tears. Her left hand went up as if she were a crossing guard telling an oncoming car to stop and let children cross the street. Her message was very clear and her head was down, staring at her lap.

Ms. Washburn took the opportunity to put her arm around Sandy in what I have seen in motion pictures and television programs as a gesture of support. But she looked at me as she made the move and her facial expression seemed to contain a question, although I could not determine what it might be. I did not respond because I could not answer a question I did not recognize.

She turned back and said softly to Sandy, "You shot Richard Handy, didn't you?"

"No, she didn't," I said as Sandy looked up with a horrified expression. "Sandy was not present when Richard was shot."

Sandy pointed at me and nodded, non-verbally confirming my statement.

"But she was involved in the black market running out of the Quik N EZ," Ms. Washburn argued. "Clearly she introduced Tyler to Richard Handy by starting his habit of going to the convenience store every day. She was behind that from the beginning. And we know Tyler didn't shoot Richard, so Sandy didn't simply put him up to it. Billy Martinez was too far away to do it. So Sandy must have been the one who killed Richard." She looked at Sandy and tried to modulate her voice to a soothing level again. "Was it because Richard was going to go to the police about the guns and the cigarettes?"

"No," I said again. "Sandy was not in the store when Richard was shot. It's clear on the audio track that Tyler did not speak in the moments before the shooting, or anytime after he entered the store, even when Molly was obscuring the view of the cameras. And Richard's greeting to whoever was near enough to shoot him was 'dude.' He would not have said that to Sandy because she is a woman."

"People that age call everybody 'dude,' Samuel," Ms. Washburn explained. "It was not a reference to the shooter's gender identity."

Sandy, interested but not participating in the conversation, watched Ms. Washburn and me in turn as we spoke, as if she were an attendee at a very well played tennis match.

"Still, I doubt Richard knew Sandy well enough to speak to her in such familiar terms," I countered.

Ms. Washburn, who is not at all beyond challenging me when she believes me to be incorrect or (in her view) stubborn, considered that and nodded her consent. "So who shot Richard?" she asked. "If it wasn't Sandy, it wasn't Tyler and it wasn't Billy Martinez, who could have done it? I doubt Molly pulled the trigger. She didn't even seem to know Richard had been shot."

"I don't know," I answered. Then I made a point of establishing eye contact with Sandy. "Do you?"

Her eyes showed nothing but fear now and she shook her head. "I wasn't there. You said I wasn't there, right?"

Ms. Washburn, facing me and out of Sandy's view, flattened out her lips and cocked an eyebrow. I took that to mean she did not believe Sandy's statement, which was wise on her part.

"Well then," I said. "I suppose the best thing to do would be to go back to the Quik N EZ and put the question directly to Billy Martinez. And I think your presence in the store will go a long way toward getting the truth from him, Sandy. Would you come with us, please?"

Sandy looked like she would rather do almost anything else. "My children," she said. "I can't leave now."

"Surely you have some contingency in place for such a situation," I suggested. "What if you had a job interview at this time? Who would you call in that case?"

Sandy stared at me for a moment but must have seen that I was not to be dissuaded. "Probably Mason, or Cindy next door," she said. "But—"

"This might keep your brother Tyler out of jail," Ms. Washburn said. "Maybe you'd better call your neighbor and ask about her taking the kids for an hour or so."

Before our eyes, Sandy Clayton Webb gathered herself into the businesswoman she must have been and the executive she hoped to be. She stood up and straightened her clothes. "There's no need," she said. "The kids are in the afterschool program and won't be ready to get picked up until five."

"You said they were coming on the bus," Ms. Washburn reminded her.

"I lied."

Ms. Washburn's look as we followed Sandy out of the house was one I would never be able to understand.

TWENTY-EIGHT

"WHEN YOU MAKE THE next left, you'll see the store on your right," Sandy Clayton Webb told Ms. Washburn despite the obvious presence of a Global Positioning Satellite device in the car and the fact that Ms. Washburn had driven to the Quik N EZ more than once before.

It had been my condition that Sandy accompany us in Ms. Washburn's Kia Spectra; she had suggested using her own vehicle "in case it gets close to when I have to pick up the kids." Given her recent record of falsehood concerning her children and my need to be sure she did not alert someone at the convenience store in advance, I had insisted.

Ms. Washburn made the turn without comment. As we approached the store, Sandy appeared to be getting nervous. It was difficult for me to see clearly because I would not turn around in the car and she was sitting in the rear seat on the passenger side, an arrangement Sandy had argued against. But I could feel the vibration from her leg, which was tapping on the floor in front of her, and noticed through the edge of my peripheral vision (I have never understood the "corner of my eye" axiom) her hand going to her head, presumably to adjust her hair in some way, which seemed odd.

"Is something worrying you, Sandy?" I asked. "Someone we should be careful about encountering once we get to the store?"

"No," she insisted. "I don't know anything about this. I don't understand why I had to come." She had made similar statements periodically throughout the ride, although the drive took less than two minutes.

"Yes, you do," Ms. Washburn said as she parked the car directly in front of the Quik N EZ, which seemed to be experiencing a relative lull in business. "You knew it when we talked back at your house and you stood up to come here and face Billy Martinez."

Sandy actually laughed. "Billy Martinez," she said.

"What does that mean?" Ms. Washburn turned off the car's engine and removed her safety harness. "Should we be worried about someone else in there? Here's your chance to warn us, Sandy."

"I don't have anything to say," she said, but it wasn't until both Ms. Washburn and I had exited the car that Sandy unbuckled her harness and opened the door in the rear. She stepped out slowly, eyes on the Quik N EZ. I am not able to say she looked terrified but there was definitely an edge to her manner that did not inspire a relaxed attitude.

Ms. Washburn stopped me out of Sandy's earshot. "How do we want to handle this?" she asked. "We don't really know what we're looking for or who we're going to find in there."

"We know Billy Martinez will be there," I said. "What we are looking for is Sandy's reaction."

"Shouldn't we have thought about defense or something? Maybe I should apply for a gun license." She lowered her voice as Sandy approached.

"Ms. Washburn," I said, reaching for the door handle, "it's a convenience store."

I held the door open for the two women, which is something I have been told is polite. In this case it seemed a bit odd, but I did want to make sure Sandy didn't decide to walk away. She did not seem to consider such a move and entered the Quik N EZ with her head held high.

Inside, the store was indeed not very busy at all. There was one customer, a woman in her late sixties by my estimate, frowning in concentration as she perused the aisle devoted to household items. I did not get close enough to determine which type of product was causing her so much consternation.

My attention was focused on the counter, where Billy Martinez was indeed manning the cash register, and was alone. Clearly management was aware this would not be an especially stressful time of day for the staff; Billy appeared to be the only employee in the store. He looked up from a comic book as we approached and first looked slightly irritated. But then he saw Sandy and his expression become one of alarm.

"What's going on?" Billy's voice was slightly hoarse, as if his throat had gone suddenly dry.

"We are here to find out more about the shooting," I said. "And we brought Sandy with us because we believe the incident was somehow connected to the black market operation you were help-ing to run from this store."

I did not look at Sandy, but I could see that Ms. Washburn was being very careful about watching her face. She mirrored what Sandy must have been doing, and shook her head negatively in a very small gesture, as if wanting not to be noticed by anyone but the person she was signaling. That was interesting, but not unexpected.

"Sandy?" Billy attempted. "Who's Sandy?" But he was staring di-rectly at her.

"I have been diagnosed with a form of high-functioning autism," I told him. "That is not a form of stupidity."

"What's that supposed to mean?"

Ms. Washburn answered before I could. "It means you're insulting our intelligence. You were selling cigarettes and handguns, among other things, off the books through this store and Sandy was somehow involved. You recognized her when we came in and you're staring at her now because she just tried to tell you not to admit to anything. But once we call Detective Hessler and invite him here to question you, it's going to be a different story. So why don't you talk now, Billy, and maybe you can keep yourself from a long jail term."

Billy had winced at a few of the words Ms. Washburn had used—*black market*, *handguns*, and *jail*, for example—and had glanced more than once at the woman in the household items aisle. For the minimum wage he was no doubt being paid, Billy was actually trying very hard to maintain the reputation of the business for which he worked.

He looked Ms. Washburn directly in the eyes. "I don't know what you're talking about and I don't see any proof. So go ahead and bring the cops here. Because I don't think you have anything to tell them."

"We know you did not fire the gun at Richard Handy," I told Billy. "That's the question we are actually attempting to answer. So if you can tell us who really did kill Richard, we will withdraw. It is the job of the police to investigate the related matters."

"I didn't kill Richard," Billy said.

"I know. I just said that. Who did?"

He looked past Sandy toward the spot where the shooting had occurred. "I don't know. I wasn't looking that way."

"Oh, come on." Ms. Washburn shook her head in disbelief. "You're standing at the counter. You have a clear view of the dairy case from where you are. Even if you weren't looking in that direction before, you were going to look up when you heard shots. So who did you see holding the gun?"

"The kid they arrested." Billy had been given his story. Even if it did not fit the facts or make any sense at all, he was going to repeat it ad infinitum. "The one who kept coming in to see Richard. The retard."

Sandy's face flinched at the last word. "Don't ever say that," she said quietly.

Billy appeared not to have heard her. "He was standing there, holding the gun over Richard's body. Just making that noise he makes, like, 'nnnnnnn,' over and over. Something wrong with him."

Sandy gave him a vicious look that needed no interpretation. "I *said* not to say things like that!" she hissed.

The moment was interrupted when the woman from the household products aisle walked to the counter and stood behind Sandy. She did not move.

We all stayed motionless and silent for eleven seconds until Ms. Washburn addressed the customer. "We're not in line," she said. "You go ahead."

"You sure?"

"Absolutely," Ms. Washburn told her. "Please." She gestured toward the counter, and the woman walked to Billy and placed a small bottle of glass cleaner on the counter.

No one said a word as Billy scanned the UPC code on the item, bagged it, took the woman's five-dollar bill and gave her the necessary change. The woman thanked him, gave the rest of us a curious look, and left the convenience store. There were no other customers present.

"That's it," Billy said once the door had closed behind her. "I'm not talking to you anymore. Why don't you just go home?"

"You're not telling us the truth, Billy," Ms. Washburn said. "We're going to have to call the police and let them know about the black market ring you had here, and you're going to go to jail. Is that what you want?"

Billy appeared confused by our refusal to leave the store when he had told us to do so. "Just go," he reiterated. He looked past my head and his mouth twitched a bit. I did not look behind me, but saw Sandy also glance in that direction.

"The contraband merchandise and the shooting of Richard Handy are connected," I said. "If we let the police know about your involvement in selling illegal goods, they will undoubtedly assume you are implicated in the murder."

Billy, his eyes still looking at a point behind my right ear, gave a tiny nod. Clearly he had heard the truth in what I had told him and was making the decision to answer our questions. He walked out from behind the counter.

Then he went to the entrance to the convenience store and turned the dead bolt in the door. Having locked it, he turned the sign now reading CLOSED from our perspective inside the building to its opposite position, meaning the CLOSED sign now faced outside. And he lowered a venetian blind on the door to shut out any light—or visibility—in either direction.

"Billy," Sandy said. Her voice was shaky.

"It's not up to me, Ms. Webb," came the reply. Billy walked back toward us but did not resume his position behind the counter. Instead, he went back to the dairy display where Richard Handy had died.

Next to the display, facing toward the counter, was a narrow door bearing a sign that read EMPLOYEES ONLY. It opened and Raymond Robinson walked through it toward us.

He was carrying a shotgun.

"It's so unfortunate," he said. "You could have just accepted the story you were given. The young man with the disability was upset because he felt betrayed by someone he thought was his friend, and he snapped. He borrowed his brother's gun and came here to take his revenge. Why was that so impossible to believe?"

I took a step toward him and Mr. Robinson leveled the shotgun at my chest. "Don't do that," he said.

I felt my head start to shake. I'm sure it was at most a slight movement from the perspective of the others (except perhaps Ms. Washburn, who knew me well) but from my viewpoint the frustration and anger at myself was palpable and made the reaction feel much more noticeable than it was. That led to feelings of embarrassment, which added to the frustration. This was not a helpful tactic but I was having difficulty controlling it.

"You shot Richard?" Ms. Washburn sounded both surprised and disappointed. "With all that money and all those businesses, you had to kill a kid because you needed to protect your little black market side deal?"

"It was the guns," Mr. Robinson said. "Those made it a federal crime and that made it more dangerous. When Richard threatened to expose the operation, he became dangerous. He never really understood. And your brother ... " He smiled a smile without any amusement or warmth at Sandy. "Well, he presented the perfect opportunity, didn't he?"

"You cold bastard," Ms. Washburn said. Her voice was angrier than I'd ever heard it, which only made me think of how she would sound if she knew about her husband's affair. That did not seem a productive thought at the moment. "Why did you even get involved in that sleazy business to begin with?"

But Mr. Robinson pointed the shotgun directly at her chest. "I'm not a Bond villain," he said. "I have no intention of explaining my evil plan to you for so long that you can figure out a way to escape. There is no way to escape."

Then he looked at Billy Martinez and gestured with the barrel of the shotgun. Billy, taking the instruction, said, "Move over here," and pointed toward the dairy section. It was easy to see the advantage of leading us into that area—it was away from any windows. The security cameras appeared to have been removed, probably in anticipation of replacement that had not yet happened.

It was the perfect place to shoot people and not be seen.

Ms. Washburn did not move and neither did I. "We're not fake victims, either," she told Mr. Robinson. "If you want to kill us you're going to have to do it on our terms. Where you can be seen. Where you'll get caught."

"I can easily cause you pain without killing you," the entrepreneur responded. "And once you're in pain, you'll go where I want you to go."

I decided it was best to stick to Ms. Washburn's plan and remain standing in the spot nearest the door. Even the blinds on the nearest window would not provide total obstruction from view. It would be risky to do anything especially incriminating here and Mr. Robinson clearly knew that because he stayed in the narrow doorway from where he had emerged, shotgun in hand.

"You found a profit source in some off-the-books merchandise that you could funnel through a number of locations," I said, basing my statement on the compiled data from Detective Hessler, our independent research, and the statements from those involved we had interviewed as well as some Internet searches. "Perhaps some of your other businesses were involved in cash flow problems, like the electronics chain you're planning on closing. Tyler Clayton works at one of those stores, doesn't he? And when you were doing one of your weekly visits as an employee, you met Tyler and found out that he liked to come here and considered Richard Handy a friend.

"Richard had been threatening to expose the contraband operation you had developed here, and you thought having his friend give him hush money in public every day would be an effective way to keep him quiet. So you made sure you met Tyler's sister Sandy, and, perhaps by pretending to have some romantic interest in her, you gained her trust and by extension Tyler's."

"Pretending?" Sandy gasped.

I did not react to her question, as I saw no reason to answer. She was beginning to understand the truth.

"Move over there," Mr. Robinson reiterated, but no one in the room moved. "*Now.*" He was alternating his aim at Ms. Washburn and me. "The four of you."

Sandy's mouth dropped open. "What do you mean, Raymond?" she sputtered. "You're going to shoot *me* too?"

"Of course he is," Ms. Washburn informed her. "He can't afford to leave any witnesses alive."

Ignoring the drama in the room and the frantic feelings of dread in my mind I forced myself to remain still, concentrating especially on my hands and head. I'm not sure my right foot did not begin to tap where I stood. "And things were going fairly well for a while," I continued as if nothing had happened since I spoke the last time. "Sandy Clayton Webb provided Tyler, as well as a place to store some of the contraband merchandise you couldn't afford to leave in your monitored warehouses."

Sandy looked stunned, blinking, not necessarily processing the situation as it happened. "I should have stuck with Match.com," she said, presumably to herself.

"But you had a problem. Richard Handy, who knew what you were doing, was worried. He had been arrested once for selling contraband cigarettes and did not want to be involved in the new operation. And the bribes he was getting, even though they were on camera and could be used to blackmail Richard, were no longer working."

"I could have gotten some of that cash, then," Billy Martinez said. No one responded to him.

"You kept Richard at bay for a while with Tyler's daily 'tips' of one hundred dollars, but he was getting nervous," I said. The longer I spoke, the longer Mr. Robinson was not shooting. "You couldn't let him leave the business because he knew about your illegal activities and you couldn't persuade him to participate again, could you, Mr. Robinson?"

It might have been a mistake to say the man's name aloud; it seemed to wake him from the thoughts on which he'd been ruminating. Mr. Robinson looked up at me. And when he focused on me, the shotgun did the same.

"I said move over there," he reminded me. Again there was the gesture with the shotgun.

"No," Ms. Washburn said. "We're not moving. Your best choice is to let us go and take your chances with the police. We don't have a confession from you about the shooting and only have evidence about the black market stuff. Take the lesser sentence and consider yourself lucky."

Mr. Robinson's face contorted with anger and he turned his attention toward Ms. Washburn, who actually started at his movement. "Shut up!" he shouted.

To draw his attention back to me, I added, "It makes no sense to shoot the four of us. The police will find four bodies where Richard Handy died and you will be the only logical suspect. You are condemning yourself to the same fate either way. When Richard threatened to go to the police, you shot him and almost managed to get Tyler implicated. How did you get him to stand there holding the gun?"

"He used me," Sandy said in a small voice. "Raymond told Tyler I would have to go to jail because of the stuff we were selling and that he'd make it look like I shot Richard. But he wouldn't do that if Tyler played along."

"How do you know?" Ms. Washburn asked her. "You weren't here when it happened."

Sandy shook her head. "No, that's true. Tyler told me on the computer after it happened. I didn't know anybody was going to get shot. I was supposed to get Tyler here to give Richard a five-thousand-dollar bribe, and Raymond said he wanted the cameras painted because that would be suspicious, so Tyler got Molly to do it." She turned toward Mr. Robinson. "You killed Richard and you shoved the gun into Tyler's hand and threatened him with me. Then you slipped through that little door of yours and got out through the basement. But you never told me anybody was going to get killed."

"Don't be a fool!" Mr. Robinson hissed at her. "They're both probably recording this for the police!"

"We are not recording the conversation," I informed him.

But Mr. Robinson did not appear to have heard me. Apparently trying to avoid implicating himself in the imagined recording, he took on a more conversational tone. "I don't know anything about the shooting." Then his eyes narrowed and his voice became hushed again. "Now. Move. Over there. All of you."

"Wait." We hadn't heard Billy Martinez speak for some time, so his voice was unexpected. Everyone turned. "You're gonna shoot me?"

Mr. Robinson did not answer him. He stepped out of the doorway just enough to maneuver without being easily seen by the street. "Get over by the milk," he said.

I decided to continue ignoring him and concentrate on Sandy, who was the one giving out useful information at the moment. "You didn't know Tyler was to be used as the sacrifice to the police?"

"Of course not. I wouldn't put him in that position." Sandy appeared offended even as she was being prepared for execution. "He was just supposed to go and do his usual thing, give Richard the tip and then get Molly to paint over the cameras. I thought they were going to fake a robbery or something and frame Richard. When he got shot I was horrified."

Mr. Robinson was not one to be denied. We had stalled beyond his patience. He fired a blast from his shotgun into the ceiling. As everyone else's attention was riveted on the origin of the loud sound, I looked out the front window toward the street.

There was no movement. Apparently the Quik N EZ had better soundproofing than one would expect.

Still, Mr. Robinson's voice did not rise above the level of typical conversation in volume. "Walk over to the dairy case or I will shoot you where you stand," he said.

I did not see the benefit to carrying out his orders. Being shot where Mr. Robinson was less likely to be caught did not have any particular advantage from the victim's standpoint over being shot in the open. It was more likely the police would catch our killer sooner if we did not move. The only possible upside to moving would be the extra few seconds of life that would afford, during which it could be theorized that a better plan might be formulated, but the statistical odds of that happening were not terribly attractive.

"I will not move," I said. "Fire." Mr. Robinson, the successful executive, must not have been accustomed to people he saw as subordinates disobeying his orders. His face registered anger and he turned toward me with one barrel of the shotgun smoking from the blast he had just fired. That meant one barrel was still full.

"No!" Even as Sandy and Billy, looking terrified, had taken two steps toward the dairy counter and now turned back, Ms. Washburn, standing her ground, shouted and distracted my intended murderer. "You can't do that! You can't just take his life because he's smarter than you!"

I did not see the logic behind that argument, but Mr. Robinson sneered at Ms. Washburn and aimed the shotgun carefully toward her midsection. "If you were smarter than me, you'd be the one holding the shotgun," he said. Ms. Washburn's eyes widened in sudden fear and she looked at me.

Then Mr. Robinson pulled the trigger.

My grasp of emotional states is not always strong, especially at the intuitive level. Normally I require some context or explanation before I can determine exactly what feeling another person is expressing. That means it is rare that I can effectively analyze a situation and anticipate another person's actions—particularly a person I do not know well—before they occur. It usually presents something of a disadvantage to me.

However, when Mr. Robinson turned the shotgun on Ms. Washburn, I did not spend any time trying to remember renderings of facial expressions or recordings of vocal modulations. My training in social skills, which had been painstaking in my teens and twenties, has helped me to some degree in such matters, but was not now being accessed. That was probably for the best, as it would have taken up too much precious time to act.

Instead, I acted entirely on instinct. I don't actually remember considering the context or the logistics of the situation at all. I can't honestly say I recall making a decision. I saw Mr. Robinson about to fire the shotgun blast at Ms. Washburn and I acted without thought.

I dove.

In retrospect, there must have been some calculation on my part, because I chose not to dive toward Mr. Robinson, who was the obvious danger in need for neutralization. Instead I took the faster and closer path.

I launched myself at Ms. Washburn and took her down in a flying tackle.

As I did I felt something in my lower left leg, not exactly pain but more akin to heat. It was not a major impediment immediately. Ms. Washburn landed on the floor next to some boxes of chocolate cake mix. I had aimed for her midsection, where Mr. Robinson had trained the gun, to better protect her from injury but had not been accurate in my dive, catching her higher up and causing her to fall backward. I landed on top of her.

"Samuel," she said.

I could not speak. My hands had inadvertently ended up in areas that are not considered appropriate when touching a woman, and I stammered. Finally I managed, "I am sorry," but it took a long moment, during which Mr. Robinson cursed loudly and reached into his pocket for ammunition to reload the shotgun.

In that split second I wondered what he would have done if we had lined up to be shot, since he could not have fired four times without reloading. Now Mr. Robinson's plan seemed quite inefficient.

"Sorry?" Ms. Washburn looked astonished as I rolled from my present position to one next to her, which seemed considerably more like what a gentleman would do. "You saved my life."

At that moment the glass in the entrance door to the Quik N EZ shattered from the force of a blow from outside and two uniformed police officers crashed their way in as Billy Martinez rushed Mr. Robinson. Billy pulled Mr. Robinson's arms back behind him, in the process forcing the weapon to the floor. And he held them there while the officers, followed by four others, wrapped the plastic ties they call "zip strips" around Mr. Robinson's wrists and ushered him out of the building, presumably to a waiting police cruiser. I did not hear a reading of the Miranda Rights, but I had no doubt Mr. Robinson would be receiving one very shortly.

"You tried to kill us!" Billy shouted as his boss was being taken out of the Quik N EZ.

"He tried to kill *me*," Ms. Washburn said quietly, possibly to herself. I was the only other person who could have heard her.

I stood up and helped Ms. Washburn to her feet just as Detective Hessler was entering the store, surveying the activity as officers began taking statements from Sandy and Billy. That was when I noticed the continued sensation of heat in my left leg.

"Samuel," Ms. Washburn said with a gasp, "you've been shot."

"Yes." I did my best not to look down. "That will require some attention."

Sandy, standing very straight, folded her arms to communicate a certain lack of cooperation, while Billy, still explaining that Mr. Robinson had been trying to kill all of us, was telling as much of the story as he knew. He was explaining to the officer nearest him how he'd only been the person to store the contraband merchandise off the store's premises and that he'd never stolen anything when Hessler walked casually over to Ms. Washburn and myself.

"Well, you were right," he told me as soon as he was close enough. "It was Robinson after all. I never would have figured it, a guy that rich. What did he need with selling black market guns? It'll get him twenty years easy."

"Detective, Samuel needs medical attention," she said, and pointed to my leg. I remained resolute in my determination not to look at the wound.

"Yeah, there'll be an ambulance outside in a minute," Hessler said. "That doesn't look bad at all." He turned back toward me. "So why'd he do it?"

"He is an entrepreneur and that is how he defines himself," I answered. "If he wasn't starting a new business he felt stagnant. When he saw Richard Handy's small-time attempt at selling a few cartons of cigarettes, Mr. Robinson was intrigued and wanted to see if he could do his employee one better."

Ms. Washburn stared at me. "Samuel, your leg ... Wait. You knew it was Robinson?"

"I did not know. I suspected. After the interview we did with him and the statistics about the black market sales, it seemed logical he had some connection. What delayed my analysis was the participation of Sandy Clayton Webb. It wasn't until Mike saw her at Billy Martinez's house and then immediately calling someone on the phone that I considered the idea she was somehow connected to the only person we knew who could have gotten Billy involved in the contraband sales. That was Raymond Robinson."

Ms. Washburn had not broken eye contact. "So you guessed."

I shrugged. "An educated guess, perhaps. Certainly it was based on the facts we had available to us."

"And you didn't tell me," she continued. "You had answered the question and you didn't tell me."

"I had not answered it," I corrected her. "I had a theory. I needed to test it."

"Well, your test turned out right," Hessler interjected. "I think we'll find that Ms. Webb and Mr. Martinez will be happy to take some plea deals in exchange for information on the guy who shot Richard Handy."

"Sandy has two children and is recently divorced," Ms. Washburn told the detective. "You have to find a way to keep her out of jail if you can."

Hessler cocked an eyebrow. "It's not up to me. It's up to the county prosecutor and maybe the FBI. The Feds don't like it when you sell guns, especially if any of the buyers were from out of state."

"We don't know that Sandy actually sold any of the merchandise," I pointed out. "All we know is she provided housing for some of the items Billy could not store under his parents' roof, and one hundred dollars a day, presumably to keep Richard Handy quiet."

Sandy, protesting that she "had two children coming home from school in an hour," was led out the door by two officers. She was not handcuffed but the officers did hold her arms as they walked.

Billy Martinez had already left, escorted by the other two uniformed policemen. He had said very little, reiterating only that Mr. Robinson had tried to kill him, which was not technically true but would have been if the scenario had been allowed to play out according to the entrepreneur's plans.

"A lot of it will have to do with how much of the profit Ms. Webb was getting, I would guess," Hessler said. "If she was getting rich off this business, prosecutors and juries are not going to look kindly on her. Using her brother, a kid with a disability ... " He said the word *disability* as if trying to sound it out phonetically. "That's not going to help either. He could have taken the rap for the murder if you hadn't shown us the evidence, Hoenig."

I do not do terribly well with direct compliments. "You would have found it yourself sooner or later, detective." I believed that to be true, although I would have probably wagered on "later" rather than "sooner" if bets were being placed.

"Wait a second." Ms. Washburn, having listened to the conversation, was beginning to piece together some of the information she had not been given in advance. "How did you know to be here, detective?"

Hessler looked puzzled. "What do you mean, how did I know?" he said. "Your pal here called me two hours ago and said I should be outside with some cops in case the 'scenario,' as he put it, didn't go as well as planned."

Now Ms. Washburn folded her arms and looked at me, although I was not returning her gaze. "And how did you know exactly when to come in?"

I undid two buttons on my shirt and pulled the collar to the right to reveal a mechanism taped to my skin, which had been extremely uncomfortable throughout this visit. "I am wearing a wire," I told her. "The detective came and put it on me when you were at lunch."

"You waited until I was away? Why?"

I could feel myself blush. "It was necessary for me to remove my clothing," I said.

"Samuel." Ms. Washburn shook her head in what Mother would have said was disbelief. "You are in your own way quite the gentleman. But this was a dangerous situation and I was walking into it. You can't not tell me that stuff."

Detective Hessler raised his hands palms out as if surrendering or being robbed in a motion picture about the American West. "I'm not getting involved in this," he said, stepping away. "I stopped doing domestic situations when I got my shield." He went to the entrance and looked out, presumably surveying the uniform officers. I heard two car doors close. He turned toward me. "EMTs are here. Your leg." He gestured to us to leave the store.

"I apologize for not keeping you completely informed," I said to Ms. Washburn. I have been told that apologies are an appropriate (if often insufficient) tool for those times when a person does something for the right intentions but in doing so hurts another's feelings. "It was meant to protect you. I did not expect the situation to become violent, and if you knew I was wearing the transmission device that could have made things less manageable."

"Wait a second," Ms. Washburn said, her face probably registering wryness. "You lied. You told Robinson you weren't recording the conversation."

That struck me as odd. "You have heard me say things that were not entirely true before," I reminder her. "But in this case I was not lying."

"You said you weren't recording him," she reiterated.

"I wasn't. The police officers were recording. I was merely the transmission device."

Ms. Washburn reached out to touch my arm and I instinctively flinched. She stopped her hand. "Sorry," she said.

"It was an impulse," I told her. "It should not be taken personally. I have a difficult time being touched."

"I know. We should get out of here." Ms. Washburn pointed toward the door. We started in that direction, careful of the broken glass on the floor. "So you called the cops two hours before we left, huh?"

We walked out into the sunshine and saw the remaining two police cruisers, with Sandy Clayton Webb and Billy Martinez in the two back seats, pull away from the street. Hessler was standing next to his unmarked car talking on his cellular phone.

"After all, Ms. Washburn," I said. "It never hurts to have a little backup."

She laughed, then pointed. "There. The ambulance." She was supporting me a bit on my left side, although I was not aware of a serious limp on my part.

We walked to the waiting ambulance where a male Emergency Medical Technician was emerging from the rear of the vehicle. "You the one who got shot?" he asked.

I felt the beginning of some pain in the affected leg. "Yes, but I do not believe it to be—"

Then I made the mistake of looking at my lower left leg, and saw blood—not very much, but certainly a result of the wound—leaking through my trouser leg.

And I lost consciousness. I do not have difficulty seeing blood. Unless it is my own.

TWENTY-NINE

TYLER CLAYTON SAT IN Mother's overstuffed chair and manipulated the screen on his tablet computer. Tyler had not yet fully regained his vocal speech, still somewhat shaken by the events that had led to Richard Handy dying from a gunshot wound and his sister, Sandy, being arrested.

My left leg, bandaged but not especially painful, was elevated per doctor's orders on a stool I had brought from home. The less said about my fainting, the better, and Ms. Washburn had not mentioned it since I had awakened in the Emergency Room at St. Peter's University Hospital in New Brunswick, where I had spent ninety minutes being treated before my discharge with what the attending doctor called, "One of the more superficial gunshot wounds I've seen."

"Why did Tyler have the gun with him if he had never expected there to be violence?" Ms. Washburn asked Mason Clayton, who was seated in the other client chair at our Questions Answered office. I was behind my desk but Ms. Washburn had walked out in front of hers and was leaning on it, closer to the client.

"As I understand it, Sandy told Tyler to bring the gun because she was afraid there might be some danger at the store. I guess it was what Raymond Robinson told her to do." Mason glanced at his brother, something he was doing with some frequency. "Is that right, Tyler?"

Tyler looked up. He did not look at Mason, Ms. Washburn, or me. Instead he looked at Molly Brandt, seated next to him in a folding chair, her eyes never leaving his face. She nodded at him and he nodded back. "Yes," Molly said.

"Did Tyler know Sandy and Robinson were running the black market sales through the Quik N EZ?" Ms. Washburn asked Mason.

Before he could answer, I cleared my throat. It did not especially need to be cleared of any obstruction. This is a way to indicate that you would like the group's attention without merely blurting out one's thoughts.

"Ms. Washburn," I said, "Tyler is here with us. You can ask him the questions directly even if he is not answering you with words. He can hear and understand."

Ms. Washburn nodded and looked at Tyler. "I'm sorry, Tyler," she said. "I didn't mean to ignore you." Tyler did not look up from his tablet. "Did you know about the black market sales?" Ms. Washburn asked.

Tyler's lips twitched a few times before he managed to say, "No."

I stood up and walked to the other side of my desk, facing Tyler and Molly. "Where did you think the one hundred dollars each day was coming from?" I asked.

Tyler could not say the name, so he wrote on his tablet computer and turned the screen toward me. *Sandy*, it read.

We had called Mason after leaving the Quik N EZ and gave him the answer to his question, which he had already gotten from Detective Hessler—it was probably Mason we had seen the detective calling on his cellular phone when we left. When Ms. Washburn called, Mason was on his way to post bail for Sandy, whose lawyer, T. Harrington Swain, had simply ended Tyler's case when the charges against their younger brother were dropped and used the retainer he'd been given to start defending Sandy. He suggested that a plea bargain was much more likely in Sandy's case but that until something was arranged and the issue of prison was settled, Sandy's children would be living with their father.

So now, three days after the arrests at the Quik N EZ, Mason and Tyler (plus Molly, who had apparently attached herself to Tyler and would not do anything independently) were gathered at Questions Answered for what Mother, who had declined to attend, called a "postmortem," which seemed appropriate only in the case of Richard Handy.

There was no point in asking Tyler where he had thought Sandy might have gotten the hundred-dollar bills he'd been giving Richard Handy to silence him; it was clear at this point that Tyler's concept of money was at best a little nebulous. Besides, in police interviews Sandy had provided the answer herself.

"She said she'd met this guy Robinson through her brother's job and thought he was the answer to her divorce," Hessler had told Ms. Washburn and me after taking our statements at the police station. "But he was mostly interested in his work, not so much her, and as it turned out, mostly in making sure her brother delivered a hefty tip every day. Your pal Sandy decided she'd become part of Robinson's work so he'd be more interested, and that ended up with her investing what savings she had in the black market scheme and storing some of the merchandise in her attic. The one saving grace for her is that she never had any of the firearms in her possession or the Feds would never let her out of jail. She only had some cigs and a few cases of Johnnie Walker blue label that Robinson was selling to special clients."

"So Sandy is telling all," Ms. Washburn noted.

"Hell hath no fury," Hessler said. This was a reference to *The Mourning Bride*, a play by William Congreve from the late seventeenth century, although Hessler was unintentionally paraphrasing the actual quote, which is, "Heaven has no rage like love to hatred turned, Nor Hell a fury like a woman scorned." Still, he had gotten his point across.

"Had she been communicating with Mr. Robinson after Tyler was arrested?" I asked. "Was she calling him when I saw her leave Billy Martinez's house?"

"Probably," Hessler answered. "She was trying to get Robinson to set up good old Billy as the shooter and get her brother off the hook, but that wasn't the plan. Tyler was afraid he'd send his sister to jail if he told the truth, so he just stopped talking entirely. And Billy knew we figured he hadn't shot Handy, so he wasn't going to drop a dime on his boss."

I asked Hessler if Billy would be in prison for a long while, and he tilted his head in a gesture of uncertainty. "He had stuff in his house. He knew what was going on. And he was there when Handy was shot, probably knew it was going to happen. That was the difference with him, withholding evidence in a murder. Sandy knew stuff but didn't know there was going to be a killing, and she wasn't there when it happened. Billy was. I don't know what kind of deal the prosecutor will offer him. If he's necessary to get Robinson, he might do okay."

There had been no further word of plea bargains over the next three days. Mason looked at Tyler in the Questions Answered office and sighed. "He's still working through all the stuff that's happened," he said to Ms. Washburn and me. "I'm not sure he understands that he didn't get Sandy in trouble; Sandy got Sandy in trouble."

Again, I pointed out that Tyler was present in the room and cognizant of what was being said about him. Mason looked sheepish— that's what Mother would call it—and nodded.

Mason stood up. "I guess that finishes our business here," he said. He reached into his pocket and produced a checkbook. "What do we owe you for answering the question, Mr. Hoenig?"

Ms. Washburn said what I was preparing to say: "You don't owe us anything, Mason. We owed you a free question."

Mason's brow furrowed. "A free question? Why?"

I walked over and addressed Tyler directly. "We gave you an incorrect answer to your question, Tyler."

Tyler looked up and his eyes met mine, the first time that had happened since the shooting had been reported.

"Richard Handy was indeed your friend," I said. "He wanted you to know that."

I removed the Tenduline, which Hessler had returned since it had no relevance to the murder prosecution, from my pocket and offered it to Tyler. Tyler reached for it, saw what it was, and drew his hand back quickly.

"It's cursed," Molly reminded us.

"Not so," I told them. "I have done some research on the supposed curse. The legend states that the Tenduline will have the power to predict a violent act, and if one were to believe in such things, its presence in Richard Handy's pocket before he was shot would prove the point."

Tyler sat back farther to better distance himself from the die. "But," I went on, "once the death had taken place, the legend clearly notes that the Tenduline is drained of its status as an omen. It becomes an item of great protection and value."

I again held the die out for Tyler. "Richard wanted you to have it so he held it out toward you when he died," I said. "He was your friend and he wanted you to be protected."

Ms. Washburn made a sound that might have been a sniff.

Tyler, staring at the item in my hand, took a breath. Then he held out his own hand in front of mine. I placed the Tenduline in his palm without making contact hand-to-hand. I knew Tyler would prefer not to be touched.

It took him seventeen seconds to summon the words. "Thank you," Tyler said.

He, Mason, and Molly left shortly thereafter, Mason continuing to offer payment and Ms. Washburn insisting that was not necessary. I was less adamant but understood her point.

We settled back into the chairs behind our respective desks. I began work on a question I had been asked before Richard Handy was murdered, one regarding the use of a cellular telephone in an airport restroom and a talking mynah bird. It was unusual but not especially interesting, I had discovered. This was one I'd answer for the money more than the intellectual challenge.

Ms. Washburn was quiet for a moment, then opened her desk drawer and extracted an envelope. She stood and brought it to my desk. "Would you notarize something for me?" she asked.

I had obtained a notary public license as an exercise when researching a question four months earlier. It was an astoundingly simple process to become a notary public, so I had merely filled out the form online and then paid the necessary fees. I had never intended to act as a notary, but for a close associate like Ms. Washburn it would certainly be simple enough.

"Certainly," I said. I had ordered the necessary ink stamp and eschewed the device which creates a raised seal on a notarized document since that is not required in the state of New Jersey. I retrieved the ink stamp from my desk. "What may I help you with?" I asked.

"My divorce decree," Ms. Washburn answered, taking the document out of the envelope and turning to the first necessary page. "I need to sign it and send it back with a notary seal."

She signed in numerous places while I watched to be sure she was not doing so in the wrong spots; of course she was not. Her attorney had marked the places to sign very obviously so a woman even considerably less intelligent than Ms. Washburn would have clearly known where to sign.

"I thought you were not certain about the divorce," I said as she signed.

"I wasn't for a while but I am now," Ms. Washburn replied. As with many legal documents, signing and initialing in the necessary areas can be time consuming. She continued with her work.

"What made you decide to go ahead with the divorce?" I asked. I have been told that my voice has less inflection than most in conversation and I was relying on that quality to hide any interest I had experienced in relation to Ms. Washburn's marriage.

"A lot of things," she answered. "For one, Simon was seeing another woman even as we were talking about reconciling." She stopped and looked me in the eye unexpectedly. "But you knew that, didn't you?"

I have some difficulty lying to anyone, but with Ms. Washburn it would be almost impossible. "Yes," I said.

She nodded and went back to signing. "And you didn't say anything."

"I felt that it was not my place to do so."

Ms. Washburn nodded. "You were right. You made a good choice, Samuel." Another set of initials was left at a designated line. "And what really did it was when you saved my life."

That did not sound helpful to me. "I was not thinking about your marriage when I knocked you down," I said.

Ms. Washburn smiled, but there was something added to the smile I did not understand. "No, you weren't," she said. "But I thought about Simon and what he would have done in that situation. He would have dove, all right, but not to save me. He would have leapt out of the way of the gun, in the other direction, and let me get shot." She sighed. "That's not my idea of a marriage."